A Dream to Trust

By

Stella Jayne Phillips

A Dream to Trust

Contact Information: info@thewildrosepress.com

Cover Art by *Jennifer Greeff*

The Wild Rose Press, Inc.
PO Box 708
Adams Basin, NY 14410-0708
Visit us at www.thewildrosepress.com

Publishing History
First Edition, 2022
Trade Paperback ISBN 978-1-5092-4084-5
Digital ISBN 978-1-5092-4085-2

Published in the United States of America

Behind the front desk of The Palace Hotel, Patrick Benton glanced up from the purchase contract for the Henderson Building into the dimly lit lobby. Waiting for the ten p.m. late arrivals, he was manning the desk and periodically glancing out the hotel's front windows, Tara Wilson and her two children were running a little late. "All I Have To Do Is Dream" played softly, honoring the beginning of The Palace's quiet time. Patrick felt a warm presence and the spirit of the hotel's resident ghost, Victoria Wyatt, appeared beside him. Her folded hands rested on the front desk on top of his purchase contract and blurred the words. A consummate inn keeper, Victoria frequently materialized beside the front desk prepared to meet new arrivals.

Lit by the old-fashioned streetlight in front of the hotel, leaves on the hotel's front porch danced in the cold January air. As a black SUV parked for check-in directly in front of the lobby window, Victoria dissolved leaving the scent of lavender.

Praise for Stella Jayne Phillips

Literary Titan Award for fist book in series novel,
SWEET DREAMS AT THE PALACE HOTEL

Dedication

Dedicated to: Christina, Penny, Sabrina, Barb, and Mary, who offered feedback and support; Melanie Billings, editor who believed in my dream; Michael, who shared his recovery story, and the generations of strong women in my family who provided inspiration with their stories of starting over.

Chapter One

The Historic Palace Hotel combines the comfort of home with royal service. Palace guests begin their day with a golden opportunity to plan the day's activities or make new friends while they enjoy complimentary breakfast items made on the premises or acquired from local businesses. Evening finds the lobby transformed into an intimate lounge serving wine and beer, many of the offered libations locally sourced. Constructed in 1917 by the original innkeeper Mrs. Victoria Wyatt, The Palace Hotel enjoys a reputation for comfort and excellence. Oh, and did we forget to mention the resident ghost?

~Creekside Chamber of Commerce.com/visitor information

****

A piano banged the last chords of a country ballad. Behind the front desk, Patrick Benton looked up from the purchase contract for the Henderson Building into the dimly lit lobby. Waiting for the ten p.m. late arrivals, he manned the desk and periodically glanced out the hotel's front windows. Tara Wilson and her two children were running a little late. "All I Have To Do Is Dream" played softly, honoring the beginning of The Palace's quiet time. Patrick felt a warm presence and the spirit of the hotel's resident ghost, Victoria Wyatt, appeared beside him. Her folded hands rested on the front desk on top of his purchase contract and blurred the words. A consummate innkeeper, Victoria frequently materialized beside the front desk to meet new arrivals.

Lit by the old-fashioned streetlight in front of the hotel, leaves on the hotel's porch danced in the cold January air. As a black SUV parked for check-in directly in front of the lobby window, Victoria dissolved, leaving behind the scent of lavender.

A woman jumped out of the driver's seat; the door slammed behind her, breaking the quiet. The back seat passenger door popped open, and a young boy jumped down, slammed the door, and raced around the car to his mother. She yanked open the other door and lifted out a little girl. Grasping the boy's hand and carrying the girl, she climbed the front steps.

"Welcome to The Palace, Ms. Wilson," Patrick commented as he held the front door open. She set the girl down; the boy took the child's hand, led her to the sofa, and helped her up.

Patrick finished the check-in procedure, helped unload the SUV, and while Tara Wilson drove the vehicle to the rear lot, he sent the bags to the attic via the dumbwaiter. The children stayed on the sofa. The little girl closed her eyes, rested her head on the boy's lap. The boy's brown eyes followed Patrick's every action. Tara Wilson paced up the front steps again. She opened and closed the door silently.

"I'll show you up." Patrick recognized a trace of fear in her eyes and gave her what he hoped was a reassuring smile. "I have to get your luggage from the dumbwaiter anyway." The boy woke the little girl.

Ms. Wilson lifted the girl in her arms and took her

son's hand. They trooped up the stairs. As they turned the corner at the first landing, Patrick recognized the '60s surf song about the safety found in the singer's room. Appropriate.

On the third floor, Patrick opened the locked door to the dumbwaiter, retrieved the luggage, and hauled it to Tara's room. She tapped her key on the electronic lock and opened the door. On the threshold, she hesitated, flipping on the lights with her free hand. The children followed her inside. The boy held the door, and Patrick carried the luggage inside and set it beside the closet.

"If you need anything, call the emergency number." He indicated a bright blue card framed beside the mirror. With a wish for a good night, he slipped out the door.

The door closed with a quiet *whoosh*, and the deadbolt clicked when it slid into place. Patrick strode down the hall to his apartment. He took his key from his pocket and glanced once more toward Tara's room. Was she afraid of all men, strangers, or him in particular? In the shadowy hall, Victoria appeared at Tara's door. She glided through the closed door and disappeared. No screams filled the hallway, so Victoria must have appeared only to him. He opened his door and stepped inside.

****

Scents of coffee and toast teased Tara when she ushered CJ and Makenna into the lobby the next morning. Breakfast the last few days was a blur, but it hadn't smelled this good. Her stomach rumbled in anticipation. Conversation, blended with Journey's "Good Morning Girl," created a low hum punctuated by occasional laughter. She stopped the children at the bottom of the staircase and scanned the room. Patrick, according to his name tag, sat behind the front desk, a coffee cup in his hand. He acknowledged them with a nod.

"Is it okay? Are we safe?" CJ whispered.

Tara squeezed his hand, and they walked to the breakfast buffet. Behind the bar, a young woman offered a good morning as she filled the juice pitcher and sliced a casserole into squares. Tara helped Makenna fill her plate.

A favorite classic rock song extolling the joy of a sunny day and being in love filled the room. Tara sighed in relief. So far, today was good. The lobby's warmth, the hum of conversation, the familiar music, and the comforting scents of breakfast filled her with peace. The first peace since her lawyer's phone call. She and CJ gathered the empty dishes and put them in the bus cart.

As they climbed the stairs, CJ whispered, "Are we going to see them today, Mom?"

"It's up to them." She ruffled his hair, and he grimaced. "I'll tell them we're here, and we'll see." CJ took Makenna's hand, strode ahead, and they played a game of stretching their legs high on every step. Makenna's four-year-old legs were no match for her brother's longer stride. CJ changed his pace to match Makenna's.

Two flights later, they reached their attic room. The children stopped their chatter and stood against the wall beside the door. Tara tapped the electronic key against the lock, grabbed the handle, and opened the door. She touched the light switch and scanned the room. Empty. She motioned the children inside. When they started running, she taught her children to stand to the side when she opened the door and wait until she gave a signal to enter. Sometimes she channeled one of the handsome spies from an old TV show. CJ understood, if she entered without giving a signal, he would grab Makenna, hide and call 911. She knew he remembered that night, the night when her five-year-old son dialed 911 and saved her life. Her former sister-in-law, Ronni Stephens, responded to her text, including a map, directions to Eckie House, the garage apartment, and an offer of lunch.

Bundled in coats, Tara and the children hustled down to the lobby. The young woman from breakfast now sat behind the front desk, collecting keys and wishing guests a good day. Her name tag read *Charlotte*, and she acknowledged Tara with, "Good morning. How can I help?"

CJ leaned against Tara, his body a warm presence. Makenna tugged on her hand. "Do you have a town map?"

Charlotte reached under the desk and set out a tri-fold map, opened it on the desk. "Let me show you where you are." She circled The Palace. "Are you looking for something in particular?"

"I can't see, Mommy." Makenna tugged harder.

Tara lifted her daughter in her arms and shook her head. "Not really."

"Then here's a few things that might interest you." She pointed out a playground, toy store, children's store, museum, and the square.

For the next two hours, they toured the small town, played on the playground, checked out the stores. A gray bank of clouds hid the sun, and their breath made little puffs of white. Safe. The other tourists meandered along the sidewalks and strode across the square. A police officer stopped to shake hands with a small boy. Tara's shoulders relaxed and released the tension in her neck.

At eleven-thirty a.m., she took out her phone, and following Ronni's directions, they meandered toward Eckie House. Children on bicycles raced down the residential street, their piping voices a song of a happy childhood.

Tara glanced at CJ. A frown appeared between his eyebrows; his glasses slid down his nose. A month ago, CJ's excitement filled her heart as he raced down the streets of Bisbee on his new bicycle. The bicycle they left behind. She reached over and ruffled his hair. He looked up at her over his glasses and rolled his eyes. She chuckled as he smoothed his hair down.

Sunlight glinted on the Eckie House windows. On the wide veranda, a porch swing and three rockers swayed gently in the winter breeze. They walked through the gate, crossed the lawn, and skirted the house.

Around a corner, a two-story building appeared. A grin lighting his face, Ronni's brother, Nathan Stephens, leaned against the door. He kissed Tara's cheek, ruffled CJ's hair, and winked at Makenna. He led them up a flight of stairs, opened the door to an apartment, and ushered them inside. The scents of chicken soup and fresh bread greeted them. Ronni set a stack of plates on the table and wrapped Tara in a hug.

"Oh, look how much you've grown." She crouched in front of Makenna. "Do you remember me?"

Makenna shook her head.

"I do," CJ piped up. "You lived in the blue house on the corner."

"We did." Ronni nodded and stood. "I'm glad you remember."

All through their lunch of soup, homemade bread, cut-up fresh vegetables, humus, and Italian dressing, conversation stayed safe. Comments about the town, the famous ghosts, Eckie House, Serendipity, where siblings Nathan and Ronni sold their art. Lunch finished, table cleared, Tina and Makenna raced to Tina's room to play. Nathan offered CJ a ride on the ATV parked in the garage below the apartment.

Encased in a comfortable chair and holding a cup of tea, Ronni blurted, "Thank you for warning us about Trey being released on probation."

"I wasn't sure if you were still in the neighborhood." Tara shook her head. "I don't know that he's even looking for you, but better to be prepared."

"After Paul died, I sold the house, and Nathan and I became gypsies for a time, itinerant artists."

"Because of Trey?"

"Not really," Ronni admitted. "Paul's parents didn't like me much when Paul was alive. After he died, they constantly criticized. My attorney heard a rumor they were going to file for grandparent visitation rights. I told Nathan I needed to disappear, and he offered to join us."

"He's a protective older brother. I'm not surprised. I can picture you and Nathan slipping away in the dark of night."

"Not quite." Ronni chuckled. "Paul's parents left on a three-week cruise. By the time they returned, we were gone." She set her mug on the coffee table. "We've made friends here, done some of our best work," she admitted. "Tina loves preschool. It's perfect."

Tara set her empty mug down. "I hope I haven't brought you trouble."

"No." She shook her head. "I think we're safe here. After all, you live in a hotel occupied by both a ghost and a police chief."

The sound of Nathan's heavy footsteps and CJ's laugh stopped the conversation. Eyes alight, a wide smile splitting his face, CJ rushed to Tara. "Mom, it's so cool. The ATV and orchard and stuff."

Tara looked at Nathan and mouthed, *Thank you.* "Good. I'm glad you had a good time."

Makenna burst into the room, Tina on her heels. "It's my turn now. My turn with Uncle Nathan."

Nathan shrugged. "Sure. I'll give you all a ride to the gate. Makenna, you ride shotgun."

****

Weak sunlight filtered through the lace curtains when Tara woke to Makenna's giggles. Makenna sat up and reached for a large gray dog sitting beside the twin bed. The dog's tongue darted out and licked Makenna's fingers. His tail thumped once on the wood floor. Tara dropped her feet to the floor. The dog bounded through the closed door. "Momma, he ran away," Makenna whined.

Tara lay down beside Makenna and covered them with the blanket. "It's okay, baby. He probably just needed to go out." Makenna nestled in Tara's arms and drifted off to sleep. Soothed by her daughter's heartbeat and her puff of even breathing, Tara relaxed under the warm quilt. Not only a famous ghost at The Palace, a ghostly dog who liked children. She closed her eyes and slept.

Chapter Two

On a bright spring morning in 1908, my brothers, Jacob and Matthew, and I started construction of the Henderson Building. Some help we hired, and others just volunteered their skills. By the time winter weather arrived, the structure was completed, and only the interior still needed work. My brothers headed back to Tucson, leaving me to finish the building and open Henderson Law.

~Practicing Law in Creekside, A Love Story by Micah Henderson

****

The alarm's annoying *beep, beep, beep* woke Tara from a dream of dancing through a spring meadow with her children. Bundled up in sweatshirts, they trooped into the lobby, enticed by the scents of toast and coffee. Animated conversations blended with The Monkees' "Daydream Believer." Patrick sat behind the front desk, coffee cup in hand. A young man, *Eric*, according to the name tag on his green polo shirt, poured coffee and handed out greetings. Tara and the children filled their plates and settled at a table by the front window. Gray clouds covered the sky, contradicting The Beatles' assertion that "Here Comes the Sun."

Ninety minutes later, Tara walked away from Emanuel Lutheran Preschool alone. Makenna found Tina a ready-made friend in Ms. Lake's class.

Creekside Elementary swallowed CJ in a fifth-grade classroom. Tara shoved her hands deeper in her coat pockets. How could she explain to Police Chief Alex Stark in a calm, rational, honest manner why she left Bisbee and her grandfather's house? Why her brother, Owen, sent her here. Just the thought of Trey and her hands shook with a potent mixture of fear and anger. She took a deep breath, relaxed her fists, closed her eyes for a second, and collided with the owner of a familiar blond head. "Oh, sorry." She looked into clear blue eyes.

"My fault," Patrick claimed. "We're blocking the sidewalk." He lifted the arm of a large, flowered sofa.

"Hey. This thing's heavy. Why'd you stop?" A large man appeared in the doorway, his dark brows drawn down in a frown.

"Tara, this grouch is my brother James Benton. James, Tara Wilson guest of The Palace."

"Sorry about that. Our fault. Nice to meet you." James disappeared inside the building.

"We'll be out of the way in a minute." Patrick lifted his end, and the two men muscled the sofa across the sidewalk and into the bed of a black pickup.

With a small wave, Tara walked away. Two blocks, one left turn, and she stood in front of a small craftsman bungalow painted navy blue. A low iron fence surrounded the tiny front yard. On the gate, a discrete sign announced, *Creekside Police Department.* Hesitantly she strolled up the sidewalk to the front door. On the door, a small sign announced, *Open. Please come in.* Tara yanked open the door and stepped between two worlds. Outside, a hundred-year-old residence restored to pristine condition. Inside a modern office, laptops on desks behind a long counter. A young woman behind the counter stared at a computer screen, her delicate brows drawn into a frown. The young woman looked up. "How can I help you today?"

A few minutes later, Police Chief Alex Stark led Tara to a small office, offered her a chair, and faced her across a scarred wooden desk. "When Owen made the appointment, he said you would explain everything. What is it you need to explain?"

A sigh escaped Tara's lips, and she read concern in his chocolate eyes. "I'm hiding in Creekside."

Alex leaned back in his chair, putting more distance between them. "What are you hiding from?"

"Ex-husband, just released from prison," she blurted in one breath. "He's been gone five years. I expected we'd have more time. Good behavior, he got out for good behavior." She laughed bitterly. "Good behavior until he drinks too much or finds a drug contact. Good behavior until he needs money." A tear slid down her cheek, and she brushed it away. Alex grabbed a box of tissues from the desk drawer and handed it to her. "Sorry. The kids were happy in Bisbee. They loved Grandpa's ancient house."

"Why Creekside?"

"Owen's idea. I suggested LA or Denver, big cities." She shook her head. "My brother said we were safer in a small town. People more likely to help. He remembered you live here. Ronni and Nathan are here, so we'd at least know someone."

"Ronni and Nathan Stephens?"

Tara nodded. "They're Trey's stepsiblings, my former in-laws." She sighed. "Last time they met Trey, he tried to break their parents' trust and take their money." She shook her head. "It didn't work. He had no claim."

"When did you last see Trey?"

"Five years ago. The night CJ saved me." Her fists clenched, and she consciously relaxed them. "All I want is a safe place for my children. A chance to hear them laugh again." She looked straight into his dark eyes. "Is Creekside safe?"

"Tara, we'll do everything we can to keep you safe."

A few minutes later, Tara strolled the sidewalks of Creekside. She traveled beyond the business area, away from the square. The gray clouds floated on, and the sun shone in a crystal sky. Craftsman bungalows and small Victorians were interspersed with modern houses large and small. Old or new most homes boasted a front porch complete with porch swing and rocking chairs.

She glanced at her phone. She'd missed lunch, and it was nearly time to retrieve Makenna and CJ from school. A few blocks from the square, she recognized the building where she'd seen Patrick hauling furniture this morning. Door closed and truck missing, she let curiosity win and walked up to the front door.

Beside the door was a small plaque, *Henderson Building, 1909, "Law is order, and good law is good order." Aristotle.* Ah, at one time a law office. She peeked in the window. The room was empty.

Tara strolled toward the preschool. She needed a place to work. For the last five years, the small parlor in her grandfather's house was her office. The attic room at The Palace was big enough for the three of them, but there wasn't enough room for a desk. While they covered their tracks by staying in a new hotel each night, she'd worked from hotel rooms, libraries, patios, parks, and lobby bars. All good temporary solutions. The advantage to running an online business was a flexible location. To maintain the clients she already had and make her business grow, she needed a dedicated place to work, a place to keep records and have private conversations. With the kids in school most of the day, wandering the streets of Creekside, working with clients from a new location every day wasn't going to keep her business alive. She did not miss the constant challenge of keeping up with the repairs on Grandpa's old house, but she desperately missed her office in the small parlor.

On the steps of Emanuel Lutheran Church, Nathan leaned against the railing. His face split in a grin when she dashed up the stairs. "Pick up time." They gathered Tina and Makenna from Ms. Lake's classroom and strolled across town. "I could have picked up Makenna and saved you a trip."

Tara shrugged as they trooped down the stairs. "Or I could have picked Tina up. I'll remember you offered, and you remember I did. It's not like I have a full schedule."

She waved goodbye and headed toward the elementary school. Makenna chattered about school, her new friends, the games they played. The school bell's ring announced CJ's release. Children raced out the door, leaped down the steps, and gathered near a bus in the parking lot or danced through the gate onto the sidewalk.

CJ, his face split in a smile, hurried toward her down the sidewalk, another boy on his heels. He skidded to a stop. "Mom, this is Zack Healy. He's invited me to his birthday party."

A freckle-faced boy with floppy hair and a sweet smile offered his hand. "Nice to meet you, Ms. Wilson."

Tara shook his hand, impressed by his manners. "Nice to meet you too, Zack. You're having a birthday party?"

"Saturday." He took an invitation from his pocket and passed it to her. An emerald green extended cab pick-up drove up beside them. Zack lifted a hand and waved. "There's my uncle." A large bearded man wearing a similar sweet smile stepped out. A few minutes later, Tara accepted the birthday party invitation for CJ.

Tara hustled her children toward The Palace as the previously clear sky turned an ominous dark gray, and the sun disappeared. They climbed the hotel's front steps, crossed the front porch, and Tara yanked open the heavy door. Warmth surrounded them. Tara tugged the children away from the door and helped them remove their coats. The scent of chocolate and cinnamon suddenly tickled her nose. As she took her jacket off, Tara glanced toward the bar. Patrick smiled when their eyes met.

"There's hot chocolate, tea, coffee, and cookies," he offered. "Your timing is perfect. My sister Nikki just put the cookies out, and they're still warm." He tugged a blue checked napkin off a silver plate, exposing an arrangement of sweets.

Tara and the children joined him at the bar. "Oh, snickerdoodles, that's the source of the cinnamon scent. Are the others oatmeal raisin?" Tara asked. At Patrick's nod, she asked the children which they would like, arranged mugs of hot chocolate and cookies on a small table, settled the children, and accepted coffee in a sturdy white mug from Patrick.

"What a lovely surprise on a cold day, sweets and coffee," Tara commented as Patrick handed her the mug.

"Nikki usually has the drinks on the bar between lunchtime and when Victoria's opens at five. Some days a baking mood strikes her, and we all benefit." Patrick sipped his coffee.

"Nikki Stark? The innkeeper?" Tara asked.

"Yep. My sister, Nikki Benton Stark. Sorry, I've lived in this small town just long enough to assume everyone knows us. I live in an apartment across the hall from you in the attic and help Nikki with the hotel when she asks. Our brother, James, the grouch you met today, lives with his fiancée in Eckie house. During the summer, my son, Scott, works in the hotel."

"The hotel's website didn't mention it was a family business," Tara commented.

"The Palace is Nik's business; the rest of us are just accessories after the fact."

By the time the children finished their snack and the dishes were placed in the bus tray, Makenna's eyes were drifting closed. With Makenna balanced on her hip, Tara led CJ up the stairs.

So the handsome blond front desk clerk was her neighbor in the attic and the inn keeper's brother. No worries about noisy neighbors or inadvertently living across from someone who recognized her or knew Trey. Did Patrick live with someone? He mentioned his brother's fiancée and his son but no wife, girlfriend, or fiancée for himself. Why did she care? Didn't her relationship with Trey prove she had no built-in radar when it came to a man's true character? Ahh, but the warm voice and blond hair were hard to resist.

Tara set Makenna on the step behind her with CJ, tapped her key on the lock at the top of the stairs, and opened the door. A faint scent of lavender drifted through the hallway. Leaving Makenna and CJ standing just inside the stairway door, Tara opened the door to their room and flipped on the light. She verified the room was empty and motioned her children inside. As she locked the door, CJ yanked open the bathroom door, glanced inside, and closed the door.

Oh dear, he checked for danger in the bathroom. She hated that her little boy understood the need to be afraid. A ten year old should still be innocent enough to live without fear. Someday they would. One day in the future, she would confront Trey and make some kind of peace. She'd find out if the rehab was a success. At one time, before the drugs and alcohol took over, he'd been charming, loving, and fun. Then he found new friends and new love. Which Trey was out on parole and how would she know the right time to find out? Not yet, not today.

After she reviewed the children's schoolwork, shared pizza and salad delivered by Willie's, and tucked both children in their beds, Tara stood under the shower and let the hot water ease her tense muscles. Dressed in a flannel nightshirt, Tara slid between the sheets and drifted to sleep. In the darkest part of the night, she woke to the shushing sound of a wooden rocker moving against a wood floor. In a rocking chair beside the bed, a woman appeared, a toddler boy on her lap.

"I know you're sad. Me too," she whispered. "But he'll be back, RJ. Your daddy will be back." The boy cuddled against the woman, his head nestled against her shoulder, his eyes closed. The ghost stood, the boy in her arms, and glided through the wall. When Tara glanced back at the rocker, it was gone. Tara recognized the scent of lavender and drifted back to sleep. *The hotel's website warned that Victoria wandered everywhere inside the hotel and only lavender's comforting scent indicated where she'd been. Benevolent spirits and friendly people, so far; the town lived up to its advertising.*

Chapter Three

Spring and new businesses are popping up all over town. Welcome to Creekside Micah Henderson. The brand-new Henderson Building, home of Henderson Law, opened with a celebration and reception on Monday. Grandma's Bakery provided sweets and coffee.
~*The Creekside Reporter, April 1909*
****

A deceptively crystal clear sky promised warmth it didn't provide. Biting cold chapped Tara's cheeks. Her hair stuffed in a blue knit cap and her body encased in a white puffer jacket, she figured she resembled a snowman except for her snow boots and dark jeans. She turned the corner. Standing in front of a store window, a tall man with red hair wiped off paintbrushes and dropped them in a plastic toolbox. He shut the box just as she reached him. She focused on the plate glass window. Her mouth dropped open. Hearts exploded across the glass, laughing, dancing, holding hands, playing instruments inside a gazebo identical to the one on the square. Some hearts wore top hats, some tennis shoes. Others carried flowers or heart-shaped candy boxes. Above the action, a cherub, Cupid, floated a smirk on his face, and his bow and arrow poised to shoot. "That's amazing."

"I may have gotten carried away." He stuck out his

hand. "Chance Pagent."

"Tara Wilson," she answered. "It's nice to meet you. I believe you know Ronni and Nathan Stephens. They've spoken of you."

He nodded. They spoke in generalities about the town, their mutual acquaintances. He picked up his toolbox, wished her a good day, and strode away. She stared at the window. How could the art for sale inside Serendipity compete with that window? A discrete chime broke the silence when she opened the door. She blinked, adjusted her eyes from the bright sun to the indoor light. Out of the corner of her eye, she glimpsed movement and turned her head toward a loft. Lovers stood at the railing, their arms wrapped around each other, their bodies melded together. Tara blinked. They disappeared.

"Welcome to Serendipity." Behind a counter, a woman with dancing red curls asked, "How can I help you today?"

Tara glanced up at the loft again. No one. She strode to the counter. "You must be Ainsley. Tara Wilson. We have mutual friends?"

Ainsley shook her hand, warm palm against Tara's cold fingers. "Nathan and Ronni Stephens." She tilted her head, and a smile lit her eyes. "Relatives of yours, I think?"

"Sort of." She nodded. "They suggested I visit you. Check out their work." They meandered through the store. Ainsley pointed out Ronni's and Nathan's paintings and photography. A mixture of paintings and photographs of The Peace Park, Mission San Xavier del Bac, Hawley Lake iced over and blanketed in snow adorned the walls. Nathan's paintings of Jerome's Spirit

Room and The Petrified Forest at twilight bore a darker stamp. Displayed on a round table in the loft, a collection of Jude Healy's colorful figures glowed with life in the sunlight glinting on glass. A small card identified the display as *Hickory Building—Life in Retrospect.* Tara recognized the lovers locked in an embrace from the railing, children played games, a mother rocked a baby, a young woman danced the Charleston, a small boy beside her copied her steps. "They're amazing." Tara walked around the display, and the colors changed with the angle of the light. "I met him yesterday."

"And Zack?" They climbed down the steps.

"Uh-huh. Looks like CJ's going to a birthday party Saturday" They stopped on the sales floor. "Thank you for the tour."

"My pleasure. If you have a moment, there's something else you might like." She led Tara to a rocking chair surrounded by baskets of colorful quilts. "You have a young daughter?" Tara nodded. Ainsley offered Tara a chair and handed her a basket. "Would she like one of these?"

Tara took out small stuffed animals, each one a unique work of art. A grinning tiger, a lounging lion, a momma elephant rocking her baby, dogs with goofy doggie grins, and cats with intelligent eyes. She withdrew one last dog, an achingly familiar gray German Shepherd. The spirit dog that made Makenna giggle. "This one."

Grocery bag in one hand, gift bag in the other Tara climbed the front steps of The Palace and yanked open the heavy door. "Welcome back," Nikki Stark, the hotel's owner, perched behind the front desk, greeted her. "Successful shopping trip?"

Tara plopped her bags on the desk. "You might have mentioned the lovers in Serendipity."

"Not everyone sees them." Nikki shook her head. "Anyway, they're usually a pleasant surprise." She nodded at the gift bag. "What did you buy?" Tara took the stuffed dog from the bag. "Ah. Smokey. Does he visit you?"

"You recognize him?"

"Wait." Nikki's hands flew over her laptop's keyboard. She turned the screen toward Tara. "The original residents of The Palace, Victoria, RJ, and Smokey."

On the screen a posed portrait of a woman, a boy of about ten, and a familiar large gray Shepard. "Your resident spirits?" Nikki nodded. "What happened to them?"

"RJ was killed in 1945 while serving in the military. Victoria died in The Palace in 1949." She shrugged. "No idea what became of Smokey." She dropped the stuffed animal in the gift bag. "Other than he still runs around the hotel."

****

Main Street disappeared in the rearview mirror when Tara turned her SUV onto a two-lane road marked with a small green sign proclaiming it *Thirteenth Drive*. The road wound through trees, one side bordered with juniper. A wooden fence marched along the other side *No Trespassing* signs hung at frequent intervals. Suddenly the road ended. On the right, a colorful group of balloons marked a gate. Tara punched in the code; the gate swung open. Heeding the directions on the invitation, she bore left on a gravel driveway and stopped in front of a three-story house right out of a fairy tale. The front door opened, and four boys rushed out, followed by a tiny white dog and a familiar large man. "You're here."

"Can I get out, Mom?" CJ asked from the back seat. At her nod, he jumped down and slammed the door.

Jude Healy appeared at her window; the dog nestled on his shoulder. "Welcome, Tara. Come in for a minute?"

She climbed out of the car and followed Jude inside.

"This is King." He nodded toward the dog. "The boys already disappeared into the playroom. We'll start there. Jefferson Lynch is helping me. His son Carson is Zack's friend."

Jude yanked open a door. Playroom, the perfect description. Large screen TV, pool table, foosball, video games, and a bar along one wall loaded with snacks and soft drinks. A tall man sporting black-framed glasses and a scruffy beard waved from behind the pool table. "That's Jefferson. My first boy's birthday party since I was a little boy. I need all the help I can get. Few minutes we'll herd them outside for mountain bike racing, corn hole, badminton, and stuff. Then pizza and cake back in here with the presents." They stepped out of the playroom and started down the hall. "We locked up the ATVs, the gate's locked, and we'll be with the boys all the time. They should be safe. Plus, my housekeeper's here, so that's another adult." They reached her car, and Jude opened the driver's door. "Thanks for bringing CJ. We haven't lived here very long, and CJ and Zack seemed to hit it off." He shut the door. "Probably because they're both the new kids."

Tara waited for the gate to close in her rearview mirror. Yeah, CJ should be safe. She recognized Jefferson Lynch; Nikki pointed him out as Creekside's only counselor. Makenna was at a playdate with Tina at Eckie House. Her children were safe. She drove the SUV behind the hotel, hopped out, and glanced down at her outfit. The navy wool pants still held their crease; her red silk blouse and navy blazer looked fresh and wrinkle free. Time to use the next few hours to find shared office space. She took the map out of her leather tote and started walking. Three hours later, she'd answered the same questions too many times. No, she did not have a permanent address. No, she could not sign a lease for more than six months. Yes, they lived in the hotel. Had she met Victoria? Not officially. She checked the time. Just enough time for coffee at CuppaJoes before she started gathering her children.

The cup warmed her. Tara inhaled the comforting scent of coffee and vanilla. Seated at a small table by the window, she withdrew a legal pad from her tote. She plopped it on the table and looked up into familiar hazel eyes. "Mind if I join you?" MaryBeth, the owner of the coffee shop, slid into the other chair and set down a mug and a plate holding two muffins. "I brought the sugar."

"Well, since you provided sugar," Tara answered and grabbed a chocolate chip muffin. "Not to mention you own the place."

"How'd it go?" MaryBeth nodded toward the legal pad. "Your search for office space?"

"Didn't find anything." She bit into a muffin. The

mixture of chocolate, butter, and sugar exploded on her tongue. "Oh, this is exactly what I needed."

MaryBeth shrugged. "Hey, sometimes only sugar and chocolate will do." She bit into the second muffin. "Did you ask Patrick Benton?"

Tara shook her head. "The office isn't open yet."

"Don't you live across the hall from him?" She frowned. "Surely he's friendly enough to talk to you once in a while."

"You have any idea when he'll open the office?" Tara asked as she sipped the last of her latte. Patrick rarely appeared in their shared hallway.

"No." She shook her head. "Bet it'll be soon, though. Nikki claims he's been bored since the first week he moved into The Palace."

"That's a good idea. I'll try to catch him at the hotel." They cleared off the table. With a wave, Tara bounced down the steps. Space in a law office was perfect if Patrick opened the office soon.

After dinner, baths, stories, and quiet time their busy day caught up with the children. CJ and Makenna snored softly, the sound a comfort. Tara withdrew the legal pad and started another list, another plan. Within a few minutes, questions filled the top sheet. Should they find an apartment? That would solve her office space problem. Were they safer in town or outside? Was Trey even looking for her? After the two weeks they'd spent traveling across California, Nevada, New Mexico, and Arizona, could he even find her if he tried? No answers. Tara tossed the pad back in her tote bag, slipped between soft sheets, and drifted into sleep. Hours later, Tara yanked herself from the familiar nightmare. Her eyes popped open. She lay perfectly still, moved only her eyes to orient herself. The breath she held released in a *whoosh*. Not the hospital, not the little condo in Scottsdale, not Grandpa's house in Bisbee. She rolled to her side and focused on the lace curtain and her children's soft snores. Creekside, The Palace Hotel. They were safe.

CJ rolled over and whispered, "Mommy."

She wondered if he'd shared her nightmare. She hoped not. Bad enough, he rescued her, a five-year-old hero. That he might relive the terror and horror of that night in his dreams broke her heart. She padded over to CJ's bed; he'd kicked the blankets off. She tugged the blanket over him, ruffled his brown hair, kissed his forehead. Makenna slept curled in a ball, buried under the covers, Smokey in her arms. Tara yanked on a pair of socks and buried herself under the quilt and blanket. She slowed her breathing and willed away the last of her nightmare. At this moment, her children were safe. She was safe. Sleep claimed her.

****

Left hand holding Makenna's tiny one, right hand clasping CJ's, Tara descended the steps in front of The Palace. Puddles glistened in the winter sun, and the breeze teased Makenna's fine hair yanking it from her ponytail. Constantly scanning the sidewalk for Trey, Tara listened with half her attention to Makenna's description of life at preschool and how the church was hers since she attended school there. CJ answered but didn't disagree.

They climbed the steps to the narthex. Pastor Tim greeted them. Inside, Tara's gaze landed on a familiar face, and she breathed a sigh of relief. Children surrounded Nikki. A baby in a pink blanket snuggled against her chest, and Chief Stark, a diaper bag on his shoulder, wrapped an arm around Nikki's waist. The artist from Serendipity's window, Chance Pagent, held a little girl in one arm, his other arm draped around the shoulder of a young woman clasping the hand of a second girl. Chief Alex caught her eye and nodded a greeting.

The door opened with a blast of cold air. A young woman carrying a toddler girl rushed in, followed by James and Patrick Benton. "Oh. We made it," she exclaimed as she handed the child to James and hugged Nikki. "See, James? I knew we'd be on time."

"Only because we jogged the whole way," James responded. He turned to Tara. "Hello again. At least this time, I didn't try to run you down with a sofa." He took the other woman's hand, tugging her to his side. "Tara Wilson, this is my fiancée Andrea Hamilton and baby Ella." Tara introduced Makenna and CJ. They strolled inside the sanctuary and settled in pews. Tara found herself surrounded by Bentons and Starks. She located Chief Alex at the end of the row. He looked at her and winked. She relaxed her shoulders. For the moment, they were safe, surrounded by friends.

Chapter Four

1912 Looking back, there were moments that stole my breath. Moments when I immediately knew a single event would change my life. And then there were moments I believed just a small piece of life's puzzle. Not particularly important. How could I guess that the stylishly dressed woman with kind eyes would indirectly change the course of my life? I jumped up from my chair and immediately wished I'd left my cuffs rolled down and my jacket on. I offered my right hand and attempted to snag my jacket with my left. "Oh no, Mr. Henderson. It's much too warm for a jacket today." A smile lit her face, and Mrs. Faith Eckie dropped gracefully into the offered chair. "I'd like your help with a small legal issue involving a plot of land."

~Practicing Law in Creekside, A Love Story by Micah Henderson

****

Tara inhaled the scents of onions, peppers, and garlic when she yanked open the door of Manuel's and hustled CJ and Makenna inside. They slipped into a booth. Tara faced the door, CJ and Makenna on the other side. Maybe they were safe in Creekside, but she wasn't ready to stop watching over her shoulder. They ordered family style, several entrées, and starters set in the middle of the table. Food filled the table, and Tara served their plates.

"It's like Santiago's, mom," CJ commented as he crunched into a chicken taco. "I miss Santiago's."

Her heart hurt for CJ. She'd uprooted him again, gave him no choice when she packed the car and drove away from Bisbee. He was entitled to miss the life they left behind. "What else do you miss?"

"Grampa's house, Uncle Owen, my friends Ben and Chris. My bicycle."

Tara took his hand across the table and squeezed gently. "I know this is tough. I wish I could make it easier." She sipped the red sangria and let the wine soothe her aching heart.

"I get it, mom. We weren't safe." He frowned; small wrinkles appeared between his brows. "Are we safe now?"

"Yeah. I think so, and you have some new friends." She winked at him. "And was that just a rumor you won a bicycle race yesterday?" A smile split his face, and for the rest of the meal, they talked of yesterday's birthday party and Makenna's playdate with Tina. Tara relaxed in the booth and let the children's animated voices soothe her.

Leftovers packed in a plastic bag, Tara herded CJ and Makenna out the restaurant door and into a blustery winter wind. Black clouds covered the sun. Few tourists blocked the sidewalks. Music and the scents of food escaped the restaurants and bars when the doors opened. "It's knocking me down," Makenna whined. Tara lifted Makenna and balanced her on her hip.

"Is it going to rain, Mom?" asked CJ. "We didn't bring an umbrella."

"If it does, let's hope it waits until we're home." They sped up. In front of The Palace, Tara set Makenna on the sidewalk, and they dashed up the steps. Before Tara could grab the handle, the door swung open, and Patrick Benton ushered them inside.

"Just in time," he greeted them. Tara raised her eyebrows in question, and he nodded toward the front door. She turned, and her mouth dropped open. A wall of rain blocked her view of the street.

CJ ran to the window. "Look, Mom, it's raining sideways."

"A perfect day for a hot drink, a sweet snack, and a good book," commented Patrick. "There's hot chocolate, hot apple cider, and mulled wine on the bar." He lifted a napkin from a plate on the front desk. "And I'm guarding the cookies." Chocolate chip, oatmeal raisin, and peanut butter cookies nestled together on the plate. He offered Tara a small tray.

Children settled in the library with books, cookies, and hot chocolate. Tara took their jackets and Manuel's leftovers and climbed the stairs. On the third floor, she opened the panel door and stopped. Two boys in sock feet and a large gray dog slid along the hallway and landed in a heap of arms, legs, and laughter. The dog barked. Boys and dog disappeared. *That's exactly what I want for CJ and Makenna, laughter and a safe place to play when it rains.*

Jackets hung, leftovers stored in the mini-fridge, Tara returned to the lobby. Comforting scents of cinnamon, cloves, and orange greeted her while Deanna Carter remembered her first taste of love like "Strawberry Wine." Perched on a stool behind the front desk, a mug in his hand, Patrick's blond head bent over a book. He looked up and nodded. Tara returned his acknowledgment, grabbed a mug from the bar, and filled it with mulled wine. She glanced in the library. CJ sat on the settee, engrossed in a book. Makenna slept, her head on his lap. Her courage restored by the sight of her children and the warmth of the mug, Tara returned to the lobby. "Patrick, do you have a minute?"

His head came up. He blinked. "What can I do for you?"

"Any idea when you'll open the law office?"

His brows drew together. "Do you need an attorney?"

She shook her head. "Not at the moment." She lay a brochure for her business on the desk. "Office space."

He picked up the brochure, and his blue eyes scanned the page. "Do you operate only online? Any face-to-face contact with clients?"

"Online and telephone contact exclusively. Clients have no idea where I am and don't care. It's the beauty of my business." *The perfect business for someone in hiding.*

Patrick nodded. "Okay. To answer your question, I'll probably open within a week, but I could use part-time help setting up sooner. Would you be interested in helping me set up if you decide to rent space?" At her nod, he slipped the brochure under the desk. "Stop by the office Monday about noon, and we'll hammer out the details."

"Thank you. I'll see you Monday."

Tara entered the library just as Makenna woke. "I took a nap, Mommy."

"Good for you. Let's put our dishes away, choose a game and a movie, and go upstairs. Looks like a great day for hanging out in our room." They trooped up the stairs as Lionel Richie crooned, "'Hello."

31

****

Puddles left by yesterday's storm glinted on the sidewalk. A cloudless blue sky stretched overhead, the cold air still. Stone steps leading to the front door of the Henderson building were dry and swept clean. A large yellow ceramic pot held pride of place beside the front door; a fern spilled out of the top. Two chairs stood beside a small table on the porch.

A deep, male voice shouting, "Come in," answered Tara's knock. Inside the reception area, the sun glinted on the polished wood floor. Other than a small rug in front of the door, the room was empty. Tennis shoes squeaking on wood heralded Patrick's arrival.

"Hi, Tara. Let's meet in my office." Patrick led her to a partially closed door, opened it, and offered her a chair.

An hour later, Tara walked out the door, a key to the office tucked in her purse. Tomorrow, as soon as she dropped off CJ and Makenna at school, Tara would wait in the law office for the furniture delivery and telephone and internet service. Her shoulders relaxed in relief, an office with access to a small kitchen and shared use of a conference room. Much better than she expected to find in Creekside. Not only was the office perfect for her business, but knowing Patrick would be checking in during the day was a relief. While she didn't need a bodyguard, knowing he was around made her feel safer.

Should she tell Patrick about Trey? Was she putting him in danger by keeping her secrets? Therapy after the assault convinced her nothing Trey did was her fault. He was an adult; he made his own choices. The drinking, drugs, and creepy friends had nothing to do with her. But did she miss the red flags she should have seen? She'd known something was wrong before he demanded a divorce; that's why she didn't tell him about her pregnancy with Makenna.

Makenna. She glanced at the time and lengthened her stride. Time to gather Makenna from preschool and head to Creekside Elementary. One excellent benefit to her new home, everything important was within walking distance. The only driving required so far was a birthday party at Jude Healy's fairytale house. How did a man who looked like he stepped from a book about lumberjacks or mountain men end up living in a house plucked from the pages of a fairy tale?

****

The glary overhead light barely penetrated the shadows in the stairway. Patrick's tennis shoes slapped on the bare wood, the only sound in the narrow space. He opened the door at the top and fumbled for the light switch. The space was clean and empty, no longer stuffed with leftovers from former Hendersons. Sunlight glinted through the sparkling windows. He marveled at the arrangement of rooms. He stood in a large room attached to a small kitchen on the West. On the east side, three doors stood open. The first led to a large room, possibly a bedroom. The second led to a bathroom. The third opened on a stairway. He climbed wooden stairs to a partial second story, including a loft and two small empty rooms separated by a bath. He leaned on the loft railing and pictured small children peering through the wooden rails at the adults on the first floor. Descending the stairs, the echo of a childish giggle followed him. He shook his head. Perhaps he spent too much time living in a hotel populated by spirits.

He touched the light switch beside the kitchen door and stopped. A young man dried dishes at the sink while a young woman washed, their voices quiet, words indistinct. The man set the dishtowel down and wrapped the woman in his arms from behind. She leaned back against his chest, and he nuzzled her neck. She sighed; her breath a soft *whoosh* in the quiet room. They disappeared. Patrick flicked the light switch. Scents of vanilla and cinnamon floated in the air of the empty room.

Patrick shut the lights off and climbed down the stairs to his office. If he turned the upstairs into an apartment for himself, would he trade one set of spirits, Victoria and her family, for another? Henderson didn't mention spirits when they negotiated the contract of sale. Either he never met them, or he thought Patrick wouldn't. As he placed a small stack of office supplies in the center of the reception area for Tara, the front door opened, and James sauntered in. "So you already have a tenant?"

Patrick rolled his eyes. "I won't ask how you know." He joined James at the door. "I'm ready to go home;. You can keep me company."

"At least she's pretty. That should improve your mood," James commented. His dark brows drew together. "And terrified."

"Do you know something I don't?" James shook his head. "So why do you think she's terrified?"

"The way she enters a room like she's expecting trouble. The way the kids stand behind her until she herds them ahead." They dodged a clump of tourists in front of Maggie's Boutique. "She channels the guy from that old spy show when she enters her room at the hotel, moves the kids against the wall before she opens the door."

"How do you know?"

James shrugged. "Went up to visit you and caught her in the hallway." As they climbed the steps to The Palace, James asked, "You don't think she's afraid?"

Patrick grasped the door. "Yeah, she's terrified."

Warmth, animated conversation, and Elvis Presley's mellow voice filled with passion claiming he "Can't Help Falling In Love" greeted them as they sauntered into Victoria's. Eric nodded a greeting and returned to serving wine to a couple at the bar. "Later," commented James. "I'm picking up my best girls." He ambled toward Nikki's apartment.

"Later." Patrick climbed the stairs. On the second floor, the familiar sounds of guests getting ready for the evening, the running showers, and voices muffled by the walls and doors surrounded him. He opened the panel door and climbed the stairs to the attic. Did Tara's fear mean Nikki was in danger? Couldn't do anything about that, a hazard of innkeeping. Alex would protect Nikki. He opened the panel door. Two boys and a gray dog raced down the hallway and landed in a pile of arms, legs, and laughter. The dog barked. They disappeared. Though he didn't miss the worry of single parenting a young boy, Patrick missed the laughter.

****

The front door of the Henderson Building propped open, Tara stood in the center of the reception area directing traffic. She'd agreed to help with the move-in and set up. The quicker the law office opened for business, the sooner she could use her new office. Plus, her generous landlord offered a free month's rent for her help. Win and win. The vendors arrived all at once, and the offices rang with the sounds of boots on wood floors as furniture, small appliances, rugs, office supplies, and technology found their way to a new home. The front door closed on silent hinges, the latch a small click. Movers gone, Tara stood in the center of the reception area and admired the polished gleam of old wood on the desk and the colorful glow from a Tiffany lamp on a side table. All that was left to do was put away everything. All? She grabbed a blade and slit open the first box.

In a rush of cold air, the door opened. Tara looked up and smiled at her landlord with the windblown hair.

"Looks good in here," he commented. "Did you get lunch?" The grandmother clock in the corner chimed the hour, one o'clock.

She shook her head.

Patrick strolled over, offered his hand, and helped her up from her seat on the floor. "Deli sandwich okay? Donaldson will be here in an hour."

They strolled to the deli. Patrick's large hand on the small of her back occasionally guided her around puddles. He opened the door and smells of spice, meat, garlic, and onion assaulted her. Tara's stomach rumbled.

At a table beside the window, they munched sandwiches, crunched potato chips, and sipped iced tea while discussing where things belonged in the office.

Sixty minutes later, Donaldson greeted them from the front porch of the Henderson Building and followed them inside. Patrick and the contractor disappeared upstairs, and Tara returned to unpacking. The reception area finished, and her office arranged; she texted Patrick she was leaving and slipped out the door.

Grateful for her warm jacket, Tara strolled toward the preschool, considering dinner possibilities. If she meant to make a home in Creekside, she needed to rent something with a kitchen and a little more space. As long as their favorites appeared regularly on the menu, CJ and Makenna didn't care if the food was homemade, frozen and microwaved, or bought in a restaurant. At least breakfast was different each day, thanks to Nikki's creative casseroles. Sighing at the mistakes that forced her to trade Grandpa's big family kitchen and three-story house for a hotel room, Tara climbed the steps at preschool. Chaos of sound greeted her, a combination of childish voices, hymns, and tennis shoes on wooden floors.

Later Tara sat on the edge of Makenna's bed, rubbing her daughter's tiny back. "Momma," Makenna whispered, "when are we moving again?"

"Why, Makenna, do you want to move?" Tara tucked the blankets tighter and stroked the hair from her daughter's forehead.

"No. I want to stay, but hotels are for a little while, not forever." Her eyes drifted closed. "Houses are forever."

Mckenna's eyes closed, and Tara listened to her breathing even. Yeah, hotels are for a little while, but for a while longer they were, according to her brother Owen, safer in this hotel.

After her shower, tucked under her covers, Tara texted Owen. —*Are we safe? Do you know anything?*—

His response: —*So far, according to his parole*

37

officer, Trey's still in California. But it's only been a short time. Please stay in the hotel.—

Tara slipped into sleep. During the darkest part of the night, she woke to the sound of laughter and a waltz played on a music box. In a shadowy corner of the room, Victoria danced, a young boy balanced on her feet. At the tune's final note, the boy giggled, and they disappeared, leaving the scent of lavender drifting in the air. Tara closed her eyes, determination her last thought as sleep claimed her. If Victoria could run a successful hotel and raise a son in a time when single mothers were an oddity, surely Tara was strong enough to raise her two children alone and keep them safe.

****

Strolling the streets surrounding the square, Tara admired the Valentine decorations in every business window. Hearts, flowers, and cupids danced across plate glass windows belonging to restaurants, bars, clothing stores, gift shops, and toy stores. Jackson's Real Estate boasted a heart wreath painted on the door, and a red neon heart lit the window of Edgeware signs. The Movie House marquee listed *Can't Buy Me Love, Love Story, The Spy Who Loved Me, Love Me Tender,* and *Falling In Love* playing on Valentine's Day and night. She climbed the steps to Henderson Building, dug out her key and the code to the newly installed alarm. Inside, she shut off the alarm and turned on the lights.

Tennis shoes squeaking on wooden steps broke the quiet. "Tara, that you?"

Tara recognized Patrick's voice. She took off her jacket. "Morning, Patrick." He stepped up to her, took her jacket, and hung it on the antique coat rack.

"Come on. I'll give you a tour of the upstairs before Donaldson shows up." He led her down the hallway to a panel door. He slid the door open, and she followed him up a narrow flight of stairs and into a large room. He flicked on the light. "What do you think?"

Specks of dust danced in the sunlight filtered through a French door, a standing Tiffany style lamp, the only furniture in the space, created a rainbow on the white ceiling. "It's amazing." She strolled to the French door and admired the Juliet balcony. "Did you buy the building to get a hold of *this?*" She turned in a circle, arm extended.

"I'd no idea what *this* was until I owned the building. The only time I looked at it, Henderson leftovers filled the entire space." She raised a brow in question. "Furniture, trunks, boxes, anything several generations of Hendersons weren't using but wanted to save."

They strolled through the space, and he opened doors, pointing out the individual rooms. "Did you have to clean it out?" She pictured him hauling years of odds and ends down the stairs.

"No, Henderson, his daughters, and sons-in-law took care of it." He led the way back downstairs. "Donaldson will use the outside stairs, but I didn't want you startled by the noise. He's starting this afternoon."

Tara strolled to the kitchen. Boxes stacked against a wall shrunk the small space. An hour later, the flattened boxes were in the recycle bin, coffee mugs, plates, and flatware dried in the small space dishwasher. A coffee maker and a pot for boiling water rested on the counter. She heard the front door open and dashed to the reception area. "Hi. May I help you?" Tara asked.

A young woman held out her hand, a smile lighting her face. "Hi. You must be Tara Wilson. I'm Catherine Jessup." They shook hands. "James sent me to set up the accounting program for Patrick. I've seen you at church and preschool. Our daughters share a teacher."

"Oh, that's why you looked familiar." Tara pictured a little girl with unruly brown curls and her mother's smile cuddled in the arms of Chance Pagent. "Hope, right?" Catherine nodded. "Makenna talks about her all the time. She's very jealous of Hope's big sister, the neighbor who draws pictures, and her dog."

"Hope's very quick to share everything she knows," Catherine admitted.

By one o'clock, the accounting program inhabited Patrick's laptop. The grandmother clock chimed. Catherine appeared in front of Tara's desk and suggested they go to lunch.

Seated in a booth at the Lone Star munching on chopped salads and warm rolls, the tension in Tara's neck eased as Lena Horne extolled the virtues of "Summertime" and Catherine entertained her with horror stories of house-training Ariel. Hope and Lily snuck the puppy into their beds at night, and sometimes, just like any baby, the puppy couldn't quite make it outside to pee.

Catherine asked Tara about living in The Palace and admitted she loved her little house but missed the breakfasts and Nikki.

At the Movie House where they would part, Catherine asked, "Noon on Saturday, we're having lunch at Eckie House, ladies and children only. Ronni and Tina will be there. Bring a dessert and join us?"

"Are you sure it would be okay? I've met Andrea only once."

"Of course it's okay. But let me ask Nikki to walk over with you since she'll be attending."

That night while Makenna watched a movie on the tablet and CJ worked through his math problems, Tara called Ronni.

"You should come," commented Ronni. "I'm glad Catherine invited you because that was next on my to-do list. If there aren't kids CJ's age, Nathan will come to get him. Nathan's giving Zack an art lesson that afternoon." Tara agreed to lunch.

Tara climbed under the covers and turned off the light. The full moon created slices of light and shadow in the room. From a corner drenched in darkness, a woman glided toward CJ's bed. Victoria. Tara held her breath. The woman reached out her hand, and CJ's brown hair ruffled as though touched by a breeze. Tara released her breath in a *whoosh*. Victoria looked up, winked, and disappeared. Apparently, the hotel's resident spirit held a fondness for little boys.

Chapter Five

Welcome to Creekside, Anabelle Lea. Anabelle Lea Curtis entered the world on February 25 at seven in the morning, the first baby born in Creekside since Statehood on February 14. She joins her mother, Margaret Curtis, at Eckie House. Momma and baby are both doing well. Welcome Home, baby Anabelle Lea and welcome to Creekside, Arizona.

~The Creekside Reporter February 1912

****

The welcoming scent of coffee, the calm tones of Tara's voice, and sunlight glinting on the antique wood floor greeted Patrick when he strolled through the front door of his office. He sighed in relief at the sudden change from chaos to peace. Today started with a frantic call from Nikki; could he handle the front desk? Baby Michelle was sick, and Eric had the morning off. He switched to a Palace polo shirt, leaving his dress shirt and his peaceful attic apartment behind, and loped down the stairs into chaos.

Michelle's whimpers filled the lobby with sadness, and Nikki struggled to comfort the baby and assemble breakfast on the bar. He shooed them away and barely finished the setup when the first guests trundled down the stairs to the sounds of "A Beautiful Morning" by the Rascals. Chatter, laughter, the clink of silver on sturdy glass plates filled the room. As he dashed between the breakfast bar and the front desk, he caught glimpses of Victoria hovering in the hallway outside Nikki's suite and then drifting to the front desk, peering over his shoulder. By the time he checked out the final departing guest, loaded the last of the dishes in the dishwasher, and made a check on Nikki and Michelle, the day was half over.

Clad once more in a dress shirt, he strode out the hotel's front door and raced to his office. He gave Tara a slight wave, which she answered with a grin, and he headed toward the kitchen and coffee. Scone in one hand, coffee in the other, he meandered through the reception area and strolled to his office and his second career of the day. Ensconced in a leather executive chair, he turned on the laptop to check his calendar and listen to voicemail. A pile of letters rested in his inbox thanks to his tenant, who sorted the mail. At the bottom rested a large manila envelope marked *personal*. The envelope bore an unfamiliar return address. Using a letter opener engraved with *PBJ*, a gift from James who thought the similarity to peanut butter and jelly funny, he slit the seal and dumped out the contents. A small book bound in green leather and a single-page handwritten letter tumbled onto the desk.

Dear Mr. Benton, Thank you again for your patience when my family and I cleaned out the apartment over the law office. It took far longer to sort and distribute several generations of left behind treasures than we expected. Please accept the enclosed copy of Practicing Law in Creekside, a Love Story. My grandfather complained the Henderson Building isn't furnished without the story of Micah and Margaret. Regards, Erin Henderson.

Patrick filed Erin's letter and lay the book on the credenza behind his desk. Hard to believe a law office was home to a love story and spirits.

"Hey, Scott, what's up?" Patrick asked as Scott plopped into the chair beside his desk.

"Grandpa's birthday," Scott answered.

"And you want to attend his party?" Patrick removed an invitation from his desk.

"Yeah. He's my grandfather. Mom emailed me asking me to attend."

"And?"

"And I want you to go with me so I can include Casey. I'd like her to meet Grandpa and Mom."

"Will Casey's parents be okay with that?" asked Patrick, grateful he had a son and not a daughter.

"If you chaperone, yeah."

"Ah, you're setting up a meet the family for your girl."

"Yep. You're willing to go, right?" At Patrick's nod, Scott rose. "Who's your date?"

"You and Casey."

"Thanks, Dad." Scott ambled out the door.

Patrick grabbed the elegantly embossed invitation, leaned back, propped his heels on the desk, and dialed the number to RSVP. Ambivalent about attending, he'd delayed until the last minute to respond. Would have sent regrets if Scott hadn't asked him to chaperone. Voicemail picked up, and Patrick left his message, Patrick and Scott Benton plus-one. He dialed James' number. "Hey, Bro'"

"What's up?" James asked.

"Can Scott, Casey, and I use your condo the weekend after next? Assuming you won't be using it."

"No problem. I'll be in Creekside. But you, Scott, and Casey seem an odd group."

Patrick ran a thumb over the invitation's raised letters. "Cyrus Morgan's seventy-fifth birthday party is Saturday. Scott wants to go and bring Casey."

"And since Cyrus is Scott's grandfather, you're tagging along?"

"Yeah. The third wheel, chaperone, whatever," he admitted. "At least it's at the Botanical Garden. Great scenery and no one will notice if I wander off."

"And a big enough venue you can avoid Amy and her latest husband. Which number is this one anyway?"

"Very funny. All I know is I was first and don't envy any who came after. Thanks for letting us use the condo." He disconnected and checked voicemail. Amy's terse command to call was followed by Whitney's polite request. He dialed the number for Amy. Voicemail. Left a message that yes, he and Scott would attend Cyrus's birthday party. If there was something else she wanted, call back. His return call to Whitney was answered on the first ring.

"Hi, Uncle Patrick."

"Hey, Whitney. How are you?"

"Good. Umm, Scott says you'll be in Scottsdale the weekend after next. Any chance we could meet Sunday for lunch or something?"

"Sounds good. The Sugar Bowl, Olive and Ivy or somewhere else?"

"Olive and Ivy, and can we eat outside?"

"Sure, I'll make a ten-thirty reservation, okay?" At her agreement, Patrick ended the call. Scott must have talked to Whitney before he asked Patrick about the party. He'd wondered about his father's other children and grandchildren. After all these years, it felt good to have at least one connection with the other family. Whitney, his half sister's child, his niece, Scott's cousin, and nearly the same age.

Personal business complete, Patrick shoved his cell phone in the drawer and used the office phone to return the next message. Tara's cheerful goodbye drew Patrick away from the notes regarding a revocable trust. He returned her goodbye, closed the file, and glanced at the clock. Three o'clock, she must be on her way to pick up Makenna. He placed the file into a desk drawer and locked it, signed off his laptop, and contemplated Scott's desire to attend the birthday party. Was it only a wish to keep a connection with his grandfather? A need to see his mother, introduce her to Casey? At least he liked Cyrus Morgan, no hard feelings. He found seeing Amy depressing, a glowing testament to his failure as a husband.

He slipped his cell phone into his pocket. Time to take another look at the upstairs apartment and make a plan. He rolled his chair under the desk, and the opening bars to Donna Summer's "She Works Hard For The Money" announced a call from Nikki. "Hey, little sister."

"Hey yourself. You on your way home soon?"

"I can be. What's up?"

"I'm supposed to be on the desk then open the bar, but Alex got called into work. Mitch and Colin are at practice. Can you cover for me?"

"On my way." He hung up, grabbed his jacket, and headed home. Home? Maybe that was his answer. He didn't need the apartment; he already had a home.

Chapter Six

You're invited! Faith Eckie and Margaret Curtis invite you to a celebration following the christening of Anabelle Lea Curtis on June 1, 1912, at noon. Lunch will be served in the Eckie House main parlor. Children are welcome at the reception. In lieu of gifts, please donate to the Creekside New Mothers' Fund.

~The Creekside Reporter

****

Flowers spilled from window boxes; their blooms barely open. Tara opened the gate to Eckie House and offered a cheery hello to Andrea and James, who shared the porch swing. Andrea lifted a bottle of wine and motioned Tara over.

"Can I interest you in a glass of wine? We've plenty and extra glasses," Andrea offered.

Tara hesitated.

"We're having a wedding conference, and I could use an ally." She nudged James' shoulder. "Can't convince James it's all about me because I'm the bride."

Tara started to shake her head.

"No, don't say no. I'll call Ronni and have her bring the girls, Nathan too if he's there. Time for Ella to wake up anyway." Ella, curled in a ball, slept on a blanket. Wine glasses marched across a table in two lines, three open bottles of white wine surrounded by ice, nestled in a plastic cooler. Bottles of red wine stood in a row on an end table beside James.

"What did you say you're doing?" Tara asked, noticing a plate of crudités on the table beside Andrea. "Having a party?"

"Not exactly. Planning a wedding reception, and we can't seem to make a decision." Andrea grabbed her phone and invited Ronni and the girls over. "We've narrowed it down to three each of red and white. Just need to pick one each for dinner."

James patted her on the arm and escaped through the front door.

"James thinks I should close my eyes and pick one." She shrugged. "They're all good."

James returned with a miniature table and three little chairs.

"Excuse me a second." Andrea picked up the now wide-awake Ella and hustled her inside.

"Perfect timing," James commented as Ronni, Nathan, Makenna, and Tina rounded the front. "Hey, where's Cameron?"

Bringing up the rear, Cameron trailed behind Nathan. "Yep." Nathan lifted his arm and dangled a large bag from his hand. "And apple juice, water, and the girls' snacks." He climbed the steps, set his bag on a chair, and swung each of the girls onto the porch accompanied by their giggles. Laughter and animated conversation floated on the air as adults debated wines and munched raw vegetables while children snacked and then played on the veranda with toys from a deck box nestled in the corner.

The sun began its slide toward the horizon, and they hauled everything inside, including chattering little girls and an exhausted dog. "Stay for dinner?" offered Andrea. "We've plenty."

As the sun tinted the sky with orange and pink, Tara waved goodbye from the front gate. Perched on Nathan's shoulders, Makenna grasped his hair and rested her chin on the top of his head, and they strolled through the quiet neighborhood. "While you didn't have to walk us home, we appreciate it." Tara flicked Makenna's fine hair off her forehead. "Your shoulder accessory is fighting sleep."

"Yeah, she very nearly landed a face plant in her dinner." He tightened his hold. "Jude driving CJ home tonight, or is it sleepover Friday?"

"Sleepover. Mom and The Palace can't compete with Zack, King, bikes, and an ATV," she admitted. "I'm grateful CJ's found a friend and an outlet for his energy."

At the steps to the hotel, Nathan lifted Makenna from his shoulders and handed her to Tara. "Want me to carry her upstairs?"

"I can walk now, Mommy."

Tara set Makenna's feet on the ground. "Guess not. Tell Uncle Nathan thanks for the ride."

"Thank you, Uncle Nathan," Makenna responded.

Nathan leaned over and kissed Tara's cheek, then Makenna's. "You're welcome." He turned around and strolled away. His dark head disappeared around a corner as the sun slipped below the horizon.

****

Coffee and a heady combination of cinnamon and sugar scented the air when Tara and Makenna stopped on the last step of the stairs in the morning. The Beatles' "Getting Better" competed with animated

49

conversation and the soft clink of silver against the dish. Makenna, balanced on Tara's hip, whispered, "Why do we always stop on the bottom step for a minute?"

Tara gazed into her daughter's brown eyes. "To find a place to sit, to see if anyone we know is here for breakfast."

"So not cause we're scared?" Tara's gut clenched. How to answer without frightening her four year old?

"When you go to lunch at preschool, do you look around for friends to sit with?" Makenna nodded. "Well, if some friends are here for breakfast wouldn't you want to sit with them?"

"Look, Mommy, Hope and Lily are over there." She pointed toward a table beside the window. Catherine glanced up from a conversation with Hope and waved them over. Tara set Makenna down with a sigh of relief and they joined Catherine. How could she help Makenna feel safe and secure? Should they have moved farther away, a larger city, maybe on the East Coast or out of the country?

As Tara took her first sip of coffee, Nikki Stark and Sam drew up two chairs and joined them. "Where's Michelle?" Catherine asked.

"Sleeping finally." Nikki took a monitor out of her pocket. "We were up all night." Nikki smiled at Makenna. "Good morning. Where's your brother?"

"At Zack's house. He got to have a sleepover so Mommy and me had wine at Miss Andrea's," Makenna announced in her piping voice.

Nikki raised an eyebrow. "You drank wine?"

Makenna shook her head, her curls bouncing. "No! Mommy had wine."

"Can Makenna come with us today, Mommy?" Hope asked.

"That's up to her mommy," Catherine answered and looked at Tara. "She's welcome to come. Sam and Lily are taking a trail ride and Hope is taking a very short lesson on the pony. Alex is driving Sam and Lily home later so we won't be gone long."

"Can I mommy?" Makenna piped up. "I've never been on a pony."

"Are you sure it's okay?" Tara asked Catherine.

"Yep. Hope's lessons are five minutes on a very gentle pony walking around the corral. We'll start the longer lessons this summer."

Coffee cup in hand, Tara lounged in an Adirondack chair on the hotel's front veranda, and Catherine's SUV disappeared around a corner. Saturday morning without children, house chores, or laundry, what should she do with a free hour? In Bisbee, Saturday morning meant laundry, house cleaning, grocery shopping, yard maintenance, and driving Makenna and CJ to lessons or playdates. Her cell phone announced a call from Owen with the introduction to "You'll Never Walk Alone."

"Hey, big brother, what's up?"

His sigh traveled across the air. "Not much. I'm sitting on my patio, coffee in hand, watching the girls climb all over the swing set like monkeys. Maybe gymnastic lessons would have been better than ballet."

"That's what Jen and I thought, but you insisted ballet was safer for your delicate little girls." She pictured Paige and Sophie hanging upside down from the swing set's top bar. "Their recital should be coming up pretty soon, right?"

"May. They're excited." He paused. "Tara, I rented

out Grandad's house."

"Are you sure that's a good idea? Trey knows about that house, it's probably the first place he'll look for me."

"I hope so. I rented it to a couple of guys on the force. Trey shows up there he'll go right back to prison."

"So you want me to stay here? Is it still safe?"

"Yeah. Alex is a good cop. Ronni and Nathan are there. How are the kids settling in?"

"Good. They've found friends, like their schools. Want a dog, but that's not possible yet."

Tara climbed the stairs. Trey was smart, clever, manipulative, and should have become an actor. He wore whatever personality made his life easier, got him what he wanted. He wanted the inheritance from her grandfather.

When they divorced and he discovered the money wasn't a marital asset, he vowed revenge. That's when she discovered a restraining order meant nothing.

She swiped the key against the electronic lock, turned the handle, and opened the door. Music in three-quarter time filled the room. A tall man, his red suspenders a slash across his white shirt, led a laughing woman in the waltz. With a flourish, the music ended. He wrapped his arms tight around her. Their lips met. They dissolved, leaving behind the scent of lavender.

Tara envied their joy in each other. Had she ever experienced joy with Trey? When they met, he romanced her with thoughtful little gifts accompanied by clever notes. He charmed her friends. After the wedding, everything changed.

Feet propped on a footstool, Tara relaxed on the

hotel's front veranda and waited for Catherine. A familiar black SUV slid into the parking space, the door opened, and Catherine popped out, a finger to her lips. Tara took the steps two at a time and stood beside Catherine as she opened the vehicle's back door. Her curls a riot, face streaked with dirt, Makenna slept in the car seat. "They crashed about ten minutes ago. One minute constant chatter the next silence," Catherine explained. Tara reached inside and lifted Makenna into her arms.

"Looks like they both had a good time," Tara commented as Catherine quietly closed the door. "Thank you."

"If you don't have other plans, come over about five-thirty. Chance is hosting a backyard barbecue using both our yards. Jude's driving Zack, so you could meet CJ there."

"Sounds good. What can I bring?"

"Just Makenna," Catherine answered as she climbed behind the wheel.

Five-thirty p.m., Tara met Nikki in the lobby and they strolled out the hotel's back door. Baby Michelle slept bundled in the stroller, Makenna's hands gripped the handles, shoving it forward with only occasional navigational correction by Nikki. "Will Sam and Lily be in time for dinner?" Tara asked as they strolled up the walk to Sanders House.

"Yeah, Alex will come back as soon as they've put the horses in their stalls. He's on very early tomorrow." Hope and Tina raced toward them, their faces wreathed in smiles. They took Makenna's hands and tugged her across the yard to a playset. Country music blared from speakers on the patio, competing with animated voices and barking dogs. Chance and James stood behind a grill in deep discussion.

A Frisbee landed in front of Tara's feet, and CJ appeared beside her. "Well, stranger, looks like you made it home after all," Tara commented, ruffling his windblown hair. "Did you have a good sleepover?"

A grin split his face. "Yeah."

"Good. Give me a hug, and you can go back to your game." With a quick hug, CJ grabbed the Frisbee and raced across the lawn, Cameron a white streak on his heels.

As the streetlights popped on, creating white circles on the sidewalk, Nathan and Tara strolled toward the hotel. "Thanks for walking us home again," Tara commented as they turned the last corner. "Makenna's going to believe you're more pack animal than uncle." Makenna, perched on his shoulders, giggled.

"My pleasure. James offered to carry Tina. Jude's hauling CJ and his stuff to the hotel. Alex showed up to walk Nikki home. Without you and Makenna, I'd feel superfluous."

"Mommy, what's superflus?" Makenna asked.

"It means extra, not needed," Tara answered.

"I need you, Uncle Nathan," Makenna piped. "I was too tired to walk all the way home."

They climbed the hotel's front steps. "Ah. There's the rest of our party," Tara commented as Jude's big truck drove into the parking space.

The back door opened, and CJ hopped out, backpack in one hand. The door slammed, Jude waved, and the truck drove away.

"Thanks, Nathan. It's time these two got cleaned

up for bed."

Nathan set Makenna on the porch and, with a wave, sauntered away and disappeared around a corner.

Children sleeping quietly in their beds, Tara let the shower's hot water ease her tense muscles. She turned off the water and stepped into the steam-filled bathroom. Wrapped in a white bath sheet, she stared at her cloudy reflection in the mirror. Using a wide-toothed comb, she straightened her long hair, gently untangling the knots. After months away from Bisbee, the blond highlights started about her ears and streaked like tiger stripes to the ends. Without the highlights for distraction, the premature white created obvious stripes against her ash brown hair. She shook her head at the reflection and used the hairdryer.

Cross-legged on her bed, dressed in flannel pajama bottoms and a T-shirt, she sipped a glass of wine. Her journal resting on crossed legs, she used a purple pen and created a gratitude list. The family and friends she'd found in Creekside, her children's laughter, the good schools, and a safe haven all made the list. Plus, a business she could operate anywhere and a warm-hearted landlord whose flexible attitude and protective nature provided a feeling of security. Wine finished, teeth brushed, lights out, she slid under the covers. To the sound of her children's even breathing, she fell into sleep.

In the darkest part of the night, she woke when something heavy landed beside her on the bed. Expecting CJ was sleepwalking again, she opened her eyes and stared into two sad brown eyes in the face of a very large gray dog. He laid his head on his paws, thumped his tail once, and closed his eyes.

Must be dreaming? She closed her eyes, and sleep claimed her.

Chapter Seven

My admiration for Faith Eckie grew each time we met. Her life's work supported women and children in need. Her most frequent legal issues involved building small houses on the twenty acres surrounding Eckie House and finding ways to legally transfer them to women and children living in Eckie House. Occasionally she arrived at our appointment accompanied by another woman, an Eckie House resident needing legal advice.

~Practicing Law in Creekside, A Love Story by Micah Henderson

****

"Morning, Patrick," Tara called as she entered the office Monday. The scent of coffee filled the air. Patrick's head appeared around the corner from the kitchen. "How was your trip?"

"Okay, but if anyone asks you, it's not comfortable staying in a condo for the weekend with your grown son and his girlfriend." He disappeared into the kitchen, and Tara followed. "But I think I was the only one uncomfortable."

"Why?"

He grabbed the carafe and poured coffee into two mugs. "I worried they'd want to sleep together. Unfortunately, I remember being twenty." He spooned sugar into one cup and handed it to Tara. "At twenty, sharing a condo with my girl opened all sorts of possibilities."

"Thanks." Tara accepted the mug. "They don't share an apartment at the university, right?

"No, and they were prepared to sleep apart on this trip. I wasted my time worrying. Scott took me aside and admitted Casey's dad told her she could go along only if they did not share a room." He grimaced. "God, I'm grateful to be the single father of a son. I'd probably totally mess up a daughter."

"Other than father panic," she teased, "was the rest of the weekend okay?"

"Yeah. I like my former father-in-law, and he's always been good to Scott."

Mugs in hand, they retreated to their respective offices. Patrick opened his laptop and reviewed notes for the next appointment.

At the party, Cyrus had taken him aside and detailed a trust set up for Scott. At least Cyrus agreed Scott couldn't access the assets until age thirty. Amy accessed her trust the day she graduated from law school. Until then, the trust paid reasonable college expenses, and Amy lived the life of most law school students, including shared housing, cheap meals, and cheaper entertainment. Cyrus paid for their elaborate engagement party, but Amy's trust allowed her a wedding to rival the royals because they wed one month after graduation. He'd loved the college Amy, believed their love was forever. The trust fund wife, he didn't recognize. Only the best for trust fund Amy. Expensive vacations, the trendiest restaurants, spa days, charitable events on the weekend.

Amy looked happy with her new husband.

According to Scott, they traveled the world for his job, she hadn't practiced law since they met, and his children lived full-time with their mother or were on their own. The first sight of Amy standing near Cyrus brought a familiar knee-jerk reaction, a mixture of fear and sadness. By the time he and Scott stood before Amy and Cyrus, the feelings disappeared. No more fear for Scott. His son was a man, not a boy and his relationship with his mother was his choice. Their marriage ended so long ago; grief for a lost dream was just a memory.

His appointment arrived, and the day slipped away in a familiar rhythm.

****

Cinnamon, sugar, and coffee permeated the air. Sunlight glinted through the plate glass, making streaks on the wooden floor. The Eagles advised that everyone "Take It Easy," and Tara, CJ, and Makenna waited on the bottom step.

"I don't see anyone we know," commented Makenna.

Plates filled, they settled at a table beside the window. The children's excited chatter provided a counterpoint to Fleetwood Mac's "You Make Loving Fun." Field trip to North Lake for CJ, and a visit from the fire department for Makenna.

Tara left CJ at the elementary school, and he disappeared inside the building. Makenna bounced in impatience, and they covered the distance to the preschool in record time.

At the door, Chance Pagent waited, one hand holding the door open, the other clasping Hope's hand.

"Morning, ladies," he greeted. "Excitement at

preschool today."

"Fire trucks are coming," the girls chorused.

"Walk to class, please," Tara reminded Makenna as she released her daughter's hand. Chance and Tara stood inside the door, and the girls speed-walked to their classroom and disappeared inside. With a wave, Chance dashed away, disappearing around a corner. Tara turned in the other direction and strolled toward the law office. When her fear subsided would she return to Bisbee or stay in Creekside? She missed Owen, Jen, and their children. She missed Grandpa's house though she didn't miss the constant repairs. What was best for CJ and Makenna? She climbed the law office steps and admired the arrangement of spring flowers perched on the table. Inside, the scent of coffee drifted through the room. Flowers clutched in both hands, she strolled to Patrick's office. "Morning, boss. Flower delivery." She set them on the corner of his desk.

"Morning, Tara." He yanked out the card and handed it to her. "They're for you."

"Oh." She opened the card. *Happy Birthday, sis. Love Owen.* She picked up the vase and strolled back to her office. She'd forgotten her birthday.

Noon lunch arrived from Rosa's courtesy of Patrick. Scents of tomato, basil, garlic, and onion filled the kitchen. They shared a feast of antipasto, bruschetta, salad, and spinach ravioli.

"You could have warned me it was your birthday." Patrick picked up a crostini decorated with fresh tomato and basil and crunched.

"Except that would have meant I remembered, which I didn't." She shook her head. "I didn't even notice the date when I checked my phone this morning, just noticed it was Friday field trip day."

"Will you take the rest of the day off to celebrate?"

"No. I will take a few minutes to make reservations for us at Manuel's. Mexican food for birthdays is a family tradition."

They finished lunch and worked together, clearing the kitchen.

"Thank you for lunch. Between you and Owen plus a birthday dinner with the kids, it's turning out to be an excellent celebration considering I forgot my birthday."

****

Arms full of Mexican food leftovers, Tara, CJ, Makenna, Nathan, Ronni, and Tina strolled toward the hotel, expertly dodging clumps of tourists near the square.

"Thank you for inviting us to your birthday party, Tara," Ronni commented as they neared the hotel. "Let's plan on a repeat for my birthday."

"For me too, mommy," Tina piped up.

"I thought you wanted a party with ponies and gifts," Nathan responded and lifted her into his arms.

"I do. I want both."

At the hotel's front steps, they exchanged hugs and birthday wishes. Tara, CJ, and Makenna slipped inside. Then, with a final wave, Ronni and Nathan strolled away with Tina as a passenger on Nathan's shoulders.

Climbing the steps, Makenna gave a piping recap of the birthday dinner and what she wanted for her birthday. When they stepped from the stairway to the attic hallway, Tara spotted an envelope taped to their door. She signaled the children to wait at the stairway and glided silently to the door. She yanked the envelope from the door and took out a birthday card. When she read the signature, she opened the door, flipped on the light, and signaled the children to follow.

"What is it, mom?" CJ asked, a frown marring his handsome face.

Tara gave his shoulder a gentle squeeze. "A birthday card from Nikki and The Palace Hotel."

Tara slipped the gift card for a bottle of wine from Victoria's in her wallet and propped the birthday card on the mini-fridge next to Owen's flowers.

Someday would they be able to accept surprises without fear? CJ still had nightmares occasionally. The therapist warned they may always haunt him. She wondered if their flight from Bisbee, the roundabout road trip to Creekside brought them back.

Children tucked in, Tara, dressed in boxer shorts and a baggy T-shirt, sat cross-legged on the bed and texted Owen a photo of her flowers and the card with the message:

—*Loved the flowers. I forgot my birthday but enjoyed the day anyway. Miss you all.*—

She turned off the lights and slid under the covers.

****

As dawn peeked into the room through the lace curtains, Tara woke to a woman speaking encouraging nonsense, a smile in her voice. In the corner of the room, Victoria kneeled on the floor, her blue gingham skirt pooled around her, arms stretched out. A few steps away, a man, his back to Tara, held the hands of a small boy balanced precariously on little feet. The man released the child's hands. With a squeal, the boy toddled the few steps to Victoria, who drew him in for a hug. The man's deep laughter floated in the air, and they disappeared.

Tara warmed at the reminder of her children's first steps and drifted back to sleep. Her last thought before sleep claimed her that some kinds of love did last forever, and a parent's love topped the list.

****

Sun bathed the attic room in a golden light, and Tara, dressed in jeans and sweatshirt, hustled her children out of bed and through their morning routine. "Hurry, hurry, it's Saturday, and we have so much to do."

They slipped out the door and navigated the stairs, Tara whispering reminders to walk softly. On the last step, they stopped as The Sandpipers crooned their intention that "Come Saturday Morning" the fun would begin.

As they filled their plates, CJ asked, "Why are we so early? We're almost the first ones here."

"It's Saturday, and we have a list of adventures for today."

A frown crossed his face. "Like what?"

"First a ride out to Windsong to talk to Becca about riding lessons. Then to Ronni's to arrange photography lessons, and then—"

"What?"

"And then the fair on the square this afternoon with games and food." Tara sat back and sipped her coffee. "A very busy day."

A short time later, they drove out of town onto a two-lane road that ran beside fields encircled by white fences. Makenna chattered, describing her one visit to Windsong in minute detail, the ponies, horses, smells, cats, and dogs. Turning under an arch inscribed with *Windsong*, a floating W, and a treble clef, they bounced along a dirt road to a large white house; its windows sparkled in the sun. Four big dogs instantly surrounded the car. Becca's shrill whistle split the air, the dogs silenced and trotted onto the porch.

Tara turned in her seat and faced CJ and Makenna. "A couple of rules before we get out." They nodded. "No running, do everything Mr. or Mrs. Mathews tells you. Got it?" They nodded. "Let's do it."

By noon, CJ's spring schedule included riding lessons on Saturday and photography lessons on Thursday after school. On Tuesday, Tina and Makenna would start dance lessons after school, accompanied by Nathan. Tara hoped when, or if, Trey showed up, they'd be such a familiar part of the town's fabric no one would think of them as that frightened woman with two children. Makenna was part of her disguise since Trey didn't know she was pregnant when he assaulted her, and Makenna's birth certificate proclaimed father unknown.

Makenna's hand clasped in one hand and the blanket tucked under her arm, Tara sauntered toward the Spring Festival at the square. CJ led the way, looking over his shoulder every few seconds to check on their progress. Darius Rucker's "Come Back Song," played by a cover band, competed with conversation and the happy squeals of children. Pungent scents of pizza, grilled meats, barbeque, and spicy tacos caused Tara's stomach to grumble.

They crossed the square; their progress slowed by greetings from friends. As planned, under an oak tree sat Ronni and Nathan. Unplanned, Jude, Ainsley, Catherine, Chance, Patrick, James, Andrea, and Nikki surrounded them. Tara released Makenna with an admonishment to stay with Tina and Hope.

As she spread her blanket, Zack joined them and led CJ toward a pick-up kickball game. "Looks like I've been deserted. Perfect time to find some food."

Catherine popped up from where she leaned against Chance. "I'll go along. Chance, please keep an eye on the girls." He nodded. The band moved into Kenny Chesney's "No Shoes, No Shirt, No Problems."

Tara imagined a world with no problems but couldn't get the idea into focus. She sighed.

"You okay?" Catherine asked.

"Sure. Just trying to picture life without problems." She admired her boots and shrugged. "I'd miss my shoes anyway." They laughed.

In the next few minutes, they gathered an assortment of food, pizza, salads, hamburgers, sandwiches, tacos, burritos. They spread the food on a blanket, and to the powerful strains of The Eagles' "Take It To The Limit," the children appeared, herded by Chance, James, and Jude. Patrick held Michelle on his lap. Parents cleaned small hands and faces using baby wipes and sanitizer, food was distributed, and as the band played Josh Turner's "Why Don't We Just Dance?" Tara prayed they were safe a while longer.

The spring air cooled as the sun started its descent. Tara folded the blanket and gathered her children. Nikki slipped Michelle into her stroller, and Patrick offered Makenna a piggyback ride.

With farewells, they strolled away from the square. Sam and CJ led the way, their conversation a mix of a recap of the day and questions about Windsong from CJ. They entered the hotel through the back door, and Nikki, Sam, and Michelle disappeared through her sitting-room door. Tara led the way upstairs.

When they arrived at the attic, Tara commented, "Makenna can walk now." She lifted Makenna from Patrick's arms and placed her on the floor. "Thank Mr. Benton, Makenna."

"Thank you, Mr. Benton." CJ took her hand.

"You're welcome." Patrick walked toward his door.

At the sound of Patrick's handle turning, Tara nodded toward CJ. Grabbing Makenna's hand, CJ led them back to the stairway door. Tara unlocked the door and flipped the lights on as she shoved it open. She signaled the children, and the three of them disappeared inside.

****

At the click of his neighbor's latching door, Patrick slipped inside his apartment. James had it right; Tara channeled the guy from that old spy TV show when she entered her hotel room. She kept the children away from the door with ready access to the stairwell, and CJ carried his cell in one hand, his sister's hand grasped in the other. Her fear explained her need to live in the attic. The door at the top of the stairwell locked on the stair side, accessible only with a room key. Only three rooms in the attic, his apartment, Tara's room, and the empty room Nikki hadn't rented since Tara moved in. No strangers on the third floor.

He stripped and climbed into a hot shower. Who or what was his neighbor afraid of? Who knew the answer? Definitely Alex, maybe Nikki, but Chief Alex never shared secrets.

Dressed in a blue Palace polo shirt and dark jeans, Patrick took the stairs two at a time and arrived at

Victoria's at exactly five o'clock p.m. He flipped on the bar lights bathing Victoria's portrait in a soft white glow and shining a small spot on the word *Victoria's*. He gave the bar a final wipe, and moved an Easter basket filled with chocolate eggs and guarded by a small, white rabbit wearing a blue jacket, yellow vest, and red bow tie to the front desk. Lionel Richie admitted he was "Running With The Night" just as heels clicking on wood floors announced Victoria's first customer.

When he closed the bar at nine-thirty p.m., Patrick lowered the music's volume as the Beach Boys extolled the virtues of being "In My Room." He strolled the hallway to Nikki's sitting room and tapped twice. A grinning Mitch opened the door, greeted Patrick, and escaped into the hallway. Patrick strolled toward Nikki, who slowly rocked a Michelle-sized bundle in her arms.

"Evening, sister dear." Patrick leaned over kissed her cheek and the top of Michelle's head. "She wasn't interested in sleep tonight?" He plopped onto the loveseat.

"Oh, she fell right to sleep after her bath, but her sore gums woke her up." The rocker's rails whispered against the thick rug.

"Good night in the bar, guests, visitors, and locals. The chocolate's gone."

She shrugged. "Of course, who can resist chocolate? What brings you to visit me tonight? Not only a bar report."

He shook his head. "What do you know about my neighbor?"

"Not much. She's divorced, two children, a brother named Owen, and my husband asked that I not rent the empty attic room to anyone I didn't personally know."

"Did he say why?"

"No, and I did ask. If she's still here in May, I'll put Scott up there and rent out his room. May to September, I need every room." She shrugged. "What do you know?"

"She's an excellent tenant who channels a secret agent when she returns to her room."

"Yeah. James mentioned that. Obviously, she's scared and waiting for the other shoe to fall."

Patrick unfolded his lanky body from the love seat, gave her another cheek kiss, and commented, "Let me know if you find out anything else. I like her, and it'd be easier to offer protection if I knew what was going on." He slipped out the door.

Chapter Eight

Autumn leaves danced down the sidewalk. My favorite client should appear in a few minutes, and I contemplated what legal issue brought her out on this breezy fall day. Filtered sunlight turned the polished wood floor into a river of honey. The silver fountain pen she gave me on my birthday glinted. Through the window, I watched her climb the steps, another woman at her side. I dashed to the door and yanked it open, welcoming her inside. My breath stopped. Faith Eckie grasped my hand; her warmth drew my attention back. "Micah Henderson, this is Margaret Curtis." I must have offered them chairs because, in the blink of an eye, they sat before my desk. Hopefully, I offered tea. Most of that meeting is a blur, not because it was so long ago. Because one smile from Margaret Curtis and I knew this moment, the moment we met, would change my life.

~From Practicing Law in Creekside, A Love Story by Micah Henderson

****

Raindrops bounced on pavement, dripped from trees, and created miniature rivers flowing beside the sidewalks. Patrick gazed through the front window of the Henderson Building's upstairs apartment at a black umbrella sporting white polka dots weave around puddles and approach the front steps. The umbrella climbed the steps and disappeared under the porch overhang. Inside the apartment, a discrete bell chimed the opening notes of the Sandpipers' "Come Saturday Morning," warning Patrick the umbrella's owner was inside the office. Patrick flicked off the lights and slipped down the stairs and into his office.

A moment later, Tara peeked her head in and wished him good morning, her hands cradling a mug of coffee.

"Morning. Please, sit down."

Tara set her mug down and slipped into the chair beside his desk.

Patrick looked into her questioning eyes and realized he was nervous. He should be. He'd never asked a tenant or neighbor on a date. He hated the awkwardness when things didn't work out. "My brother's getting married."

Tara nodded.

"I'm his best man."

She nodded again.

"Would you like to go with me as my plus-one?"

"Um."

"No, wait," he stopped her. "Whatever your answer won't affect your lease. This is not coercion. If you say yes, you'll sit beside me at dinner. If you say no, my brother, soon-to-be sister-in-law, or my sister will choose my dinner partner." He grimaced. "I hate that. The women are always perfectly nice but have perfectly reasonable expectations I won't meet."

Tara frowned. "Expectations?"

"Yeah. That there will be calls, texts, a follow-up date." He shook his head. "Not going to happen, especially with friends of my family. When things don't work out, and they never do, everyone is angry with me." He smiled. "If you go with me, we'll have a good time. You already know the main players and a number of the guests. Monday, I'll come to work, you'll come to work, and things will return to normal." He shuddered. "Can't picture you sending me texts asking when we can get together again."

"So you are asking me to accompany you to avoid a setup date?"

Patrick nodded.

"Because setup dates never work for you?"

He nodded, again.

She picked up her mug and sipped, set the mug down, and admitted, "I was invited to the wedding. I'll go with you, and I would never see an invitation from you as a threat to my lease." She picked up her mug, rose, and disappeared through the doorway.

****

By the time Tara slid under the covers, the rain stopped, and the moon glinted through lace curtains creating a snowflake pattern on the wood floor. She chuckled at Patrick's nervous stammering when he invited her to be his plus-one. Obviously, he didn't make a practice of asking his tenants or neighbors out. Creekside was a small town, so dating someone local was risky, could cause hard feelings, and damage his reputation. It wasn't a date, just one neighbor helping another avoid a potentially awkward situation. Still, it was as close to a date as she'd had since the divorce, almost five years ago. Progress. Almost a date, like their lunch on her birthday was almost a date.

In Bisbee, she'd avoided dating, going out with friends in groups when she was ready. The men she might have been willing to go out with were friends. In a small town, a date created expectations, and she didn't have any expectations. For so long, her dreams were limited to a walk in the neighborhood without looking over her shoulder, a night's sleep without nightmares. The combination of therapy and her brother finally let her feel almost normal.

She turned off the light and fell into sleep. In the moments before dawn, she woke to voices in a whispered argument. Tara stilled and forced her eyes open. Beside the window, Victoria, RJ balanced on one hip, faced a tall man.

Her voice filled with regret, she said, "We can't. If we go out to dinner in Creekside as a family, the news would get back to your family in a blink. Plus, the good people of Creekside know I have a lover because of RJ, but I'm not going to rub the fact in their faces."

His voice pleading, "Then let's go to Prescott. Take a trip together. I'm not ashamed of us."

Victoria handed RJ to the man and wrapped her arms around them both. "Never ashamed. But your family won't accept our decision, and you know it. They'd pick and pick at us until we gave in, or you cut yourself off from them. Right now, they know nothing about RJ."

"My brother knows."

"Yeah. But Welles is special, the most tolerant man I've ever met." Victoria stepped out of his arms. "Come on. Dinner is set up in my room."

"Oh, Vicky. All I want is us to be a family."

As they disappeared through the wall, Victoria whispered, "We are a family. Just not the usual family."

Tara slipped toward sleep. Her last thought, she

and Victoria had something in common. Their families were not the usual family since hers consisted of a brother and his family and her ex-husband's step-siblings. The scent of lavender drifted through the room.

****

The warmth of the sun caressed her shoulders; a flirty breeze teased her hair, plucking it out of the low ponytail as Tara strolled to her office. Early today, few tourists waited in line outside the restaurants for breakfast or blocked the sidewalks in clumps. Nikki's sons offered to walk CJ to school, Catherine volunteered to escort Makenna to preschool. Her phone vibrated. She glanced at the caller ID. Chief Alex. She climbed the front steps, unlocked the door, and shut off the alarm. Her purse stored in the desk drawer, Tara made coffee and waited for the first cup. She accepted procrastination was her game plan; any text from Chief Alex meant bad news. Coffee with two sugars cooling on the corner of her desk, Tara called the Chief.

"Morning, Tara. You at the office?" When she agreed, he announced he was on his way, "Be there in a couple of minutes."

Tara's stomach cramped. The front door chime yanked Tara away from her circling thoughts.

"Tara." Alex nodded. "You alone today?"

"Patrick will be here in a little while," she answered. "I'm a little early."

Alex slid into the chair beside her desk. "Owen called me this morning. Trey missed an appointment with his PO. He called in that he was sick. PO's been around a long time, and PO had a gut feeling, so he did a surprise visit. No Trey."

Tears dripped down her cheeks. "What does that mean? Where is Trey?"

"Don't know. PO called him; Trey claimed he stayed with friends who offered to take care of him while he was sick." Alex shook his head. "Not where he claimed. PO's put out a warrant." He took her hand. "They find him; he's going back to jail."

Tara's mind ran in circles. Were they safe here, unsafe? Run or stay? "What should I do?"

"You leave; you could be running toward him rather than away. Creekside's a good place to hide in plain sight." He handed her a tissue. "You could confide in Patrick. Might be safer for both of you if he knows what's going on."

She shook her head. "He's my landlord. I'm not his problem."

Alex rose and released her hands. "Up to you. I'll let you know if I hear anything else." With a wave, he sauntered out the door.

Tara blotted the tears and straightened her spine. No more tears over Trey. She needed to come up with a plan B if Trey showed up. A way to keep CJ and Makenna safe. She grabbed a yellow legal pad and started a list just as a rush of cool air entered the office along with Patrick.

"Morning, Tara," Patrick greeted as he poked his head into her office. "What did Alex need?"

"A moment of my time," Tara answered and looked up into his concerned blue eyes. "No big deal." She slid the yellow pad into the desk drawer. "Coffee's on, and Nikki sent over cookies." Patrick headed to the kitchen. Tara focused on solving billing issues and updating her calendar, comforted by the sound of

Patrick's voice on the phone from his office.

Tara felt the sensation of being watched and looked up.

Patrick stood in front of her desk. "It's my birthday. Let's go to lunch." They locked the office and strolled in the spring sunshine to Wellingtons.

Tara teased him about his advanced age, birthday presents in the form of cookies, and a lunch date with his tenant for celebration. He retaliated with a reminder that at least he remembered his birthday. He understood anyone not wanting to give away their age, but no way would he object to family offering gifts. For a brief while, Tara relaxed, forgot to worry about Trey. When Patrick put his warm hand against her waist, guiding her inside the restaurant, Tara recognized the spark of desire. Ahh, so that part of her wasn't quite dead.

He teased her about Mexican food for birthdays, and she asked, "So what are you doing for dinner to celebrate?"

"Birthday dinner at Eckie House with the whole family." He shook his head. "James drove up this morning since he loves reminding me I'm an old man."

"There's not much difference in your ages, right?"

"No. But he hated being younger. Always coming in second, second to start school, switch to middle school, start high school, learn to drive. He hated it so much my mother arranged for us to attend different high schools."

"Were you a hard act to follow?" Tara asked, imagining living in the shadow of a handsome older brother. She and Owen were five years apart, so it didn't seem to matter that he was first.

His brows drew down in a frown. "Is there a good

way for me to answer that? If I say yes, you'll think me arrogant. If I say no, you'll wonder why since I am older."

She chuckled. "Well, since you put it that way, I retract the question. I was never competitive with Owen. Probably because we're further apart. What about Nikki?"

"Nikki was and still is her own person. James and I changed from seeing her as a fragile doll to protecting her. There were a great many heated conversations where she claimed we were smothering her."

"I felt that way about Owen sometimes," Tara admitted. "I guess it's a younger sister thing."

They finished lunch and strolled to the office, dodging people stopped in front of window displays and waiting in line at ice cream shops and restaurants. "Thank you for sharing my birthday lunch, Tara."

"Thank you. Your birthday, and you wouldn't let me buy."

"Hey, you picked up the tab for dessert; that was more than enough." Patrick opened the door and shut down the alarm. "It was great to have company," he admitted as he strolled down the hallway to his office.

At three o'clock, Tara called goodbye to Patrick with, "Happy Birthday!" and strolled toward the preschool. What was it like to have a crowd for dinner on your birthday and know that each guest had a claim on you as a connection? Her family included Jen, Owen, their children, and her children. Though their connection was slim, she considered Nathan, Ronni, and Tina family. When she was safe, would she return to Bisbee or stay in Creekside?

Her children retrieved from school, their

assignments reviewed, dinner consumed, and baths taken, Tara settled next to Makenna on the bed. Together they read the counting book. Makenna counted monsters, chicks, puppies, kittens and commented about what kinds of pets they would make. She wanted a pet desperately, as she explained every single day.

When Makenna's eyes closed, Tara kissed her forehead and picked up CJ's book from the floor where he dropped it when he fell asleep. She turned down the lights.

Shadows filled the corners, the antique furniture bulky, black shapes. Makenna whimpered in her sleep, then her breath settled into a soft snore. Cross-legged on the floor, Tara focused on her breath, her eyes closed, and she counted the inhales. All her relaxation rituals failed tonight. Her heart pounded, and her muscles stiffened. As a last resort, she changed into a nightgown and poured a glass of red wine.

Settled in the comfortable reading chair, sipping wine, she let the circling thoughts about Trey's possible location take over. Subtly, she changed her thoughts, moving them from today's worries to this moment's blessings.

The quiet room, her children's even breathing, smooth red wine slightly sweet on her tongue, and a small town filled with friendly neighbors, family, and benevolent spirits. Wine finished, she crawled between the sheets and drifted into sleep.

A heavy weight landed beside her on the bed. She forced open one eye. At the foot of her bed lay a large gray dog, his head resting on his paws. Smokey. Tara closed her eyes and returned to sleep.

Chapter Nine

New School Opening–Monday Mary Beth Easley, a graduate of Bryant & Stratton College, will accept applicants for the Easley Secretarial School. Courses taught include typing, shorthand, business letter writing, basic bookkeeping, and office etiquette. The admissions office, located next door to The Opera House, opens at nine in the morning.
~The Creekside Reporter May 5, 1914

****

Click of boot heels on the wooden floor, and Chief Alex appeared in the doorway of the library. Tara looked up from her novel.

"Hey, Tara," Alex greeted her. He sauntered into the room, his teenage sons Colin and Mitch following.

Mitch settled in a chair beside CJ at the library table. Makenna, her lips moving silently, reciting the words to her favorite picture book, looked up when Colin settled on the arm of her chair. The boys greeted her children. Mitch offered CJ help with his math homework, and Colin asked Makenna questions about her book.

"Do we need to talk, Alex?" Tara asked.

"Yeah," Alex answered. "Step into the lobby?"

In the lobby, animated conversation joined The Zombies' lament that "She's Not There." Alex drew out a chair for her beside a small table near the front desk.

Tara's stomach clenched, tension tightened her shoulders, and she dropped into the chair. The minute Alex settled across from her, she asked, "What is it, Alex?"

"Trey showed up for his PO appointment armed with letters from a doctor and some friends confirming his location and illness on the date of his missed appointment. The PO canceled the warrant."

"What's that mean?"

"Trey's back on parole, same rules as before." Alex shrugged. "Illness is a legitimate excuse for missing an appointment."

"Still think I should stay here?"

He gazed into her eyes. "Yeah. Stay alert, but at least for now, it appears Trey's decided to play by the rules a while longer."

The final notes of "Turn, Turn, Turn" echoed in the stairwell as Tara hustled her children up the stairs.

Following the rules? Trey? Tara shook her head. If he'd followed the rules outlined in the order of protection, her life wouldn't be haunted by fear. He threatened and harassed while the lawyers negotiated termination of his parental rights, division of the property, and all the other details demanded by divorce. He wanted everything, her trust, CJ's college funds set up by Grandpa, all the equity in their house. The attorneys convinced him no judge would approve a one-sided settlement, especially one that took money from children. He ended up with half their assets, nothing of the trust, nothing from the college funds, and no responsibility for CJ's support because he signed away his parental rights.

One week after the divorce was final, he forced his

way inside her house. She woke in the hospital, determined not to be blindsided again. At the top of the stairs, she touched the key to the electronic lock and opened the door. A quiet, empty hallway lit by wall sconces welcomed her. Holding hands, CJ and Makenna stopped at the stairway door. CJ grasped the cell phone in his free hand. Tara slid the electronic key against the lock, opened the door, and flipped on the light. Silence. She signaled her children, and they trooped inside.

****

Steam from the hot shower filled the small bathroom, frizzed the ends of Tara's hair, and misted the mirror. White-knuckled grasp on the vanity, Tara grimaced as the muscle spasms in her back sent shocks of pain up and down her right side. It hurt *so* much. Familiar pain, but definitely not a friend. She focused on tightening and releasing the muscles in her core. The steam dissipated; the room cooled, but the pain continued. Back spasms. A knock on the door.

"Momma, I need to go."

Tara tightened the belt on her red bathrobe and opened the door. "Okay, Makenna." She forced tiny steps, breathed deeply against the pain.

CJ looked up from stuffing papers into his backpack as she lowered herself carefully onto the chair. His eyebrows drew together in a frown. "You okay, Mom?"

She shook her head. "Please get me the pills from the top shelf and my phone."

He hauled a chair in front of the closet and lifted down a small box. Then he grabbed her phone from the charger.

80

Tara texted Patrick she wouldn't be in and called Nathan, who promised to walk CJ and Makenna to school. As Nathan hung up, her cell chimed with a text. "CJ, please open the door for Mr. Benton."

Patrick stepped inside the room. "Good morning. Thought I'd offer to walk CJ and Makenna to breakfast."

Another spasm pulsed in her back, and a tear escaped. Not exactly the professional image she wanted Patrick to see. She flicked the tear from her cheek, sucked in a breath, and slowly exhaled, consciously relaxing each muscle.

She gazed into Patrick's concerned blue eyes. "Thank you. That would help. Nathan will be here in time to walk them to school."

While the children gathered jackets and backpacks, Patrick used the little kettle provided in the room and brewed a pot of tea.

As the door clicked shut on Patrick and the children, Tara took the muscle relaxer and sipped her tea. Hot sweet tea and the pills soothed her muscles, and the spasms stopped. Carefully, she set the mug down, grabbed the chair's padded arms, and propped herself up. Taking slow, careful steps, she traveled the short distance to the closet.

This must be what walking on eggshells feels like.

She slid underwear, jeans, and a sweatshirt from the drawers, making her choices based on what was easiest to reach and put on, no fashion statement today. Grasping the back of the chair for balance, she dressed and slid into the chair, exhausted.

The room spun, a result of the pills. She leaned her head against the chair's tall back and closed her eyes. A soft knock and familiar voice woke Tara. Disoriented, she glanced around the room, and the door opened.

"Did I wake you?" asked Nikki, who entered holding a basket on one arm. "I've brought brunch." She cleared the teapot and cup from the side table and set out a cup of coffee, a bottle of water, buttered toast, a small dollop of peanut butter, a serving of breakfast casserole, and a small bowl of fruit. "Patrick said you seemed in no condition to navigate the stairs." She shrugged and plopped down on the desk chair. "I had the breakfast and front desk today, so I waited until everyone left and brought you brunch."

"That was so nice of you. Where's baby Michelle?"

"Andrea's. Alex dropped her off on his way to work." Nikki popped up and flitted around the room. "I told Patricia not to clean in here today in case you were sleeping. I'll straighten up and make sure you have everything you need." She made the bed, fluffed the pillows, checked the bathroom. "Patricia will deliver fresh towels and change the sheets tomorrow, but for now, at least you can chill in an orderly space. Be right back." She strolled out the door and returned seconds later with replacements for the tea and coffee and clean hand towels. "Do you need me to call a doctor?"

Tara shook her head. "The spasms happen sometimes, so I have everything I need."

Nikki withdrew a card from her pocket. "My cell number is on the back. If you need anything or change your mind about the doctor, call." She gathered the dishes from brunch, wiped off the table, and, with a wave, disappeared through the door.

Tara propelled herself up, struggled three steps to

the bed, and carefully lay flat on the colorful quilt. She lifted her cell phone and checked the time. The first notes of "Sail Away" announced a call from Ronni.

"Hey, Tara, how are you?"

"Better, but moving very slowly."

"Nathan will pick up CJ and Makenna and deliver them here after school. We'll return them to you after dinner. Should we bring you dinner?" Ronni asked.

"Thank you."

"Are you sure you don't need a doctor? Not being able to get downstairs is pretty frightening."

"Tomorrow, I may be able to carefully traverse the stairs. For sure by the next day. Between the pills and the exercises, I usually feel pretty good in a couple of days."

"Do the spasms happen often?"

"About once a year, sometimes less. I'll be fine. Thanks for taking care of CJ and Makenna after school."

Tara carefully set the phone on the bedside table; the movement sent another spasm into her back. She settled the soft quilt over her body and closed her eyes. The pills didn't take away the pain but made her brain fuzzy enough she could ignore the spasms and relax. She floated in the twilight world between sleep and wakefulness. The mattress dipped, and a weight landed against her leg. She forced open her eyes. Stretched his full length against her leg, his head resting on his paws, Smokey breathed what sounded like a sigh and closed his eyes. Tara's heavy eyelids closed, and she slid into sleep.

Chapter Ten

After our first meeting, I noticed Margaret Curtis everywhere. Sunday Services became both pleasure and pain. I arrived early and waited in the Narthex until the mothers and children from Eckie House arrived. It allowed me an opportunity to greet Mrs. Eckie and smile in acknowledgment at the women she'd brought to the law office over the two years. Rarely could I focus on the liturgy or the sermon; my attention always caught by Margaret Curtis.

~Practicing Law in Creekside, A Love Story by Micah Henderson

****

From behind the front desk, Patrick watched Tara gingerly descend the final stairs to the lobby. CJ and Makenna followed, holding hands. Tara stopped on the last step and surveyed the busy lobby. CJ beside her, they walked to the bar, filling their plates with breakfast. A guest joined Patrick at the front desk, and he worked through the check-out process. Judging by Tara's careful movements, she wasn't quite free of pain. The lobby door chimed, and Nathan bounced in. With a brief nod toward Patrick, Nathan grabbed a mug of coffee and plopped into a chair beside CJ. The children carried their empty dishes to the bus cart and headed up the stairs with Nathan.

Patrick refilled his coffee and joined Tara. "How

are you feeling?"

"Much better, thank you." Tara sipped her coffee. "Made it down both flights of stairs and managed breakfast, so I know I can make it to the office."

The chatter of children and shoes on the wood floor announced Nathan's return.

"Mommy, Uncle Nathan tied my shoes. They need to be super tight today because we have races on the playground," announced Makenna in a piping voice.

Patrick rose as Tara handed out kisses and hugs to CJ and Makenna with a final admonishment to listen to Uncle Nathan and have a good day.

As Nathan and the children trooped out the door with a wave, Patrick offered, "If you wait a couple of minutes, I'll walk you to work." When Tara agreed, he dashed to the stairs and disappeared.

****

A soft breeze teased the flowers into a slow dance. Bright sunlight glinted on sparkling store windows, and the delicate green of the grass in the square contrasted with the bright white of the gazebo. Patrick and Tara strolled through town. Patrick shortened his stride to match Tara's careful steps. "I appreciate the escort, but you don't need to wait for me," Tara commented. "I will get there eventually."

Patrick shrugged and took her elbow when they stepped off the sidewalk to cross the street. "No worries. Never hurts to slow down and enjoy spring." They moved to one side of the sidewalk to let a jogger pass. "That is why I moved here, to slow down a little."

"I gather practicing law in San Diego was a rat race. That's a disappointment. I always picture San Diego as one long beach vacation, sun, sand, surf, and time to lounge under an umbrella." They climbed the three steps to the law office front door.

Patrick unlocked the door, turned off the alarm, and held the door for Tara. "Beach vacation is only true if you are on vacation. Not the same when you're a single parent with a busy law practice." He helped Tara take her jacket off and hang it up. "I'll make the coffee." He strolled to the kitchen.

By the time he set a mug of coffee and a bottle of water on her desk, Tara barely acknowledged him, her focus consumed by whoever was on the phone and the laptop's screen. Patrick strolled to his office and groped for the light switch. He stopped. In the shadowy corner, a couple embraced. The woman drew away; the man slowly released her. In a whisper, he asked, "Is that a yes?" She shook her head, turned, and glided toward Patrick. A warm rush surrounded him. She disappeared. Patrick glanced at the corner. The man was gone.

Patrick plopped into his chair and picked up *Practicing Law In Creekside*. As his fingers touched the green leather binding, the phone rang. He answered, and the workday began. No time for distractions from embracing spirits or love stories. While he worked, a part of him wondered about the spirits. The man was probably Micah Henderson, but who was the woman? He'd barely started reading *Practicing Law in Creekside,* so he wasn't sure how the story ended.

Patrick walked his final appointment for the day out to the reception area. As they passed her office, he glanced at Tara and grimaced. She looked exhausted; while her voice still held its smiling tones, her eyes looked a little glassy. She typed something into the computer and wished the client good day. When she set the phone down, her lips turned into a frown.

"Let's go home," Patrick suggested when he stopped at the office.

She gazed at him with tired eyes. "But there's still much to do."

"Yep, and it will be there tomorrow."

When they left the building, Patrick took her elbow on the stairs, then offered his arm for support. She shook her head. "Thanks, but it's better if I take it slow on my own."

Patrick matched his stride to hers. They wandered through town. "I gather Nathan's picking up CJ and Makenna?"

"Don't know what I would have done without Ronni and Nathan. CJ and Makenna are invited to dinner; again. They may object when they're forced to eat with only me."

"Tough for you to compete with the Stephens' household?"

"Oh, yeah. Ronni is an expert at 'kid food,' and the family includes a dog. Much better than eating in a hotel room with mom. Plus, Ronni always sends food for me home with the kids, so CJ has no guilt about being away from me at meals."

"CJ feels guilty if he doesn't eat with you?" Patrick asked as they turned down the last block toward the hotel.

"Yep. CJ feels responsible for me, wants to take care of me." Her brows drew together in a frown. "I don't know if that's normal oldest child or a result of our shared past."

"Maybe both?" Patrick shrugged. "James and Nikki frequently accused me of trying to be their father.

I can't tell you whether it's because our father left, I'm the oldest, or if it was my take-charge personality."

"Or all three?" Tara teased.

He nodded. "Or all three." He took her elbow, and they climbed the stairs to the hotel lobby.

"Thanks for the escort, Patrick." Tara climbed the stairs.

Patrick watched her slow progress until she made the turn at the landing. He wanted to pick her up and climb the stairs with her in his arms. She wouldn't allow it, of course. They were landlord and tenant plus neighbors. His attraction to her was moot. He wouldn't act on it. He hoped their relationship headed toward friendship. Sometimes, he felt a near overwhelming need to protect Tara and her children. Not a feeling he understood. They weren't family. Family in his case included a herd with little to no blood relationship. Didn't mean the bond wasn't as strong. He strolled down the hallway to Nikki's suite and knocked softly.

The door swung open, and Nikki greeted him, "Hey, brother. You're home early. Law office closed for a mental health day?" She ushered him inside. Michelle sat in her bouncy chair, a not quite toothless grin lighting her face.

Mitch, Colin, and Sam, surrounded by books and papers spread across the table, looked up and chorused, "Hey, Uncle Patrick."

Patrick returned the greeting and plopped onto the sofa. "You bartending tonight, Nik?"

"Yep, and before you ask, Alex is working. But I have all this wonderful help with baby Michelle, so we're covered." Groans came from the table of boys. Nikki chuckled. "They're not thrilled with being responsible for baby sister, but it's good for them."

Patrick popped up from the sofa. "Well, if you don't need me, think I'll chill in my room. There's a game on."

"Not so fast." Nikki grabbed his hand. "Can you man the bar for a while, about eight o'clock, so I can check on Michelle and say good night to Sam? If I take too long, can you close for me too?"

He shrugged. "Sure. After all, I almost got a chance to offer to take your shift, but you have it covered." He kissed her cheek and sauntered out the door.

****

Streetlights in front of the hotel competed with the encroaching dark. He arrived at the lobby bar early, hoping they'd have a few minutes to chat before Nikki hustled off to put Sam to bed and check on Michelle. When Patrick joined her in the lobby, her face split in a mischievous grin.

"You're early. Excellent." Before he could protest, she handed him the register key and strolled down the hallway.

Patrick's mood lightened at the sight of a familiar blonde head at the door. "Hey, Shelby. How's the newspaper business?"

Shelby perched on a bar stool, a young man on the stool beside her. "Hi, Patrick. You remember RJ Wyatt?"

"Of course." Patrick shook the offered hand. "How's the research going, Professor?" Patrick poured their wine. Shelby and RJ leaned toward each other, shoulders touching.

"Slow but good," RJ answered. "Someday, *The*

Reporter will be digital but not yet. Picture a basement stuffed with boxes filled with old newspapers. Each box marked only with a year."

Shelby tapped RJ lightly on the shoulder. "Hey, at least the boxes are marked with a year."

RJ turned toward Shelby. "I am grateful for the year." He grinned. "And that's not all I'm grateful for." Shelby blushed.

"What yanked you away from all those piles of back copies and into Victoria's?" asked Patrick.

"Wanted to share something with Nikki. Thought she was on tonight."

"You just missed her. She's putting the kids to bed." Patrick walked to the end of the bar and poured wine for other guests. Then, he circled the lobby, gathered glasses, and offered drinks.

By the time he returned behind the bar, Shelby and RJ stood by the front door. With a wave, they stepped outside. RJ took Shelby's hand. Their blond heads glinted briefly as they passed under the lights, then they disappeared. Patrick appreciated the couple's obvious affection. He enjoyed his one date with Shelby almost two years ago. Her intelligence and enthusiasm brightened a meal that could have been one more boring business dinner. He glanced at his reflection in the window. Yep, Shelby made that one date fun, but she also made him feel old. Patrick loaded the last wine glass into the dishwasher under the bar, as Nat King Cole announced, "The Party's Over."

Patrick glanced up at the sound of the front door's tinkling chime. "Hey, James. Andi toss you out?" he teased.

James leaned against the bar. "Yep. Ella's asleep,

and Andi needed one more hour to finish her current project." He nodded at Patrick's silent offer of a glass of wine. "Correction, one hour without any distractions, including me."

"Everything ready for the wedding?" Patrick asked as he flipped off the lights spotlighting Victoria's, grabbed a glass of wine, and signaled James to follow to the library. They plopped into club chairs.

"Guess everything I can do is done. Andi's working on the children's activities tonight." James sipped his wine. "There may be as many children at our wedding as adults."

"You okay with that?"

James shrugged. "I'm okay with whatever Andi wants. Anyway, quite a few of those children are relatives. I didn't see how we could leave them out." James' shoulders slumped.

"So what's wrong?" Patrick asked.

"Andi's mom sent her regrets. She's not attending."

"Is Andi upset? Was she surprised?"

James shook his head. "No, she wasn't surprised but disappointed." He set the wine glass down and faced Patrick, his dark brows drawn together in a frown. "How does a mother see anything is more important than her daughter's wedding?"

"Sorry. I've no answer to that one. Never could understand Amy's priorities, and I lived with her for years. Mrs. Hamilton's so far outside my expertise it's like she's an alien being."

"Oh yeah," James agreed. "Well, apparently, that alien being is no longer Mrs. Hamilton. Included with her regrets was a marriage announcement. She's now

Dorothy Marie Phillimore, and the happy couple will be on a honeymoon in Europe on our wedding day."

"So not only is Mrs. Phillimore not attending the wedding, she chose an impersonal method to let her daughter know she married," Patrick commented and cringed at the pain in his brother's eyes. "And there's nothing you can do to fix this for Andrea."

"Not a damn thing I can do." James tossed back the rest of his wine. "Except return home and offer myself as a distraction." He handed the empty glass to Patrick and loped out the door.

As Patrick placed the wine glasses in the bar dishwasher, Victoria's warm presence materialized at the end of the bar. "I'll bet you were a good mother. You keep comforting orphan Bentons seventy years after death."

A smile briefly crossed Victoria's face. With a nod and a slow wink, she disappeared.

Chapter Eleven

Graduation Reception–The graduating class of Easley Secretarial School cordially invites you to a reception in celebration of our graduation. Mrs. Faith Eckie, Miss Mary Beth Easley, and friends are hosting the reception at Eckie House tenth of June nineteen hundred and fifteen. Adeline Edwards, Margaret Curtis, Hope Jackson, Rose Mosely, and Madeline Stephens completed the required coursework for certification as Executive Secretaries. The ceremony begins at two o'clock with a reception following.

~The Creekside Reporter

****

Setting sun streaked the sky with crimson and orange. His sister strolling beside him, Patrick breathed the scents of spring, new grass, and the perfume of flowering fruit trees.

"Nik, will Alex join us at the rehearsal dinner?" Patrick asked as they meandered away from the business area onto a residential street.

"Yep. Alex and the children," Nikki answered as they dodged a young skateboarder on the sidewalk.

"Ahh. So a large rehearsal dinner after all. Not what James told me a while ago."

Nikki shrugged. "Rehearsal will be small, but hard to invite only one member of a family to dinner. One reason Alex and I avoided a rehearsal dinner."

"Makes sense, except you replaced it with an adult after party."

"And Andi replaced the after party with brunch the day after the wedding. She wanted one more chance to hang out with everyone before the guests left town."

Patrick opened the front gate of Eckie House and motioned Nikki ahead. "Weddings sure have changed in the last twenty years."

"True, but I think some of it is our ages. When I married Aaron, children at the wedding and reception were the last thing on my mind. Scott was the only child in the family. By the time I married Alex, we had three children between us, and most of our friends have children."

As Patrick touched the doorknob, the door swung open.

"There you are. You're the last ones," Andrea commented as she ushered them inside.

Patrick strolled past the staircase and glanced up in time to watch a young girl, her braids flying behind her, slide down the banister. When she reached the final stair, she disappeared, leaving only giggles floating in the air. Didn't matter who Andrea invited to the wedding; looked like the spirit children planned to attend.

They gathered with Pastor Tim, who opened with a prayer of thanksgiving for friends, family, and the greatest gift of all, love. Patrick stood between James and Scott. Andrea's brother, Drew, walked his father's friend Virginia to her chair in the first row and moved beside Scott. The rehearsal zipped by. Spencer walked Andrea down the aisle. Baby Ella, fourteen months old, in his arms. In a piping voice, Ella insisted she could walk. When Spencer set her on her feet, she toddled to James, her voice ringing with "Dada, up."

Informal rehearsal dinner in the formal dining room, Patrick drew out the chair across from Scott. "Where's Casey?" he asked, nodding toward the empty chair on the other side of Scott.

"She took Ella to bed. Carly and Whitney tagged along to help."

"Let's see. That's your girl, your half-cousin Whitney, your soon-to-be half-cousin Carly and your soon-to-be cousin Ella." He shook his head and sipped the wine. "This family gets more complicated by the day."

"Yea. Complicated but still less weird than Andrea's family. Where's Aunt Andi's mom?"

"On her honeymoon." Scott winced. "Does that sound familiar?"

"Yep." Scott stared into his father's eyes. "Do you think Mom will show up when I graduate college or get married?"

"No idea. She did show up for Cyrus' birthday and your high school graduation."

Scott looked down at his plate. "Doesn't really matter. It's times like this I miss Grandma. She would have been here for Aunt Andi."

The chattering of young female voices stopped their conversation. Casey plopped into the chair beside Scott after greeting Patrick. Carly and Whitney took the chairs across from Patrick. He asked about Ella, and dinner continued with anecdotes from the girls describing Ella's antics as they dressed her for bed. Casey leaned against Scott's shoulder. Scott took the hint and placed his arm on the back of Casey's chair, his fingers resting on her shoulder.

Sometimes Patrick worried about Scott's relationship with Casey. Their youth frightened him; people could change drastically between sixteen and twenty-two, dreams shifted. Scott planned two internships with hotels in Flagstaff next year. After working in a large hotel, would he return to Creekside to work the summer for Nikki? If he returned, would the reason be a desire to work for his aunt or because Casey returned home for the summer?

"Hey, Uncle Patrick, okay if we sit here?" asked Nikki's son Mitch as he set his plate on the table and drew a chair out. At Patrick's nod, Mitch, Colin, and Sam plopped into chairs.

"Where's your dad and Michelle?" Patrick asked.

"Dad's at work. We handed Michelle off to Nikki," Mitch explained as he cut his steak. "It's her fault we're late."

"Nikki's?"

"No, Michelle." He grimaced. "Dad changed her before he left, but I changed her again before we left."

"She was stinky," Sam piped up, a disgusted look on his face.

"Good job cleaning her up before passing her off," commented Patrick.

Mitch shrugged. "She's my sister, embarrassing to show up at a party with a stinky sister."

Scott drew Mitch's attention away with questions about the baseball team. They might be an unusual blended family, but Patrick admitted it said good things about the blend that a teenage half brother willingly cleaned up his baby sister before passing her off to his step-mom.

****

Black velvet sky filled with stars, and a crescent moon greeted them as Patrick and James stepped off the front porch of Eckie house after the rehearsal dinner.

"So she tossed you out the night before the wedding, bro?" teased Patrick.

"Yep," James responded as he opened the gate. "It's kind of awkward sleeping with Andi when her dad's staying at the house anyway."

They strolled down the quiet street. "Really? Even though the wedding's tomorrow?"

James nodded. "Yeah, but awkward doesn't stop Spencer from sharing a room with his girlfriend, Virginia."

"Could have been worse. Andi's mom might have ended up under the same roof if she decided to show up."

"Awful thought." James shuddered. "You're bringing your tenant to the wedding? Thought you didn't mix business with personal stuff."

"Hey, I'm continuing with tradition. My assistant Constance was my plus-one to all the weddings involving members of the law firm and their families. She was the perfect plus-one."

"But Constance is more than twenty years older than you, and no one ever considered there could be a personal relationship. Tara is younger and good-looking." They climbed the steps to The Palace; James entered the code on the door and yanked it open. "You don't think arriving at a wedding with Tara will cause talk?"

Patrick shook his head as they climbed the stairs. "Nope. I'm just a nice guy who offered to accompany a woman and her two kids to a wedding. After all, she was attending anyway."

At the attic, Patrick slid open the hallway door. "Good luck with that. Anyway, don't forget the ring tomorrow. That's your most important job. I expect perfection."

Keeping a straight face, Patrick placed his hand on the doorknob and looked over his shoulder. "Didn't you hear? I lost it." James' eyes widened then narrowed to slits.

"You lie, and that's not funny."

Patrick shrugged. "You're right. I lie." He stepped inside his room and closed the door.

On his wedding day to Amy, in the groom's room at the country club, James, his best man, frantically patted his pockets, a horrified look on his face. He couldn't find the ring. A quiet knock on the door, and their mother glided inside.

"What's wrong, James?"

He admitted he couldn't find the ring. She slipped her fingers into her tiny purse. She took his hand, held it palm up, and dropped the ring in his palm.

"You gave it to me so you wouldn't forget it." She went up on her toes and kissed James' cheek. Then she wrapped Patrick in a hug.

Twenty years later, he could still smell the perfume she wore, feel the warmth of her arms around him, and hear her whispered, "Be happy."

His cell phone chimed; he glanced at the screen. From James: —*Guess I deserved that. Thanks for the memory.*—

Across the hall, Tara tucked the sheet around Makenna and rescued CJ's blankets off the floor, the children's even breathing a comfort. A few minutes ago, rumbling male voices in the hall startled her until she remembered James' plan to spend the night before his wedding in the hotel. Tomorrow they'd walk to Eckie House early with Patrick. He'd do whatever best men did, and she would entertain Tina, leaving Ronni and Nathan free to focus on the photographs. She crawled between the covers and flipped off the lights.

As she drifted toward sleep, memories of feelings flitted through her heart. The giddy sensation of believing love would last forever. The warmth of a lover's arms in the night. The all-encompassing love the moment the doctor placed CJ in her arms. Those first years with Trey, the engagement, wedding, pregnancy, and CJ's birth, she lived in a happiness bubble.

On CJ's third birthday, the bubble broke. Trey didn't show up for the birthday dinner. She sensed the pity rolling off the other parents. Trey sauntered through the door at midnight, drunk and with no apology.

The next months were a roller coaster, sober Trey one day, drunk the next. Broken promises, missed appointments, mornings she woke he still wasn't home. Then it was over.

Tara inhaled and released the breath in a slow exhale. Starting with her toes, she consciously relaxed each muscle until her body melted into the mattress. She drifted into sleep.

A shift in the air woke her. She glanced around the shadowy room. Smokey stretched across the foot of Makenna's bed, his big head resting on his paws.

Beside CJ's bed stood Victoria; her hand reached

toward his mussed brown hair. His hair ruffled as though touched by a gentle breeze. Victoria slowly dissolved. Tara closed her eyes. Good to know a couple of spirits watched over her sleeping children.

****

Cell phone's chime startled her as Tara swiped mascara on her lashes. A glance at the screen announced Patrick waiting in the lobby. She responded with:

—We're on our way.—

"Let's go, CJ." She yanked open the door and hustled CJ toward the steps. At the bottom of the stairs, she stopped. "Wow. A whole lobby filled with handsome men."

"Thank you, Mrs. Wilson," chorused Mitch and Colin.

"Makes me feel like a rock star with my own entourage," she commented as James, wearing a classic black tuxedo, opened the front door, and they trooped onto the veranda and down the steps. Her arm looped with Patrick's, they strolled toward Eckie House. "Best man duties included accompanying the groom and your nephews to the wedding?"

"Yeah. Promised Andrea I'd keep James from showing up too early." He shrugged as they strolled away from the center of town toward the residential area. "Figured waiting for you, CJ, Mitch, and Colin would work as a delay. Wished The Palace had a gym to work off some of his nerves. We ran this morning, but he still drove me nuts with the pacing."

Surprised by James' nerves, Tara asked, "Is he nervous about the wedding?"

"Not so much nervous as anxious. He's ready for

marriage, ready to officially begin this chapter as husband and father," Patrick answered. "Nik and I didn't believe he'd ever marry, and now he can't wait."

Patrick opened the iron gate to Eckie house. "Why wouldn't James marry?"

As they climbed the porch steps, Patrick answered, "That's a story for another time." He held open the front door, and they crossed the threshold to pre-wedding chaos.

Chapter Twelve

On a bright June afternoon, I strolled from the law office to Eckie House. For months at the end of each workday, I refined the plan. By the time I left the reception, I planned to have Margaret's agreement to become my Executive Secretary. The door opened immediately at my knock, and the plan disappeared.

Gazing into familiar hazel eyes, I stumbled through my congratulations. Margaret's smile lit the room as she welcomed me to Eckie House. For the next two hours, I struggled to focus on conversations with other guests. My eyes constantly returned to Margaret as she meandered about the room accepting congratulations, making the guests feel welcome. As I turned to leave, Faith Eckie offered her escort to the door.

She followed me onto the front porch. "Micah, are you ready to hire a secretary?" she asked before I could thank her again for the invitation. I admitted hoping to talk with Margaret. "Then I'll send her to you for an interview on Monday, shall I?"

~Practicing Law in Creekside, A Love Story by Micah Henderson

****

Purple shades of twilight peeked between the trees as night descended. Darius Rucker claimed tonight was "History In The Making" as Spencer twirled Andrea about the floor for the father-daughter dance.

After the first verse, James and Nikki joined them, and within a few moments, the dance floor filled. Definitely history-making, James getting married. Until he fell in love with Andi, James' longest relationship lasted a couple of months. Patrick admired their courage. It's not like James and Andi were raised in homes with great examples of loving marriages, but they'd promised each other forever.

"Hey, Patrick." Catherine Jessup greeted him with a hug. "Did you lose your date?"

"Yep, she's on the dance floor with Jude Healy. What about you? Where's Chance?"

"On the patio with his twin." She nodded toward the French doors leading to the dining room. "I stay far away when Ainsley gets that look."

Patrick spotted the twins on the patio. "Are they bickering?" Patrick asked as Chance grabbed Ainsley's hands.

"As usual. Guess it's a twin thing. Ainsley's not happy with her brother, the artist, right now."

"Any particular reason?"

"A painting he gave her to sell at Serendipity. She's refusing to hang it in the shop. Instead it's hiding in her apartment."

"Thought Chance's paintings sold almost as fast as Ainsley hung them," Patrick commented as he filled a wine glass and offered it to Catherine. "What's wrong with this one?"

"Remember the picture of James and Andi at Drew's wedding? Ronni captured exactly what they felt for each other, right?" Patrick nodded. "Well, Chance's painting is like that; only the subject is Ainsley." Catherine placed the empty glass on the table. "Oops.

He's headed this way; think I'll drag him out on the dance floor and dissipate some of his frustrated energy before we head home."

Patrick leaned down and kissed her cheek. "Good luck with that plan." Whitney Houston's "I Wanna Dance With Somebody" blasted from the speakers.

Catherine met Chance halfway and drew him onto the dance floor, where they disappeared into the crowd. Jude guided Ronni onto the floor, and Rose and Nathan joined them. Guess the picture taking was over for a while.

Patrick ambled over to Tara and led her onto the floor. Her emerald dress floated around shapely legs; blonde curls danced in the moonlight. Why did he think taking her to the wedding a good idea? It wasn't a date, but when they sat next to each other and talked during dinner, then danced, it felt like a date. He did not mix the business and personal, ever.

Unfortunately, spending time with Tara away from the office increased his attraction. He liked her sense of humor and witty observations. He liked her laugh and the way she looked in the dress. Knowing Ronni danced nearby reassured him. Ronni couldn't catch his revealing expression without her camera. James and Andrea appeared beside him.

"Great party, Andi. Is your next career wedding planning?" Patrick teased.

"Only if I can afford to hire half the town to help me. This was definitely a group project." They danced away, blending into the crowd.

At the song's last notes, they left the dance floor. The DJ announced the cake cutting, dessert to follow. Ronni and Nathan appeared beside the dessert table, cameras in hand. Pictures taken, Nikki and Catherine appeared behind the dessert table, cut the cake, and arranged slices on small plates.

Patrick grabbed plates of cake, added a couple of tiny chocolate cheesecakes and mini eclairs from the dessert table. Tara retrieved Irish coffees from the coffee bar, and they strolled to a table. He drew out Tara's chair and plopped into the one beside her. Tara lifted her fork, cut off a small piece of cake, and slipped it inside her mouth. Her eyes closed, and a quiet moan escaped.

"That is so good. Tastes nothing like wedding cake." She forked up another bite, lifted it to eye level. "More like a cloud or something. Who made this?"

Internally Patrick groaned. First the flirty emerald dress, then the look of ecstasy when she bit into the wedding cake. Could be difficult seeing Tara as strictly neighbor and tenant on Monday.

Alex and Nikki joined them before Patrick could respond. "Grandma's Bakery," Nikki interjected. "Is it too wonderful for words?"

"Oh yeah," Tara commented. "I didn't think the bakery did wedding cakes."

Nikki took a bite of cake; her expression softened, eyes drifted shut. "It's even better than the sample Clair gave us." She cut off another piece and slowly placed it in her mouth. "Clair agreed to make and frost the cake, but no decorating. Not her thing."

"The cake was beautiful, elegant." Tara's eyebrows drew down in a frown. "Who decorated it?"

"Ainsley and Jude. He made the topper. Ainsley did everything else," Nikki admitted as she forked up another bite of cake. "Only Andrea could manage a couple of artists as cake decorators and a couple more as photographers. Andrea wanted as much local participation as possible. The wine is from White Cloud, food from local restaurants and caterers, and the desserts all Grandma's Bakery. Only the groom was from out of town."

"Hey," Patrick responded, "James is local. He owns part of your haunted hotel. That makes him local." Alex leaned over and whispered in Nikki's ear, stood, and with a nod, strode away. "Where's Alex off to?"

"Work. Lots of interrupted meals when you're police chief of a small department." She sipped her wine. "You up for walking your sister home?"

"Always. Where are your children?" Patrick asked.

"They're at Beth's with everyone else's children. Mitch, Colin, and Beth are supervising at least eight children, including a couple of babies. There is going to be a crowd hiking the few blocks to Beth's when the party ends."

"Times like this I'm truly grateful the only child I'm responsible for is swaying to Bette Midler's "The Rose," arms around his girl, and perfectly capable of getting himself home," Patrick commented as he spotted Scott and Casey on the dance floor.

"So how's that working for you? The not worrying?" Nikki teased.

"It's easier when he's in Flagstaff. If I can't see the way he looks at her, I can't worry about it. What about you? I hear Mitch has a girlfriend."

"That's already ended. It's hard to watch your kid hurt," Nikki admitted. "Who knew stepmothers could feel their children's pain."

Patrick took her hand. "Maybe not all stepparents, but we were programmed to feel for others, to empathize. Had the very best teacher."

"Yeah. Our mom." She gazed into his blue eyes. "And not one of us would change a thing."

Andrea's brother, Drew, joined them, "Hey, Andi wants one more picture of the wedding party. Leave the plates and head to the meadow."

Under a full moon and a black velvet sky punctured with stars, Nathan tugged the bridal party into a semi-circle of couples around James and Andrea. Ronni flitted between the couples, giving directions. Nathan stood behind the video camera tripod. Ronni planted herself beside Tara and Chance, outside the circle.

"Let's do this, then we can all get dessert," quipped Nathan.

The first notes of Elton John's "Can You Feel The Love Tonight" filled the meadow; the couples bowed to their partners, James and Andrea waltzed three steps and spun in a circle. At Nathan's cue, the others followed. The meadow filled with graceful dancers, flowing dresses, and laughter.

Patrick held his baby sister in his arms and asked, "Do you remember when?"

"I do," Nikki answered, "I remember learning to waltz with my feet on yours and Mom calling out the counts. And I remember James partnering Andrea and his mumbled complaints."

Patrick twirled them across the grass. "Well, he was eighteen, and she was twelve, to him a pesky child."

They drifted through the other couples and twirled

beside the bride and groom. "He's no longer complaining." At the music's end, the dancers drifted away, leaving the bride and groom locked in an embrace.

Patrick and Catherine joined Tara and Chance at the edge of the meadow. Patrick glanced over his shoulder at James and Andrea and stopped.

At the edge of a swath of moonlight, another couple waltzed in the meadow. A small cloud drifted by the moon, changing the shadows, and the couple disappeared. Of course, George and Faith Eckie wouldn't be able to resist a waltz in the moonlight.

Patrick shrugged. After all, they were here first. He wished for James and Andrea a love like Faith and George, love strong enough to last beyond death do us part.

A full moon, the scent of new grass, and early spring flowers carried on a soft breeze, a stroll through a quiet neighborhood. Perfect for romance, except Patrick strolled beside Chance Pagent. In front of them, Nikki, Tara, and Catherine chattered, reliving the excitement and romance of the wedding. The ladies' dresses floated in a colorful dance, Catherine and Nikki in shades of pink and Tara's emerald green counterpoint. Romance and Tara in the same thought, not a good idea. Patrick recognized the signs of physical attraction, the tightening of muscles, the need to stand close. The admiration for a pair of trim legs and a bright smile. Inappropriate attraction for a tenant, a single mother living with fear.

Nikki's mother-in-law, Beth Stark, opened the door before Nikki could knock. She ushered them inside. An animated movie played quietly on the television, children sprawled across a colorful rug and the overstuffed sofa. Mitch, Colin, CJ, and Zack played a card game on the coffee table. As they hustled the herd out the door, the rumble of Jude's truck announced his arrival. With a cherry good night and thank you, Zack raced to his uncle's truck and hopped in. At the corner, Catherine, Hope, Lily, and Chance waved goodbye.

Sam pushed Michelle in the stroller; Mitch walked beside them, Colin beside CJ. Patrick offered Makenna a ride, and they strolled toward home.

With a quiet "Good night," Nikki herded her crew into the owner's apartment.

Patrick, Makenna asleep in his arms, climbed the stairs behind CJ and Tara.

At Tara's door, she took out her key card and turned toward Patrick.

"Let me," he said, taking the card from her hand. He tapped the lock, opened the door, and flipped on the lights. He placed the card into Tara's hand and led the way into the room. Gently, he placed Makenna on the bed. "Thanks for being a great almost date. Good night." He disappeared through the door, closing it with a soft thud. In the hallway, he paused until the deadbolt slid home with a click.

Chapter Thirteen

By nine o'clock Monday morning, I'd been awake for three hours, changed my tie twice, and poured two cups of coffee I didn't drink. Sun glinted through the sparkling windows, a result of yesterday's frantic cleaning. The mahogany desk, in what I hoped would be Margaret's office, shone with wax. The brand-new Underwood typewriter held center stage. New typewriter, waxed desk, sharpened pencils all part of my plan. A soft knock on the wooden door stopped me. I dashed to the door, took a deep breath, plastered a smile on my face, and welcomed Margaret Curtis to the Henderson Building.

~Practicing Law in Creekside, A Love Story by Micah Henderson

****

A chilly spring breeze blew into the reception area accompanied by Police Chief Alex Stark.

"Good morning Chief," Tara greeted from the doorway to the kitchen. "What can I do for you today?"

He didn't return her smile. "Patrick free?" Tara nodded, and Alex disappeared ambled down the hallway. Their deep voices rumbled. They'd left Patrick's office door open, but the words were indistinct. She answered her ringing phone, and by the time the caller disconnected, Patrick and Alex stood in front of her desk.

"Let's use the conference room, Tara," Alex suggested. At a nod from Patrick, Tara led the way to the conference room.

Her shaking hands clasped together in her lap; Alex's chocolate eyes met hers across the conference table. "Is this about Trey? Is he missing again?"

"Tara, Trey died yesterday."

Click, the antique mantle clock turned to the hour. Muffled by the old wooden door, the familiar low rumble of Patrick's voice drifted through the room. Her heart pounded in her chest; a salty tear landed on her lips. "He's dead?"

From the credenza, Alex grabbed a box of tissues and set them on the table. "He left work early with a headache. Collapsed at his apartment. His roommate called an ambulance."

Tara swiped ineffectively at her tears. "But he died," she whispered. "I wished him gone, wished he'd forget me, wished he'd move to another country." She tried again to stop the tears. "But I never wished him dead." She forced herself to calm. "What happens now?"

"Probably an autopsy, sudden death of young man not under doctor's care." Alex patted her clenched fist, resting on the table. "Shall I walk you home? Call Ronni or Nathan for you?"

She shook her head. "I'll walk to Ronni's now." She looked down at her shaking hands. The tears splashed on the conference table. "As soon as I get myself together." *How should she tell CJ?* She rose, and so did Alex. "Thank you for telling me about Trey." Alex opened the door and escorted her into the hallway. "Please let Patrick know I'll be back in a minute." She turned right and drifted down the hallway.

Tara stared at the face in the mirror. Mascara left black smudges under her red eyes. Not the first time she stood in this restroom in front of a mirror and attempted emergency repairs. She used the damp paper towel and wiped the mascara off. Trey was dead, unreal.

Looking in her rearview mirror at Grandpa's house in Bisbee a few months ago, she pictured returning someday, unafraid. Not like this, though. Not because Trey died at forty-seven. A splash of cold water brought a little color to her cheeks. She patted them dry and yanked open the door.

A few minutes later, the law office's front steps made a lonely hollow sound as Tara clomped down them in her low boots. As she left the area around the square for the residential district, her cell phone rang with the first bars to Lea Bryce's "I Don't Dance."

"Hi Owen," she answered.

"Hey, Tara. You okay?"

"Yeah. Okay," she answered.

"Good. Gotta go, I'm on duty. I'll call you later. Let me know if you want me to drive up there tomorrow. Love you, sis."

Okay? What did that mean? Her heart beat, she breathed, the April breeze cooled her face, scents of flowers and new grass floated in the air. Beautiful day but her emotions swirled in a cauldron of confusion. The man she'd loved and feared, the father of her children, dead.

She punched in the gate code at Eckie House, stepped through, and let it close with a clank and a click. Gravel crunched as her boots hit the path around the house.

When she arrived at the garage, the door stood open. Inside, Ronni faced a giant painting, a brush, and a rag in her hands. She greeted Tara with a smile. "Hey, was I expecting you?"

"No. I should have called first."

Ronni shrugged and stood the paintbrush in a glass jar. "No problem, just cleaning up."

"Is it finished?" Tara asked as she wandered into the studio.

"For today. Go on upstairs and pour us some tea. I'll be up in a minute." Ronni turned her easel toward the wall.

The scent of chicken soup filled Ronni's upstairs apartment. Tara found green tea in the refrigerator and set it on the table with tall, ice-filled glasses. The front door opened, and Ronni strolled in.

"Mmm. Can hardly wait," Ronni commented as she entered the kitchen. "Let me wash up. I'll be right back." She disappeared down the hallway.

Tara filled her glass; the green tea sparkled on the ice cubes. The cold liquid soothed her throat as she sipped. Not ready to sit down, she wandered about the living area. Sunlight streamed through the windows turning the polished oak floors a warm toast color. A soft-bodied doll perched precariously on the arm of the pastel-flowered sofa.

Ronni appeared in the doorway, grabbed the glass of tea from the kitchen table, ambled into the room, and with a soft plop, dropped onto the sofa next to the doll. "Have a seat, Tara, and tell me what's going on." She sipped the tea. "Not like you to show up mid-week, mid-day, aren't you working?"

"Left work early," she answered as she perched on

the edge of the wing chair. "Trey's dead."

Ronni's eyes widened. "What the hell happened?"

Staring into her glass of tea, Tara answered, "Yesterday, he left work early, collapsed, and died. That's all I know."

"Exactly like his father. Though Walter was seventy instead of forty-seven." Ronni curled her legs up onto the sofa and sipped her tea. "It's weird to think of him gone, Trey, I mean. When Walter died, no question Nathan and I grieved right along with Mom."

"He married your mom when you were still young, right?"

"Yeah, thirteen and fifteen. He was a good guy. Kind, loved my mom, set up trust funds for Nathan and me. Wanted us to graduate from college debt-free."

"Is that the money Trey tried to take from you?

"Yeah. I can't decide how I feel about his death." She tilted her head to the side and closed her eyes. "I wanted to like Trey, he was Walter's son, and I loved and respected Walter." She dropped the doll on her lap. "Trey's arrogance and sense of entitlement made it difficult to like him." She picked up a box of tissues from the end table and tossed it to Tara. It landed on her lap. "If my feelings are confused, yours must be chaotic."

Tara grabbed a handful of tissues and dabbed at her tears. "Yeah. I wished him gone, out of my life. But I never wished him dead."

The hollow sound of boots on wood stairs interrupted. The door swung open on a breath of fresh air. "Hey, am I still picking up Tina?" Nathan asked as he clomped across the threshold. "Oh. Sorry, didn't realize you had company, sis. Hi Tara."

"Yep. Please pick up Tina." Ronni glanced at Tara. "Okay if he picks up CJ and Makenna as well?" Tara nodded.

"Are we having a party?"

"More like a wake," Ronni answered, "but there's plenty for dinner. Go get the kids and I'll explain later." The door clicked shut, and the sounds of Nathan's boots on the wooden stairs faded. "Does CJ remember his father?"

"He remembers his father beating me to a pulp." She shook her head. "He was four when we separated. Awful thought that may be his only memory."

"My good memory of Trey, probably the only one, is the day he visited us with you and CJ. CJ was tiny, like a doll. Trey glowed; he stared at CJ as though he couldn't believe the miracle of his son."

"Yeah. He wanted a son." She sipped her tea. "He was the perfect partner while I was pregnant, loving, supportive."

"Which Trey was the real one? The perfect partner, the father focused on his child or the violent bastard who beat up his wife?"

"All of them. I left because he found a new lover. Since he wanted the divorce to marry her, I had no clue he'd make it difficult."

The pounding of feet on the stairs and Tina's piping voice ended the discussion.

Tara escaped to the bathroom to clean up. When she returned to the living area, the children gathered around the kitchen table for snacks. Makenna and Tina competed for attention with stories from preschool. Tara and Ronni tried to include CJ, but his answers were brief, his smile forced. Ronni herded the girls into the living room for a board game and CJ spread his homework on the table.

"Need some help?" Tara offered.

CJ's pencil moved furiously over the paper. "Nah. It's a review for the quiz. Boring." He flipped the pages of his math book. "Mom, how come we're here for dinner?"

"Ronni invited us. It's hard cooking dinner in the hotel."

CJ gazed into his mother's eyes. "We're not running again, right? We're still pretty safe?"

Tears threatened. Tara stood behind CJ and wrapped her arms around him. "We're safe, CJ. Not running."

He patted her arm. "Good. I don't want to move again. I like it here, and Zack invited me to stay over next weekend. His uncle's going to take us out on the ATVs."

"Sounds good." She ruffled his hair and joined the girls in the living room.

Nathan breezed in with an offer of pre-dinner fun on the ATV. CJ and the girls trooped down the stairs behind Nathan. Working in tandem, Ronni and Tara straightened the living room, set the table, slipped rolls into the oven to warm, and tossed the salad. "CJ okay, Tara?"

"Yeah. He worried a sudden dinner at Eckie House meant running again." Tara added napkins to the table setting. "He wants to stay in Creekside."

"There's no reason you can't stay. You've got an office; the kids have friends."

"True. If we stay, we need something bigger than the hotel room."

"Definitely. What you need is something like Rose Cottage. A couple of bedrooms, small backyard, and a cottage dog."

Cameron's squeaky yip announced the dinner guests. The children and Nathan bounded across the threshold, Cameron in CJ's arms. If they stayed in Creekside, CJ needed a cottage dog.

****

Five o'clock, Patrick straightened up magazines in the law office reception area, dumped leftover coffee in the sink, and cleaned the pot. He avoided thinking about Tara's tears all afternoon while he worked with a client on a dissolution of marriage. The couple agreed on everything except the definition of fidelity. Only the final paperwork and judge's signature remained on the to-do list, and their seven-year life together was over. Does love die with the signing of a piece of paper? Or did the betrayal kill love? Or was love an illusion that never existed?

Coffee cups were rinsed and loaded in the dishwasher. Patrick meandered through the reception area. At the conference room door, he perused the room, checking everything was put away, and the trash emptied. Hand on the light switch, he stilled.

Beside the credenza, a young man dressed in clothing of the last century reached for a woman wearing a shirtwaist and black skirt. The man gently drew her into his arms; her head rested on his shoulder. Sadness filled the air, her sobs swirled in the room, and she whispered, "He died before we could make up. He never heard me say I forgave him."

"But you forgave him, and that's what matters. You reached out; that's all you could do." He withdrew a white handkerchief from his pocket and placed it in her hand. She blotted her tears and stepped back. He placed a finger under her chin and lifted it, so she faced him. "You did what you could. Now all you can do is release the regret."

She stepped away. "You're right. Thank you." The couple dissolved, leaving behind only the quiet echo of her sobs. Did Tara's tears draw the spirits into the conference room today?

Weaving around clumps of tourists on the sidewalks surrounding the square, Patrick nodded to acquaintances. Children's piping voices blended with the lower ones of adults. As patrons opened restaurant doors, music and appetizing scents floated in the air. "On your way home for dinner?" Patrick asked as Chief Stark joined him.

"Yep. Dinner break." He matched his strides to Patrick, and they hustled across the street. "You joining us?"

"Nope. I'm manning the bar so you can enjoy a family dinner, spend a little time with your wife." They climbed the hotel's front steps.

Alex tapped Patrick on the back. "Thanks for that." He leaned over the bar, nodded to two customers perched on barstools, and kissed Nikki on the cheek. "I walked your relief home. Let's eat."

With a mouthed *thank you* for Patrick, Nikki disappeared down the hall, Alex's deep rumble a counterpoint to her higher tones. Patrick took her place behind the bar and made conversation with the two ladies perched on barstools sipping wine while Lena Horne extolled the virtues of "Summertime."

The front door's chime announced Tara's return.

She waved to Patrick and hustled the children up the stairs. Out of the shadow behind the front desk, Smokey materialized and, tail wagging, silently bounded up the steps behind Tara. Patrick shrugged and poured wine. If you lived in a hotel, Smokey was the perfect pet since he didn't require food, water, or walks. Wham! requested you "Wake Me Up Before You Go-Go," and guests trooped in for a final glass of wine or beer. Patrick poured, served, and bused tables. The distinctive keyboards for Journey's "Faithfully" filled the lobby, and Patrick announced, "Last call."

By nine-thirty p.m., only the low light of the front desk's Tiffany lamp lit the lobby, and Patrick loaded the final wine glass in the dishwasher. He checked the door locks to the rhythm of Kenny Chesney's "Better As A Memory," and climbed the stairs. After a last check of the second-floor veranda, he climbed the final flight to the attic. He slid open the pocket door to the third floor.

Spread across the dimly lit hallway, two teenage boys, pencils furiously writing, spoke in low voices. Victoria rocked nearby, the chair's curved wooden rockers a *whoosh* on the bare wood floor. Smokey bounded into the hallway, creating a chaos of scattered papers and laughing boys. The group dissolved, leaving only the echo of laughter and a faint scent of lavender. Apparently, the attic was a favorite playroom in RJ's time, no tears tonight at The Palace.

Chapter Fourteen

From the first day, Margaret sat behind her desk, hands poised over the typewriter keys, my work life changed. The tenor of my practice could be divided into two distinct phases. Before Margaret joined the firm, clients entered with legal problems. Careful probing was often required to determine their reasons for a request and their hope for the outcome. When clients arrived and were greeted by Margaret, her warmth and understanding put them at ease. By the time they joined me in the office, they were ready to talk. Secrets and dreams spilled freely.

I loved practicing law, but running the business end frustrated me. Raised by a single father immersed in several businesses, Margaret understood how business worked, why some succeeded, and others failed. Her father taught his sons about business, grooming them to take over when he died. While he never intended Margaret to run any of his companies, as the youngest child and only girl, she was included in the conversations at dinner. Margaret took her dinner table knowledge, combined it with her education at Miss Easley's, and improved Henderson Law.

More than an executive secretary, she became the heart of the office.

~Practicing Law in Creekside, A Love Story by Micah Henderson

****

The clean scents of soap and baby shampoo surrounded Tara as she wrapped Makenna in a towel and yanked the drain from the bathtub. She hustled Makenna out of the bathroom and pointed CJ toward the shower.

By the time CJ appeared, Makenna wore her pink ballet dancer jammies, clutched Smokey, and fought to keep her eyes open. CJ stretched out on his bed and opened a book.

The old hotel settled around them. Tara turned most of the lights off and glided into the bathroom.

The hot shower pulsed on tired muscles, and the tension in her neck released. The problem of how or what to tell CJ and Makenna and where to go next remained. But with the scent of vanilla body wash surrounding her and the shower's pulsing hot water on her back, for tonight, she let the immediate problems go. No need to make a snap decision. Trey's death gave her the luxury of time.

The worn sweatshirt caressed her skin, its scents of soap and sunshine a reminder tomorrow the sun would rise. CJ's book lay face down on the floor. She marked his page and set it on the table. His soft snore reassured her he slept peacefully, and she kissed his cheek, something he rarely allowed in daylight. Lights off, she climbed into bed, stretched, and relaxed each muscle starting with her toes. Sleep claimed her. A breath against her cheek and a small hand patting her arm woke her.

"Mommy, I nightmared."

Tara forced her eyes open and drew Makenna under the covers. "Shush, baby. Momma's here. I'll keep the nightmares away." She curled around Makenna's soap-scented body and listened to her breathe. As Tara drifted into sleep, she resolved no more nightmares, no sudden changes for her children. They deserved the same security she grew up with. The only question was how best to provide it.

****

Intense sunlight blinded her as Tara strolled toward the Henderson Building. She detoured across the square to the gazebo and plopped down on a bench inside the fairy-tale structure. She dug her phone from the bottom of her bag and punched in her brother's number.

"Hey, Tara," he answered after the first ring. "How's Creekside?"

"Good. Talk to me, Owen. What exactly do you know about Trey?"

"He's dead. No idea from what. Roommate called the ambulance. He was pronounced dead about an hour after he arrived at the hospital."

"Will they tell you what they find out from the autopsy? Chief Alex said it would be required."

"Don't know. My contact is the PO. He probably won't bother to follow up since Trey died. He's got enough live parolees to worry about."

"Can't blame him. I'd like to know for the medical history. What if it's something hereditary CJ and Makenna's doctor should watch for?"

"That makes sense. Let me see what I can do," Owen offered. "Do you need me up there, sis? I can take family leave."

"I'd love to see you, but let's wait until I've figured out what to tell the kids."

"Okay, remember I'm available. Love you. Gotta

go. My turn to drive the kids to school."

Tara dropped her phone into her bag and left the gazebo. Several ominous gray clouds drifted across the sky, changing the light from intense to subdued. As she stepped onto the front porch of the Henderson Building, the first raindrops hit the ground.

Inside the office, she followed the scent of coffee to the kitchen. Patrick sat at the table, his phone pressed to his ear, and a mug of coffee held suspended in the air. He acknowledged her with a nod, and Tara filled a mug with coffee, tossing in a little extra sugar to make up for her recent shock. Wasn't sugar the treatment for shock? Too bad a box of chocolate donuts wasn't on the kitchen counter. The last couple of days definitely called for chocolate. The trilling of the office phone yanked her back to the present.

****

A half hour before she needed to pick up her children, Tara arrived in Patrick's office. "Do you have a moment?"

He nodded "Sure, how can I help?"

"Seems like a good time to explain how I ended up in Creekside and the latest in the weird drama my life's become." She gazed into his concerned blue eyes and grimaced at the frown lines between his blond brows. "Alex suggested I tell you a while ago, but I wanted to keep the drama away from the office."

"You don't owe me an explanation, Tara."

"Maybe not." She caught her hands together to keep from wringing them. "My ex was sent to prison. A few months ago, he was paroled, and I panicked." She straightened her spine. "Grabbed my kids and ran. We ended up in Creekside because Ronni and Nathan are here, and my brother Owen knows Chief Alex."

"What changed that you're telling me now?"

"Trey's dead." Tears fell on her clasped hands. "I don't get why I'm crying. Shouldn't I be relieved he's gone? We don't have to be afraid anymore."

Patrick grabbed the tissue box from the credenza and set it in front of her. "Relief, maybe? Shock? Confusion? Worry about telling CJ and Makenna?"

Somehow her chaotic emotions sounded sane in Patrick's warm voice. "All of the above. As to why I'm telling you now, maybe I'm practicing for my conversation with CJ?"

"What about Makenna?"

What about Makenna? Did she explain they didn't need to be afraid anymore when she'd done all she could to hide her fear from Makenna? "Makenna never met Trey."

"Is there anything I can do to help? Other than being a practice audience." He turned away, withdrew bottled water from the miniature refrigerator in the credenza, and set the bottle in front of Tara. "We at Henderson Law provide very inexpensive law services to friends."

"I appreciate the offer." She glanced at the clock on the wall and slid her chair back. "Time to face CJ." She stood and forced a small smile. "Thanks, Patrick, for listening. It's not your problem."

Patrick stood. "Anytime, Tara. You're not only my tenant but a neighbor, and I hope friend."

She glided out of his office with a nod and slight wave.

****

The tissue box landed with a plop when Patrick

tossed it back on the credenza. He settled into his chair and woke his laptop from sleep. Familiar sounds of Tara opening the desk drawer for her purse and the *click* when it shut, then her soft "Bye, Patrick," and she was gone. The confusion in her eyes, the worry, and the tears haunted him while Patrick worked through a prenuptial agreement for a client.

The law could protect assets and secure financial support for children, but nothing protected a spouse's heart or the heart of a child. Mixed feelings when someone died not a surprise. Patrick grieved when his father died, not for the man he was, but for the father he remembered when they were little. He and James remembered. Nikki didn't. Her birth coincided with the divorce, and his father lost interest in visiting soon after. His father's other family in Tucson was a bigger attraction than two sons and a daughter he didn't want. Did Nikki feel the loss more or less than he and James? Could you miss someone who disappeared from your life when you were under a year old? He saved the document and his notes and shut down the laptop.

A glance at the clock told him Scott should be out of class. Feet propped on the corner of his desk, he punched in Scott's number.

"Hi, Dad. Everybody in Creekside okay?"

"Yeah, how you doing?" He grimaced. *Do I call so rarely a call means something is wrong?*

"It's all good. Only a couple of weeks left of school, all projects completed. A couple of tests left next week, and I'm done."

"How about Casey? She almost finished?"

"Yep. We're both ready to come home. Her dad's bringing their truck to cart her art stuff home. So why the call?"

"Just touching base about your plans." Scott's deep chuckle rumbled in his ear.

"What's up, Dad? I met you a couple of weeks ago, and we talked about summer. Not like you to call for no reason."

"Only wanted to remind you I love you. Realized I don't tell you often enough."

"Love you too, Dad. See you in a couple of weeks."

Patrick signed off. That was awkward, but his mood lifted. His feet dropped to the floor, and he closed up the office. Boot heels making a satisfying clunk on the wooden steps, Patrick stepped off the front porch into the springtime chaos of tourists wandering the sidewalks of Creekside. Weaving in and out of clumps of window shoppers, he made his way home. No surprise Scott's first question about everyone's wellbeing. The day he dropped Scott and his possessions off at the university, they made a deal. Scott texted or called once a week. If he forgot, Patrick called to check on him. Scott rarely forgot. He encouraged Scott to call anytime, for any reason. Patrick refused to become a "helicopter parent," hovering over a grown son. James and Nikki accused him of helicoptering over them, big brother always watching. He gave Scott all he had, all his support. But sometimes, when he was with mothers and children, he was sorry he hadn't been able to provide a loving mother.

He yanked open the hotel's front door and held it for a mother and her young daughter. He waved to Eric at the bar and started up the steps. When Nikki set up the hotel's website, she noted that the hotel welcomed children, but as a historic building, the rooms were small, and cribs and a rollaway bed did not fit. Five years later, the permanent residents included four children, nine months to sixteen years, and the connecting rooms, two bedrooms with a shared bath, were booked months in advance. If parents of older children missed out on the connecting rooms, they booked two rooms next to each other. Nikki managed to turn a haunted hotel into a place families felt safe.

In the attic hallway, Tara's gentle voice melded with CJ's excited tones. "What does that mean, Mom? Are we going back to Bisbee? Moving again? What's going to happen next?"

Tara's voice, lower and calmer, answered him, the exact words indistinct. *Yeah, Tara, what next?* They opened the law office together. Though she didn't work for him, her presence added warmth; her muted voice from the office next door reminded him he wasn't alone. He wasn't ready to let her go. Patrick touched the key card to the reader and stepped inside his room. In a shadow near the window, Victoria faced a man dressed in an overcoat, a leather bag on the floor beside his foot.

"Ask me to stay, Vic," he pleaded and took her hand.

"You can't, so I won't," she answered and stepped closer, raising a hand to his cheek. "You have so many great things to do. Your skill is necessary."

He wrapped an arm around her shoulder and drew her close. "Then come with me." He took a white handkerchief from a pocket and dabbed at the silver tears on her cheeks.

"I have a hotel to run; and child to raise. I can't."

"Can't or won't?" He dropped his arm and stepped away. They dissolved, leaving behind the scent of lavender and the essence of sadness. Her palpable sadness made Patrick wonder if Victoria regretted her decision. She appeared to him frequently standing at the window of room 15, staring out at the town stretched before her. Did she watch for the man who couldn't stay?

****

Hot water sluiced against Tara's skin, the vanilla scent of her favorite body wash surrounded her, and steam filled the bathroom. She shut down the water, grabbed a towel, and climbed from the shower. Silence from the other side of the door meant what? That CJ fell asleep reading or that his confusion and pain were so great he'd withdrawn? Trey's death hit CJ hard, but she was unsuccessful reassuring him that everything would work out. Then, Nathan arrived with Makenna nearly asleep in his arms, and CJ withdrew. Withdrew from their discussion, withdrew from her. He asked difficult questions she couldn't answer. The hardest question—What next?

Children should come with a manual, including a section titled *How To Tell Your Child His Father Died.* Tough enough, but when the child's memories included watching that father hit his mother, impossible. Practicing on Patrick hadn't helped much. She'd stumbled through telling CJ his father was dead and was unprepared for his immediate question delivered rapid-fire.

Dressed in her favorite pajama bottoms decorated with tiny flamingos, Tara kissed Makenna's cheek and tugged her covers up. Marking CJ's abandoned book with a random receipt, she laid it softly on the bedside table and straightened his blanket. She ruffled his soft brown hair. Tonight, they slept, their light snores reassuring. The only outward sign of CJ's confusion, clenched fists.

She crawled between soft sheets, closed her eyes, and focused on relaxing each muscle starting with her toes. Sleep claimed her.

Rain pattering against the windows, and a whispered, "Mom" woke her. She folded back the sheet and welcomed CJ under the covers. He nestled against her, his head on her shoulder.

"Mom, I'm sorry."

"Oh, CJ, you're forgiven, but there's nothing to be sorry for."

"I shouted at you. I asked questions and didn't let you answer."

"CJ, you just found out your dad died. Maybe shouting was the best response for you." She drew him closer and placed a light kiss on his forehead. "You have a right to your feelings."

"But I shouted at you, and it wasn't your fault. I wasn't angry at you."

"I know. Since you were little, haven't I always reminded you to use your words?"

CJ nodded.

"You did exactly that. Nothing to forgive. I'm proud of you, CJ."

He sighed against her shoulder. Eventually, his soft snore whispered against her cheek. A second presence landed on the bed and curled against her leg. At the foot of the bed lay a large gray dog. Tongue hanging out, ears up, he stared at her, then plopped his big head on his paws and closed his eyes. Smokey. Comforted by the ghostly canine presence and CJ's even breathing, she slept.

****

A world washed clean by late-night rain greeted Tara, CJ, and Makenna as they strolled toward Creekside Elementary. Makenna's chatter competed with the squawk of birds. Only the sidewalk's puddles gave evidence of the storm. Grateful tomorrow was Saturday, Tara dropped her children at their respective schools and strolled toward the law office. Jude and Zack invited CJ for the weekend. Saturday, Makenna would attend an overnight with Tina at Catherine's for Hope's birthday. Time without her children, time to think, plan, and adjust to their changed circumstances.

"Good morning," she greeted Patrick when she entered the law office kitchen a few minutes later.

"Morning. Happy May Day," he answered as he took a second mug from the cupboard and filled it.

May Day? Already the first of May? She took the offered coffee and added sugar. "Happy May Day to you. Where did the time go?"

"You know that song about how the older you are, the days get longer, but the years are short?" She nodded. "Well, I'm at the age where the months and years are too short, not to mention the days." He ambled out of the office kitchen.

Tara wrapped her cold hands around the mug. She needed the next month to move at snail speed. Too many decisions to make. Choosing one meant losing something else. Opportunity costs, not only for her but for Makenna and CJ. The phone's annoying ring forced

A Dream to Trust

a dash to the desk, and the workday began.

Focused on the spreadsheet displayed on the monitor, Tara grabbed the ringing phone. "Good morning, TW Enterprises. How may I help you?"

Low-voiced chuckles responded. "Little sister, I'm hoping I can help you."

"Hey, Owen. What's up?" She checked her cell phone. Yep, three unanswered texts from Owen. "Looks like I missed a few of your messages."

"No problem. Figured you were at work. We're coming your way next weekend."

"Excellent. Do I need to make reservations?"

"All done. We're staying in Phoenix with Jen's sister Friday night, at The Palace Saturday night. You're staying in Creekside the whole weekend, right?"

"Yep. Let me check with Ronni and Nathan. Maybe we can do something together Saturday."

Her phone signaled an incoming call, and Tara said her goodbyes.

At three o'clock, she waved to Patrick from his office doorway and strode out of the building into a sundrenched day. This weekend, time to plan. Next weekend, a chance to bounce ideas off Jen and Owen.

She dashed up the steps to Emanuel Lutheran Church and yanked open the door. With a cheery greeting, she joined Chance and Nathan at the door to Ms. Lake's classroom, and they entered the chaos. Ten minutes later, they strolled out of the church with three little girls in tow.

"What are we doing now, Mommy?" Makenna piped as she and Tara climbed the stairs to their room.

"First, wash your hands and face, then a snack, then we'll wrap Hope's present, and you can sign the card." At the door to their room, Tara touched the key card to the lock, opened the door, and flipped on the light. Makenna stood against the wall beside the door.

"Is it safe?" she asked.

"Yep." Tara took Makenna's hand, tugged her into the room, and pointed her toward the bathroom. Makenna wasn't as unaware of the danger as Tara hoped. Tara took out the tissue paper, gift bag, and card they'd bought for Hope yesterday and set them on the small table. As she poured snack mix into a cup and removed a juice box from the mini-refrigerator, she contemplated how much to tell Makenna about Trey. Somehow, she needed to explain there was nothing left to fear.

Chapter Fifteen

****

A gentle breeze ruffled Makenna's fine hair, plucking tiny wisps from the pink clips. In one hand, her fingers clasped the gift bag handles. Backpack, packed with Makenna's important stuff, slung over her shoulder, Tara held Makenna's other hand as they strolled toward Hope's birthday party. "Mommy, can I have a birthday party?"

"Sounds like a good idea." They turned the corner leaving the commercial district behind. "When is your birthday?"

"June first. You're silly. You know my birthday."

"Oh, that's right, June first." They stopped at the corner, Tara exaggerated looking both ways, and Makenna mimicked her. "Big birthday. You'll be five years old."

"I know that. Next fall, I get to go to kindergarten."

Tara opened Catherine's front gate, and they climbed the steps to the front porch.

"Will we still live here at my birthday?"

The front door opened, and Catherine swept them into the party. Assured by Catherine and Chance that the adults outnumbered the party guests, Tara strolled toward The Palace. No answer to Makenna's question yet. Would they still live in Creekside in June? What about kindergarten?

If they returned to Bisbee, Makenna would attend school with a few children she knew in preschool last fall. After nine months away, would the others even remember her? It was hard making the switch from preschool to kindergarten, with more children in the classroom and fewer adults.

In Creekside, Makenna had friends who would make the transition with her. CJ loved Creekside, especially his riding lessons, art lessons, and his best friend Zack. She yanked open the hotel's front door.

"Hey, Tara," Nikki greeted her as she handed her brother Patrick a filled glass. "Can I interest you in some iced tea?"

"Definitely."

Nikki poured a glass and handed it to Tara. "I'm taking a break on the veranda. Join me?" They strolled outside and settled in Adirondack chairs. "How's the birthday girl?"

"Surrounded by children, adults, and dogs."

"Having a great time then. Is this Makenna's first sleepover birthday party? Was it hard to leave her?"

"Yeah. I won't be surprised if she calls tonight

wanting to come home. The first time she's stayed the night somewhere without me. Where are your kids? I think this is the first time I've seen you without at least one child in tow." Tara sipped the cold tea, and her body relaxed into the comfortable chair.

"Michelle is visiting Grandma Beth. The boys are at Windsong helping Becca, and Alex is working. Patrick offered to cover the front desk, so I'm taking a little time to be. A mental health day."

"Mental health day. That's a good way to put it." Tara sipped her drink and admired the dance of the first blooms on the crepe myrtle planted beside the steps. "Nikki, how old was Sam when his mother died?"

"Almost four. Sherri's death changed both our lives. Thank God for counseling and grief support."

Tara stared at the clear blue sky without seeing it and sipped her tea. She needed counseling, and so did CJ. Probably grief support as well, though it seemed strange to grieve the man she hid from. Without the therapist in Bisbee, she might still be locked in Grandpa's house, afraid to go outside. Would she ever have heard CJ's laugh again without the excellent trauma counselor Jen recommended? Her own emotions were a mass of confusion. CJ's must be chaotic, and he was still a little boy. But, what did she tell Makenna? Her paternity couldn't be kept a secret; too many people already knew, including CJ.

"My grief wasn't a surprise when Sherri died," Nikki continued. "When Patrick told me, our father died, my tears surprised me. I had no memories, good or bad. Why was I crying?"

Tara glanced at Nikki's bewildered expression. "Did you figure it out?"

"Yeah. I cried not for the loss of my father, but for the man he could have been, the father I wished for." She gathered their empty glasses and rose. "I'm going inside, finding a romance novel, and immersing myself in the character's problems, knowing no matter how bad things get, they always find their happy ending."

Happy ending. Tara pictured a perfect happy ending for Owen and Jen, their daughters grown, Jen's curly black hair streaked with silver Owen almost bald like their grandfather. They'd sit on the hanging swing on their back porch cuddling and watch the sunset. What did her happy ending look like? For CJ and Makenna, she pictured them grown up, passionate about their work, and supported by a loving partner. Was it possible the same happy ending could be hers? The clump of boots on wooden stairs yanked her thoughts to the present.

"Evening, Tara," greeted Chief Alex. "You okay?"

"Yep. What's in the bag?" The scents of tomato and oregano drifted from the white bag emblazoned with Rose's signature red and green R.

"Dinner. Nikki's mental health day included no cooking. There's enough if you want to join us?"

"Thanks, but I think I'll pick up something from Manuel's." Tara rose and followed Alex through the front door.

Twilight painted the sky a mix of blue and purple by the time Tara left Manuel's with a plastic bag containing her leftovers. The combination of a full stomach and red sangria slowed her steps, and she meandered toward the hotel. Time without her children, an opportunity to plan her next steps. She'd looked online and left a phone message for Jackson Realty about available rentals. If they were staying in Creekside, they needed a home larger than a hotel room. In the hotel's lobby, she bought a glass of wine. Balancing wine and leftovers in one hand, she climbed the two flights of stairs to the attic. She tapped the key card on the door at the top of the stairs and entered the hallway. The door closed behind her with a soft *whoosh*. At the door to her room, she tapped the key card on the lock, opened the door, and flipped the light switch. She stopped and examined the space. Her head understood she no longer needed to fear a surprise visit from Trey, but her heart pounded, and her muscles tensed until she verified the room was empty. When she recognized her body's anxious response to entering the hotel room, she suddenly understood Makenna's instinctive knowledge that she should be afraid.

She shoved the leftovers into the mini-fridge, set the glass of wine on the table, and stripped. Steam from her hot shower created a mist-filled room scented with vanilla. A few minutes later, dressed in her favorite flamingo pj's, wine in hand, she curled up on the easy chair. Before she made any decision, she needed feedback from both Makenna and CJ. Whatever choices she made would be in her children's best interest. They had both time and options. No midnight packing and wandering route through several states this time.

****

Tim McGraw admonished everyone to always be "Humble and Kind," and Patrick walked through the lobby, bar, library, and onto the veranda, bussing the tables. He offered last drink to the few remaining customers.

As he loaded glasses in the dishwasher, he tried to

imagine what he would be doing on a Saturday night in May if he still lived in San Diego. Not tending bar. He spent most weekends with Scott until his son developed an independent social life. He dated some in San Diego, mostly attorneys from other firms or women he met through networking organizations. The relationships stayed casual, probably his fault. He was too busy being an attorney and a single father to invest time in building a future with a woman.

After Amy, he lost confidence in his ability to identify someone who could love him and Scott. Someone who would stay. Beyond family members, Constance Hemmings, his assistant, was his most consistent relationship with a woman in San Diego. The day he strolled out of the office for the last time, she walked at his side. At sixty-two, she claimed no desire to train a new boss. He held open the driver's door of her lipstick red convertible. She dropped her briefcase on the passenger seat and wrapped him in a hug.

"What now?" Patrick asked. "What have you planned for your next act?"

"What now?" Constance responded. "Now I fill my days with fun and spend my money living my dream." She patted his cheek. "You do the same." She perched polka dot sunglasses on her nose, climbed into the driver's seat, and zoomed out of the parking garage, her shoulder-length blonde hair flying.

Live his dreams? A long time ago, he dreamed. Dreamed of a successful law practice, a loving wife, and children. After Amy left, he dreamed Scott would become a happy adult, the law firm would continue to flourish, and Amy wouldn't demand Scott split his time between them. All his dreams came true. The downside to achieving a goal was the necessity of deciding what next. He didn't have an answer.

Patrick made a second pass through the library. He placed his foot on the bottom step of the stairway as Luke Bryan proclaimed, "Most People Are Good," and glanced up.

Victoria appeared on the landing, her hands on her hips. She drifted toward him, disappearing as she placed a foot on the last step. A warm breath and the scent of lavender lifted the hair on Patrick's arm. He climbed the stairs, wondering if Victoria's spirit headed toward room 11 or to check on Nikki. When he entered the second floor, Smokey suddenly appeared in the hallway and bounded toward him. Patrick moved away from the stairs, and the ghost dog loped down the steps, his feet silent on the wooden stairs. If Nikki's theory was right, Victoria haunted the hotel by her own choice, a choice to experience important moments in her life again inside the hotel. If he bought his childhood home, would he feel his mother's presence there, hear her laugh? On the third floor, he tapped the card key against the lock and yanked open the door. When he flipped the light on, he spotted a note anchored on the fridge with a magnet.

Tonight's menu: Rosa's famous lasagna. Enjoy, Nikki.

He took the container out and set it inside the microwave. He didn't need to buy the old house to sense his mom's presence. Nikki's laugh, her nurturing, even her handwriting brought Mom's memory to life.

****

The birds' chatter competed with Makenna's piping voice as she and Tara strolled toward The Palace on Sunday afternoon. Makenna recounted each minute of the last twenty-four hours. The wonder of so many presents on a table, a cake decorated with a drawing from Chance Pagent's picture book *Princess to the Rescue,* and the scary time when she woke up in a strange place.

"What did you do when you woke in a strange place?" Tara asked, surprised Makenna admitted being afraid.

"I crawled into Tina's sleeping bag. She wasn't asleep either," Makenna answered as she skipped beside Tara. "Ariel came over and slept on our feet. I want a dog for my birthday."

"We'll see. I'm not sure a dog would like to live with us in a hotel."

"But Sam has a dog in the hotel. I need a dog."

"Sam's mom owns the hotel, and they live on the first floor. Georgie never visits us in the attic because she can't climb the stairs. Let's put your stuff in the room and visit the square. There's a fair today."

The scent of cinnamon sugar and fried bread drew Tara toward a food truck parked on the edge of the square. Treat in hand, Tara led Makenna to a picnic table near the gazebo. They sat, and Tara tore the warm bread apart. When only a few grains of sugar remained on the plate, and they'd guzzled a bottle of water, they wiped their hands with napkins, and Tara gently cleaned her daughter's face. "Momma, did you know Hope's daddy died just like Tina's? Hope said she wished her daddy could be at the party. She remembers he loved birthdays."

"That's a special memory for Hope." Tara grimaced; Makenna never met her father. "Let's start back to the hotel." She took Makenna's hand, and they ambled across the square.

"Tina said she couldn't remember her daddy. She has a picture beside her bed."

They crossed the street and climbed the steps to the hotel's veranda. "Let's sit in the swing." Tara sat and used her feet to hold the swing still.

Curled against her mother, Makenna asked, "Where's my Daddy?"

Tara patted Makenna's arm and pushed with her feet, setting the swing into a gentle glide. What had the counselor advised about tough questions from a five year old after Trey's attack? Only answer the specific question. Don't elaborate or overwhelm a child with too much information. Give enough of the truth to satisfy the child. How much would satisfy Makenna? "Your Daddy died, too."

Makenna's brows drew down in a frown; her lips made a straight line. "But I didn't go to the funeral, did I? I don't remember. Tina and Hope went to their daddies' funerals."

"No. We didn't go to the funeral." *Should I have taken the children to Trey's funeral? Did they need closure? I might be able to find out where he's buried. Maybe they can visit the gravesite? Would Makenna grieve the idea of a father like Nikki?* A slamming truck door, pounding feet on the front steps broke her reverie.

"Hey, Mom. I had the best time," CJ said as he plopped on the end of the swing. Jude and Zack hopped out of the truck. Zack climbed the steps and stood before her.

"Thanks for letting CJ come for the weekend."

"You're welcome." She tapped CJ's arm as a

reminder. He glanced at her.

"Thank you for having me over this weekend," he responded, grinning at Jude. The boys bumped fists and chorused, "See ya Monday."

After dinner and showers, Makenna drifted into sleep in the middle of Chance Pagent's *Under the Sea*. CJ lay on his bed reading, and Tara searched the room for the monitor. Retrieving it from the back of one of the drawers under the bed, she plugged it in near CJ and checked the receiver before stuffing it into her pocket.

"What's that for?" CJ asked when she turned the volume up.

"I'm going downstairs for a while. If you or Makenna need me, talk loud, and I'll run up."

"You're going down without us?"

Tara nodded.

CJ's gaze met hers. "So we don't have to be afraid anymore?"

Tara sat beside him on the bed. "No. Just the same careful anyone living in a hotel needs." She ruffled his hair. "I won't be late."

Outside the door, she listened for the *click* announcing the lock secured. In Grandpa's three-story house, the children slept on the third floor. She didn't worry about leaving them upstairs while she worked downstairs, even in the basement laundry. The monitor let her know they needed her, but they rarely did. She wanted to remind them it was okay if they were in different rooms after five months of sharing a single space.

As she turned the knob on the door to the stairs, Victoria appeared beside her. Trailed by the scent of lavender, the spirit glided to Tara's room and disappeared through the door. Ahh, so the children wouldn't be quite alone.

The lobby's wood floor gleamed the color of warm honey in the low light. Behind the bar, Patrick's blond hair shone gold in the reflection from the small spotlight on the drawing of Victoria. Tara sauntered up to the bar as Neil Diamond's deep voice lamented, "Love on the Rocks." Perched on a barstool beside Shelby, Tara requested a glass of white wine and helped herself to the snack mix. Patrick poured the wine and Shelby asked, "Where are your children?"

"Upstairs hopefully asleep." Tara withdrew the monitor from her pocket and set it on the bar. "They both had a busy weekend with friends and crashed early. How about you, Professor? Don't you have class tomorrow?"

"The advantages to teaching at the college level. I have office hours tomorrow but not until two o'clock," RJ answered and bumped shoulders with Shelby. "I've plans to sleep in."

"How's the search for your great-grandfather going?" Tara asked. "Any new leads?"

RJ's eyes lit. "Yep. I've solved the mystery. The only thing is I need to understand why it was a mystery before I share the information. Need to figure out if the answer could hurt any of the living."

"And if the knowledge could hurt someone, will you keep it to yourself? Aren't you a historian, isn't that what historians do, share knowledge from the past?" Tara asked as she sipped her wine.

"Yep. We share history so the living can learn from the past, and I'm a proponent of transparency. Sometimes I think we encourage people to become their best selves when we admit our most revered heroes made mistakes. A single decision, a moment in time, can turn a flawed human into a hero."

"But this is different because he's not a hero or because the flawed human involved is family?" Patrick asked.

RJ downed his wine in one gulp. "Because the living are family, because he was a hero, and I'm hesitant to reveal our relationship without knowing how they'd feel."

"And family changes everything," Patrick commented. "Doesn't matter if they are people you've known your whole life or sudden additions; they're still family."

****

As Tara dressed for bed, family and heroes swirled in her thoughts. Other than a blood or marriage connection, what made a group of people family? Owen, Jen, and their children were her family. Since she moved to Creekside, Nathan, Ronni, and Tina became family when they could have written her off after the divorce. No blood relation but her former father-in-law's stepchildren and grandchild. Tina, Makenna, and CJ shared a grandfather, so they were cousins. Jen had three married sisters who each had three children, a mix of adopted and birth.

Funny how she'd felt so alone after the divorce, but the feeling wasn't truth. Their couple friends in Scottsdale disappeared as though divorce might be contagious. But the town of Bisbee, where she'd been raised, circled the wagons when she returned pregnant and wounded. Friends from high school offered rides to the grocery store so she wouldn't have to go alone.

They stopped by with meals and invitations for playdates for CJ. She'd only been alone when she wanted to be. They were family too, the people who took you in when that's what you needed most.

What was the best answer? Stay in Creekside near Nathan and Ronni and the new friends she and the children made or return to Bisbee and the friends of her childhood, the friends who stepped up when she needed them most. Heroes. Like Owen, who put his life on hold long enough to rescue his sister from the hospital and haul her and everything she owned to Bisbee.

Tara climbed between soft white sheets, turned off the bedside lamp, and dropped into sleep to the sound of her children's even breathing and the settling of the old hotel.

She woke to the sound of whimpers from Makenna. A hint of dawn peeked through the lace curtains. Tara slowly sat up and grabbed the sheet. Before she could tumble out of bed and comfort her daughter, a large dog landed beside Makenna, and her whimpers stopped. In her childish voice, she whispered, "Nice doggie." And the room was silent.

Tara closed her eyes. They needed more space, but some things about The Palace were irreplaceable.

Chapter Sixteen

One week after Margaret's father died, the visits began. From my office, I heard the doorbell chime, Margaret's usual greeting, and then a deep voice speaking quickly. Thinking a potential client might be in trouble, I strolled into the reception area. In the chair beside Margaret's desk, a giant sat in a pose of supplication. His head bent forward; his forearms rested on his thighs. He glanced up and spotted me as I strolled toward Margaret's desk. He rose; I held out my hand. "Good morning. I'm Micah Henderson. How can I help you?"

He took my hand. "Oscar Curtis, Margaret's brother." I looked at Margaret, she rose, and in her eyes, I read her wish that I just disappear. "Nice meeting you, Oscar. Come see me when you've finished, Miss Curtis?" She nodded, and I strolled down the hall toward my office. But I didn't go in.

"Oscar J.," Margaret said. "I heard every word you said. I read every word of the letter you sent me after the funeral. I'll take it under advisement."

"Thank you."

"You're my oldest brother; I love you. But Oscar, whatever I decide will be in the best interests of Annabelle. She comes first. Now go away." The front door chime rang. I dashed to my desk and plopped in the chair.

~*Practicing Law in Creekside, A Love Story* by Micah Henderson

****

Wednesday, Tara strolled toward the preschool under a clear blue sky. A soft breeze caressed her cheeks. She greeted familiar faces with a smile, but inside, her heart thudded, and her stomach cramped. Nathan promised to pick up CJ and Zack at school for their art lesson, leaving time for a mother-daughter conversation with Makenna. How much do you tell a four year old about a father she never met? A father who didn't know she existed? All the research perusing the Internet, the conversation with the pastor, and still she felt unprepared.

Standing on the steps in front of the preschool Ronni greeted her with a warm smile, a hug, and a whispered, "You got this." The doors opened, and children spilled into the fenced yard.

"Would you like a cookie for after-school snack?" Tara asked as they rambled toward the hotel.

"Yes, Momma. We had fruit for afternoon snack at school, but cookies are better," Makenna answered, skipping along the sidewalk beside her mother.

They grabbed cookies and a tiny carton of milk from Grandma's Bakery and settled on the steps of the gazebo. "I'm making you a present for Mother's Day," Makenna said as she swallowed the last of the cookie. "I don't have any money to buy you cookies."

"That's very exciting. Are you making it in preschool?"

"Yep. Ms. Lake is helping me. Ryan is making a Father's Day present instead because he doesn't have a mother. I'm glad Father's Day is in summer because I don't have a father."

"But you have Uncle Owen, and he's a father." *Good thing she wasn't following a script since the conversation was totally off the rails already. How to bring it back under control?*

"Hmm. Hope says Chance wants to be her father."

"What does Hope think about that?" *And what does Catherine think? Does she know her daughters are aware Chance wants to be more than the next-door neighbor?*

"She wants Chance to be her second father since her first one died. She says lots of people have more than one father. Did I have more than one father?"

"No. You had one father, Trey."

"Did he die a long time ago, because I don't remember him?"

Makenna's tennis shoes made a clunking sound as she kicked them against the wooden step. The gentle breeze carried the scent of grass, the sounds of twittering birds, and the hum of conversation.

Tara held her breath, then let it out in a sigh. *How to explain the unexplainable?* "No, he died a couple of weeks ago."

"Didn't he want to meet me? Didn't he want to be my daddy?"

Tara gazed into her daughter's eyes as tears formed. She tugged Makenna off the step and onto her lap. "Oh baby, he didn't know about you. He had to go away after the divorce, and he wasn't free very long before he died." *Would there have ever come a time for Makenna to meet her father? If he hadn't died, would she have found a way to believe in her own safety and the safety of her children? Who was the real Trey? The man she married or the man she feared? Now she'd never know.*

Makenna climbed off her lap. "Is it time to go to Tina's yet? Are we having dinner there?"

Tara rose off the step and took her daughter's hand. "Yep, time to go, and yes, we're invited for dinner." Serious conversation over, Tara's shoulders dropped in relief. No doubt Makenna would have more questions as she grew up, as she overheard adult conversations about Trey. But for now, the black cloud of worry was gone.

After dinner, Nathan and the children played games in the meadow outside the garage while Ronni and Tara cleaned up the kitchen. Tiny glasses of chocolate port in their hands, they settled on the sofa.

"How did it go?" Ronni asked as she sipped the sweet wine.

"Sometimes parenting breaks my heart," Tara admitted. "Makenna asked if her daddy didn't want to be her daddy."

"At least he didn't know about her, so you could answer honestly he didn't know. I wonder if Michelle will someday ask that question and how Andrea will answer."

"Will she realize James isn't her birth father? She's so little, and he's been there since the beginning." *Would it be better to believe your father didn't know you existed or that he knew but gave you away?*

"I think Michelle will eventually realize James isn't her birth father. Too many people in the family know about her father, and she'll have a relationship with her half sister, Carly. Anyway, you know what they say about secrets. If more than one person knows, then it's no longer a secret."

Sounds of tennis shoes pounding on wooden stairs ended their conversation.

****

Tara and her children strolled through the quiet neighborhood toward the hotel, CJ in big brother mode, holding Makenna's hand when they crossed the street. Inside the hotel, Tara acknowledged Patrick behind the bar with a wave and herded her family up the stairs. At the door of the attic, CJ stopped Makenna and took his cell phone from his pocket.

Tara touched his shoulder and whispered, "It's safe, CJ."

They walked the few steps to the door together. She touched the lock with the electronic key, turned the handle, and ushered her children inside.

Her children settled for the night, Makenna asleep, and CJ stretched out on the bed reading. Tara set up the monitor, dropped the receiver in her purse, and with a last ruffle of CJ's hair, left the attic room, closing the door quietly behind her and listening for the *click* of the lock.

Mid-week and almost closing time, the lobby bar was quiet. Patrick poured wine for two senior citizens perched on barstools, and two couples sharing a bottle of red wine surrounded the game table. Tara ordered a glass of white wine and settled into the morris chair in the library.

The mellow sound of Sinatra's "Summer Wind" floated in the air, and Tara consciously relaxed her shoulders and unclenched her jaw. She contemplated the answers to questions swirling in her head about where they should live, what arrangement she should make for the children over the summer, and what Owen would advise. She and her children needed the weekend with their Bisbee family, a reminder of what they left behind. It might help her children figure out what they wanted and needed.

"Ready for another wine?" Patrick asked, breaking into her whirling thoughts.

"Thank you." Startled by his warm voice, she handed him her glass, his fingers a brief warmth on her hand. From the other room, his voice rumbled a wish for his customers' good night, and then sounds of footsteps echoed in the hallway behind her. The optimistic sound of Luke Bryan crooning "Most People Are Good" filled the air, and Patrick appeared holding two glasses of wine.

"Mind if I join you?" He indicated the wing chair beside her.

"It's your hotel. Of course not." She took the wine from his hand, and he dropped into the chair. "Bar's closed? Hotel locked tight?"

"Yep. Your kids down for the night?" He sipped the wine and peered at her over the glass.

"Uh-huh. I'm gonna miss this. Somehow a last glass of wine before bed alone in my kitchen is not quite the same as being served by a friendly bartender and drinking in a cozy library."

"Are you planning a move?"

"Not exactly planning. At the moment, I'm checking out my options. While I love The Palace, a hotel room is not quite enough space for a mom and two kids in the long term." She sipped the wine and gazed into Patrick's deep blue eyes. "Now there's no reason to stay cocooned in The Palace under the watchful eye of a police chief and benevolent spirits."

"Now's your time to turn into a butterfly and fly away?"

"Not quite, since I've two children with me." She sipped the wine. "Did you move much when you were a kid?"

"Nope. Mom was pregnant with James when we moved into the house where I grew up. I only know we lived somewhere else first because I was born in Tucson. James and Nikki were born in Scottsdale. Moved to California for college and decided I needed the ocean."

"Until you needed something or someone else more?"

"Yep. With Scott grown up didn't want to miss out on the next generation's childhood. What about you? Did you move around much as a child?"

"Until I was eight, we lived all over the country. When our parents died, Owen and I moved in with Grandma and Grandpa in Bisbee. Owen returned right after college." She skipped the part where she fell in love with Trey her last year in college and married him the day after graduation.

"Did you miss the moving? Did you feel trapped in a small town after living all over?" Patrick asked.

"Summers while my parents were alive, we stayed weeks at my grandparents. When they died, we were already part of the community, had friends."

"So what next?" he asked. "Return to Bisbee and your brother?"

"Don't know yet. Not going to move at all until I'm sure it's the best decision for CJ and Makenna. No jumping suddenly from one place to another." She finished her wine and handed the glass to Patrick. He rose and offered his hand, helping her from the chair. "Since you're my landlord, you'll be one of the first to know when I decide what's next. Night, Patrick."

She strolled out of the library and disappeared down the hallway, her light footsteps a muted thump on the wooden stairs; her mind pounded out the question *What next?* With Trey gone, the choice was hers alone. If she stayed in Creekside, would she build something more than friendship with Patrick of the sparks and warm voice? Did she dare?

****

"They're here!" Makenna's piping voice bounced off the walls when Owen's bright blue SUV appeared through the lobby window. Tara took her daughter's hand and then opened the hotel's front door. CJ right behind her.

The driver's door opened, and Jen popped out, her face wreathed in a smile. In a flurry, the other doors opened, releasing Paige, Sophie, and Owen. In a cacophony of greetings, Owen drew CJ to the back of the SUV. "That looks like my bike," CJ said, and the group quieted.

"It *is* your bike," Owen answered. "After we unload the other stuff from the car, you and I are taking your bike to Ronni's. She tells me there's lots of room to store it and whole neighborhoods for you to ride."

The day flew by with hours spent on the square at the End of School Celebration. Vendors lined the street, selling everything from water toys to camping gear. Local organizations manned booths, offering information about summer camps; lake camp, horse camp, bike camp, sports camps, art camp, theatre camp, fitness camps for children and adults. Paige and Sophia teased CJ about living in a haunted town though Bisbee had its own famous spirits. Eventually, Nathan, Ronni, and Tina found them on the grass with the remains of lunch. Money contributed by the adults in hand, twelve-year-old Paige herded the children toward a section of old-fashioned games of chance. The adults tossed the trash and settled on the grass to keep an eye on the children and listen to the band, who immediately started playing a cover of "Teach Your Children."

Owen propped himself up on his elbows and asked, "So little sister, what's your plan? Bisbee, Creekside, Scottsdale, San Diego, Tucson? With Trey gone, your next home is limited only by your imagination and your funds."

"No pressure," Jen added, "but we hope you'll return to Bisbee."

"Except Grandpa's house is leased until next spring, but we could probably find you something nearby," Owen added.

"No pressure here either," Ronni commented. "It's great having family close, so we'd rather you stay in Creekside."

"The only pressure I can't ignore is my children. CJ wants answers," Tara admitted. "I'm not sure what answer he's hoping for, especially now since you brought his bike. That was on his short list of what he missed from Bisbee."

"When Nathan said there was plenty of room for CJ to ride near where they live, it seemed wrong to let the bike sit unused in my garage," said Owen. "I didn't think about swaying CJ's opinion of your next move."

They gathered the children and strolled toward

Eckie House for dinner. Nathan started the grill, Nikki, Alex, and their children arrived accompanied by James, Andrea, and Michelle. Slamming truck doors announced Zack and Jude's arrival, and the air filled with the scents of grilling food and the sounds of animated conversation. As the sun set, they consumed dessert and completed clean-up.

The sun disappeared completely, and stars decorated the sky. Owen, Jen, Tara, and the children strolled toward the hotel. Jen commented, "Looks like you and the kids found friends in Creekside."

"Yeah. Makes it harder to decide what to do next. The kids are happy with their friends, and Creekside's full of activities," Tara admitted as they neared the hotel. "I'm afraid we've been gone long enough Bisbee won't feel like home to them, especially since we can't return to Grandpa's house. The problem with Creekside is we need more space, and there's very little available to rent close to the square."

"The local realtor wasn't much help?" Owen asked.

"He says competition is fierce for the summer rentals near the square because Creekside's cooler than the valley but close enough for a quick commute."

They climbed the stairs to their hotel rooms, Owen's room next door to Tara's, and agreed the adults would congregate in the library when the kids were settled.

By tacit agreement, they sprawled on comfortable chairs in the hotel's cozy library. A bottle of rosé, its translucent pink color glinting in the subdued lighting, was nestled in a cooler surrounded by three glasses. After Jen poured the wine, Owen sipped and gazed at

Tara, a troubled expression crossed his handsome face.

"It's good to see you, sis. Seeing you calm and determined to make your next move about the kids' happiness puts my mind at ease." He glanced at Jen. "Besides delivering the bike and seeing my favorite sister, I do have another mission."

Jen tapped him on the shoulder. "You're not helping by dragging this out. Just spit it out."

He frowned at his wife and removed an envelope from his shirt pocket. "I have a message for you from Trey's Uncle Matthew." He handed Tara the envelope. "He contacted me a couple of days after Trey died. I assume he was listed as Trey's next of kin."

Tara took the envelope and dropped it on the table beside the wine. "I don't remember meeting Trey's uncle though Trey mentioned him once in a while. He lived in New Mexico. What does he want?"

"Trey bought a life insurance policy when CJ was born. When you divorced, he made CJ the sole beneficiary and Mathew responsible until CJ is eighteen."

"Why? Trey signed his parental rights away to avoid child support. This makes no sense."

Owen poured more wine. "Who knows? Mathew checks out, sis. He is Trey's uncle, Walter's much younger brother. He'd like to meet you but understands if that doesn't work for you."

"Did you tell him about Makenna?"

"Nope, not my place. No pressure. Read the letter when you're ready. And sis, inside the envelope is also a letter forwarded from Trey's PO. He told me what it was and left it to me to decide what to do with it."

Tara withdrew a small envelope from the large one.

"Looks like Trey's writing. What's this?"

"Addressed to you, so I didn't read it. Trey's PO claims Trey wrote it as his amends as part of his rehab program. You don't have to open it now."

Tara gazed into the concerned eyes of her older brother. Bookended by two people who loved her, she carefully tore the end of the envelope and drew out a folded sheet of paper and a cashier's check. Finished reading the brief letter, Tara dropped it on her lap and took her brother's hand. "He apologized. Took responsibility for destroying our family. Wants to make amends by giving back the money. He planned for the letter to be sent when he'd finished probation. Do you think he meant it? That he was sorry?"

Owen picked up the letter. "Sounds like it. Making amends is part of the rehab program. Guess we'll never know if he could stay clean."

"I don't know what to do with this. Do I burn it? Save it for when CJ is older? Show it to him now?"

Jen took the letter and check and returned them to the envelope. "Cash the check. Put the letter away. You may stumble on the perfect time to show it to CJ or to burn it, but for now, put it somewhere safe."

"Yeah, sis. Someday knowing his father had regrets may matter to CJ. Especially knowing making a bad choice hurt everyone, even himself."

They gathered glasses and the empty bottle and dropped them off at the bar. With a brief good night for Patrick, they climbed the stairs to their attic rooms. Tara tapped the key against the lock and opened her door. Makenna curled in a ball in the center of the bed, only her fine hair on the pillow a testament to the little body hidden under the sheet. CJ sat up in bed. His glasses slipped down his nose, his focus on the pages of his book. Tara sat down beside him. "Must be a good book; you're still awake."

He looked up at her and nodded. "Yep. Just need to finish this chapter, okay?'

She ruffled his hair and strolled to the bathroom, taking her nightclothes with her. The warm water soothed her tight muscles. She didn't understand Trey's actions. Their first years together were loving and happy. CJ's birth deepened their love. A few short years later, Trey told her he found someone else and wanted out.

Dressed in baggy gym shorts and a tank top, she wished CJ a good night, turned off the light, and crawled between cool sheets.

At one time, she'd been giddy with love for Trey. Amazed a charming, successful, sophisticated older man chose her. Loved her. Then CJ was born, and she was no longer giddy with love but overwhelmed with love for a tiny human. Her giddy love for Trey died, a slow death caused by broken promises and violence. Her love for CJ would never die. Nothing that happened, nothing he did or did not do, would steal her love. In some part of her, she understood Trey's wish to make amends. He'd lost everything, his freedom, his wife, his son. Sleep claimed her.

In the moments before dawn, light snuck through the lace curtain, and Tara woke to the low rumble of a man's voice. In the shadowy corner of the room, Victoria wrapped her arms around a tall man wearing a long coat, a leather bag at his feet. "Doesn't matter where you go; my heart goes with you."

He returned the embrace, his arms holding her

against his chest. "I'll need it since I'm leaving mine with you. I'd stay if I could."

She released him, taking his hands in hers. "But you can't. Be safe and come back when you can."

He lifted her chin with one finger and placed a brief kiss on her lips. He stepped away, picked up the leather bag, and disappeared.

For an instant, Victoria stood in a shaft of early light. Her image slowly dissolved, leaving behind the scent of lavender and a floating tinge of sadness.

Tara closed her eyes and returned to sleep—her last thought that life was filled with painful partings even in the spirit world.

Chapter Seventeen

Before the month was out, all the Curtis brothers visited Margaret in the office. Afraid I wouldn't like what I'd hear, I avoided eavesdropping. I didn't need to hear; I understood the family wanted her and Annabel back in Fortuna. The world was changing, the possibility of war on the horizon. Margaret's brothers were debating signing up to fight, and they wanted her back with the family before the war yanked any of the brothers away. After each visit, Margaret's eyes contained a weary sadness. I badly wanted to wrap her in my arms and offer comfort. I understood she grieved the death of her father, in part, because their parting was filled with accusations and angry words.

~Practicing Law in Creekside, A Love Story by Micah Henderson

****

Tonight, the first summer visitors crowded the sidewalks. With the earliest of the schools out for the summer, families thronged the sidewalks. School ended for CJ and Makenna in a few days. Today she signed them up for summer programs in Creekside. A few days ago, Patrick offered her the apartment above the office. If she accepted Patrick's offer, she'd be able to let the kids stay upstairs between their activities just like when they lived in Bisbee. If she needed to work after she hustled them to bed, she could by using the monitor.

160

Would Patrick be okay with a dog if she found a little guy like King or Cameron? Lots of places to walk a dog near the Henderson building. The biggest question— could she live above the office, work in the office next door, and not give in to attraction? She recognized the heat in his eyes and the spark in the casual touch, but was he interested in her as a person or as another damsel needing rescue? Was a relationship, even a brief one, with her landlord a good idea or a heartache waiting to happen? Was the convenience of living in the same building where she worked worth the risk?

Her children's happy chatter entertained her as they strolled through town. On the street where Ronni lived, a couple of boys on bikes zipped by, greeting CJ with, "Get your bike, and let's ride!"

As she opened the front gate at Eckie house, Tara commented, "Go ahead, CJ, get your bike. Be back in an hour."

With a shouted, "Thank you!" CJ raced ahead. A few minutes later, he zoomed by them headed back toward the street. At the studio, Nathan leaned against the ATV, his arms full of art supplies.

"Where's Cameron? Where's Tina?" Makenna asked.

"What's this? No hello for Uncle Nathan?" Nathan responded. "Only the missing matter?"

"Hi, Uncle Nathan. Are we taking the ATV?"

The clatter of footsteps announced Tina's arrival, and the drawing students climbed into the ATV. Cameron in her arms, Ronni joined Tara to wave them off. "How's the hunt for a house coming?" Ronni asked as they climbed the stairs to the apartment.

"I may have found something; I'm just not sure it's

a good idea," Tara admitted when they'd poured glasses of peach iced tea and settled on the sofa.

"What's the problem? Too big, too small, too far out of town?"

"None of the above. The location is perfect, and the size is plenty for us. Downside is no yard and the landlord." Tara sipped the tea, letting the cold, sweet liquid cool her throat.

"I can see why you'd prefer a yard, but what's the problem with the landlord?"

"The apartment is above Patrick's law office."

"He's already your landlord, so what's the problem? Plus, you'd be working where you live, which should make child care easier." Ronni sipped the tea and lifted an eyebrow. "Oh, you're attracted to Patrick."

"Yep. Right now is probably the worst possible time for me to get involved with someone. I see him all the time; we live across the hall from each other at the hotel and work in offices in the same building, offices right next door."

"And you think you'll see more of him if you're living above the office?"

"Maybe." Tara set the tea down and frowned. "That sounds stupid, huh? I guess I counted on moving somewhere that I wouldn't see him as much. Remove temptation."

"Hey. Here's my unasked for advice. If the space works for you, take it. You're both single adults. You get to choose whether you act on the attraction or not."

"You're right. It's been so long since I felt any attraction to a man. I guess it took me by surprise. But I'm an adult; I can handle it." *Hopefully, that isn't a lie.*

****

From his perch behind the bar, Patrick watched Tara hustle her children up the stairs. What decision would she make? Would she take his offer of the apartment above the office? Did he want her to? If she moved over the office, would the erotic dreams she starred in stop? After the first summer Scott spent in Creekside working for Nikki, Patrick accepted he needed a change when Scott left for college. The house was too big for him. Though he had friends in San Diego, he'd been too busy being a single parent while building his law practice to deepen the friendships past the superficial. In reality, his best friends were his siblings.

Faced with an empty nest, he jumped from San Diego to Creekside. He meant to live in the attic of The Palace temporarily, long enough to help Nikki with the hotel while Michelle was little. With four children, a haunted hotel, and a husband who worked odd hours, Nikki still needed him. She'd waited a long time for motherhood. He didn't fault her for wanting to spend as much time as possible with the children.

At nine o'clock, he stepped onto the front veranda, walked among the tables and chairs, and picked up glasses on a tray. The sky was black. Not a single star or even the crescent moon penetrated the clouds. He hauled the heavy patio furniture toward the building in anticipation of a storm. Back inside the lobby, he locked the front door as the clouds opened, dropping sheets of rain. Pedestrians ran to shelter, clearing the sidewalks in less than a dozen heartbeats. Grateful he wasn't the one out patrolling the streets in the rain, he strolled down the hallway accompanied by The Cascades "Rhythm of the Rain." A soft warning tap on the sitting room door, and he let himself in. Nikki, Michelle wrapped in a blanket on her lap, rocked in the wooden rocker. "Storm wake her up?" Patrick asked as he plopped in the wingback chair and propped his feet on the hassock.

"No. She was already awake. Did you have a good night in the bar?"

"Yep. Perfect timing. I locked the front door as the storm hit. Alex get called into work, again?"

"As usual, and both boys are home now, but they were at a school function. Beth dropped by the school earlier and picked them up since Alex couldn't. Thanks for taking the bar. We thought everything was covered, and then suddenly it wasn't."

He held out his arms, and Nikki handed him the warm bundle of his niece. "You're welcome. I like the bar, certainly like it better than breakfast. Hey, backing you up is my reason for living in the attic."

"Hmm. When you told me you were moving into the attic, I figured you'd last a week. Going from high-powered attorney to bartender, culture shock. But here you are, and I'm grateful."

"Were you surprised, Nik, by how quickly your priorities changed?" Patrick rested his head against the chair's high back, Michelle nestled against his chest, and he let his eyes drift shut.

"Yeah. The shift started with Sam. By the time Michelle entered the picture, the children and Alex were first and The Palace a distant second. I could spend more time working, but I want more time with family instead. I don't want to be that parent who missed everything. Not too long, and Mitch goes away to college, and Colin will follow two years behind."

Patrick rose, returned Michelle to her mother's arm, and bent over Nikki, placing a soft kiss on her forehead. "Well, anytime you want me to fill in on the hotel, just say. My parenting duties are almost down to writing checks and dispensing advice."

"And the worry?" Nikki asked with a grin. "Is the worry still there?"

His hand on the door, Patrick admitted, "The worry changes, but it never goes away. I may have regrets, but I don't regret even one minute I spent parenting Scott." He slipped outside, closing the door with a soft *click*.

As he climbed the stairs to his room, he remembered he hadn't told Nikki about offering Tara the apartment above the office. Guess it wasn't important until Tara made up her mind. Nikki sounded grateful he lived in the hotel, readily available to fill in. Loneliness still haunted him, but at least he felt needed. He wondered if Tara would accept the apartment. As he strolled by her room, he could hear the shower running, and a flash of heat hit him. At least if she moved above the office, the combination of his vivid imagination and physical attraction would stop haunting him with erotic dreams and mental images of Tara wrapped in a small towel, her skin pink from the warm water. He hoped.

****

Clear sky, puffy white clouds greeted Tara and her children as they descended the stairs from the front porch of The Palace. Tara took sunglasses out of the pocket of her light jacket and perched them on her nose.

"Are you sure it's okay, Mommy?" Makenna asked for the tenth time in the last ten minutes as they strolled toward the elementary school. "Are you sure it's okay my party is not right on my birthday?"

They waved CJ off, and he raced to the playground. Tara and Makenna turned right, ambling down Exeter toward the church. "It's better than okay, Makenna. Since you and Tina are having the party together, the date is halfway between and a weekend. I'm sure more friends will be able to come on Saturday than if the party was a weekday."

Makenna danced up the church steps and twirled in a circle in front of the doors. "Good. I'll give out my invitations, and Tina will hand out hers, and everyone will come."

Tara opened the heavy church doors, and Makenna skipped, hopped, and twirled her way to the classroom, disappearing inside with a last wave.

Tara crossed the street and meandered toward the office. Tomorrow was the last day of school. Makenna had a program at noon, parents invited. One excellent advantage to self-employment, she never requested time off. She just took it. When she moved home to Bisbee after the assault, she couldn't force herself to travel the short distance to CJ's school for the first months. Between therapy and family support, by the time CJ was in second grade, she attended every event, all the field trips, class parties, holiday lunches in the cafeteria. Tomorrow CJ had an end-of-school field day. No parents were invited. His first years in school went by so fast she was grateful for all the opportunities she took advantage of to be a part of his school experience.

She climbed the law office steps and touched the front door handle. A blue ceramic pot filled with succulents sat on the patio table, a florist's stake with a small card stuck out of the bowl. Balancing her bag on one shoulder and carrying the pot in the other arm, Tara managed to yank open the office door and step inside before it closed with a thump. Patrick peeked his head out of the kitchen and strode up to her, offering to take the pot. "Where'd this come from?" he asked and set it on the front desk.

"The table on the front porch. There's a card."

Patrick yanked the card from the stake, opened the tiny envelope, and burst into laughter. He picked up the potted plants, grabbed his coffee, and ambled toward his office.

Filled coffee mug in hand, Tara plopped into the chair in her office. She turned on her laptop, and the system came to life. She left the office and strolled next door. Cell phone against his ear, Patrick motioned her inside. "Saturday, then. Can hardly wait." He set the phone on his desk. "What's up?"

"Apartment still available?" Tara asked. "If so, I am interested."

****

Saturday, James and Patrick lounged in Adirondack chairs on the hotel's front veranda. Already a steady stream of cars slowly cruised the streets around the square and filled the parking spaces. The sidewalks teemed with children and adults. "So what time are you expecting Constance?" James asked as he sipped his coffee.

"If they left Phoenix when they planned, any minute," Patrick answered and set his mug on the table. "It's amazing she's getting married."

"Because she spent so many years caring for her ill husband?"

"Yep. She claimed, 'Never again,' and I believed her. The last years with Milo, she was constantly exhausted, though she hid it well. When he died, she sold everything, bought a small townhouse and a red convertible, and announced, beyond the office, she planned to take on as little responsibility as possible."

"That why she retired when you left the law practice in San Diego?" James asked. "Because you were one of her last responsibilities?"

"Probably, though I didn't see it at the time. I think she stayed after Milo died because she figured I still needed her," Patrick admitted. "She ran both my practice and my life, though she was subtle about it."

"They say second marriages are the triumph of hope over experience. Think you'll ever be that hopeful?"

A red convertible roared into the parking space in front of the hotel. Patrick and James rose as a familiar woman, her eyes hidden behind polka dot sunglasses, jumped out from behind the wheel, and a silver-haired man climbed gracefully from the passenger's seat. His aviator sunglasses glinted in the sun, and a smile lit his face. Patrick and James hurried down the steps. Constance collided with Patrick and, roaring with laughter, wrapped him in a hug.

Chapter Eighteen

An autumn wind rattled my office window. The front door chime banged, and I glanced at the clock. Faith Eckie was early for her appointment. I waited a few heartbeats, enjoying the feminine voices drifting from the reception area to my office. Grabbing my jacket from the coat tree in the corner, I stuffed my arms into the sleeves, shot my cuffs, and strolled to Margaret's desk. The ladies turned my way, and it hit me; these two women brought all the color into my life. A few moments later, Faith sat before my desk, a teacup in her long-fingered hand. She took a sip, set the cup in its saucer, and looked me in the eye. Her delicate dark brows drew together.

"Micah, today I'm breaking my own rule."

"What rule?" I asked. She had many rules, most pertaining to how she treated the women and children of Eckie house.

"My personal rule about meddling in other's lives, about giving unasked for advice." She reached across the desk and took my hand. "The day I lost George was exactly like a hundred other days. We breakfasted with our children. He popped his hat on his head, then buzzed our daughter's cheek, letting her knock his hat off. He wrapped me in his arms and said, 'I love you, Faith. See you at lunch.' And kissed me. I responded. 'I love you, George. Enjoy your morning.' He died that

day, and my comfort was he knew, knew I loved him. From the beginning, we never left the words unsaid."

~Practicing Law in Creekside, A Love Story by Micah Henderson

****

Weaving between the clumps of tourists on the sidewalks surrounding the square, Patrick and Constance meandered toward the Henderson Building. "I almost feel guilty leaving your companion at the hotel," Patrick commented.

Her arm twined with his, Constance patted his hand. "Don't. Ardy can entertain himself. One of his greatest attractions is his ability to be happy socializing or content in his time alone. We invited him along. He preferred to hang out at the hotel."

They strolled two blocks from the square and climbed the front steps of the Henderson Building. Patrick unlocked the front door, yanked it open, and tapped in the alarm code. In the shadows of the reception area, a young man hovered over a young woman as she withdrew a sheet of paper from an old-fashioned typewriter. The woman stood and held out the paper. The man reached forward. Instead of grasping the paper, he took her wrist and tugged her into his arms. The paper fluttered to the floor. "Margaret," he whispered, "stay, please?" They disappeared.

Patrick flipped the light switch.

"Well, Patrick, you didn't warn me the office was haunted," commented Constance. "According to the Chamber of Commerce website, Creekside brags about their spirits. Didn't realize that included your law office."

He led her toward the kitchen. "Unlike the other businesses, I don't advertise the Henderson Building spirits. Didn't think they would help my credibility as an attorney."

"Did you know the building was haunted before you bought it?" Constance opened the hidden dishwasher. "That's clever," she commented. "Living in a haunted hotel, did you even think to ask?"

"I didn't care one way or the other. The spirits in Creekside are benevolent, no mean tricks or trying to scare the living."

As they wandered through the first-floor offices, Constance asked, "So what kinds of law do you practice in this tiny town?"

"Everything except criminal. I've become a true general practice attorney, and I still have time to help my sister at the hotel."

"How do you help? Unasked for advice or hands-on?"

"Both. Since Michelle's birth, more hands-on than advice. Mostly I'm a front desk clerk and bartender." Patrick flipped the light on in the conference room.

"Great. The plants arrived." She slipped one finger into the soil. "They look good on the conference table."

"They do. Now, if I can only remember to water them enough to keep them alive." Patrick punched in the lock code for the stairway. "Come on. I'll show you the apartment before my tenant moves in next weekend."

Patrick opened the door at the top of the stairs and flipped the switch for the standing Tiffany lamp in the corner. Constance asked, "Why didn't you move up here yourself? Seems a perfect fit for a small-town lawyer." She opened the doors to the Juliet balcony. "What a delightful view."

"I leave the hotel, and I lose breakfast and the dinners Nikki sneaks into my fridge. Plus, when she needs help, I'm closer living in the hotel."

"Won't it be weird having your tenant enter the apartment through the office?" Constance asked.

"There's an outside stair, but my tenant also leases the office next to mine downstairs to operate her virtual assistant business." He led her around the apartment, pointing out the hidden appliances in the small, efficient kitchen and the upstairs bedrooms. "We're used to sharing space. For the last few months, Tara and her children have lived across the hall from me at the hotel."

"Tara. The blonde hustling two children out of the hotel when we arrived?"

"Yep." Patrick ushered her out the door at the top of the stairs. As the door closed behind him, a giggle floated in the empty room and was suddenly silenced by the *click* of the locking door. Would the giggling spirits enjoy having more children in their space?

As they stepped onto the wooden front porch, Constance asked, "So will she be your plus-one at the wedding? Obviously, it won't be me since I'm the bride."

"Doubtful. I haven't asked her, the wedding's tomorrow, and she has two children to take care of. You didn't exactly send me a formal invitation indicating a plus-one was welcome."

As they strolled across the square, she answered, "Not a formal wedding, no formal invitations. Anyway, your brother and sister-in-law are hosting the wedding at Eckie House. They mentioned if you couldn't find your own date for the reception, they'd be happy to find one for you, even last minute."

"Sounds like they're into matchmaking again."

"Naturally. The happily married always want that happiness for their friends and family. Kids, no problem. Apparently, my photographer is Tara's sister-in-law, sort of, whatever that means. She offered to arrange for Tara's two to join hers and her plus-one's child at a friend's house. Seems they've set this up before."

"Probably Catherine. She and my brother-in-law's mother handled child entertainment at James' wedding."

"How about that. Swept into town a couple of hours ago and already solved all your problems. Some things never change." They wove among the clusters of tourists crowding the sidewalk around the square. "Now, all you need to do is invite your date."

On the hotel's veranda, Constance plopped into a chair beside Dr. Ardavon Ament, and he poured her a glass of iced tea from the carafe on the table. Patrick ambled inside and approached his sister.

"Welcome home, brother," Nikki greeted from her perch behind the front desk. "Tara's in her room if that's what you were about to ask. Makenna did battle with the grass on the square, and the grass won. They're doing clean up."

"Makenna okay?"

"Yeah. Just a couple of skinned knees and a little hurt pride. She raced across the square with a friend. She tripped, so the friend won."

"What makes you think I want to talk to Tara?

Could it be because you and James are playing matchmaker? After all the grief you gave me when I simply provided you with the benefit of my wise council? Never did I play matchmaker."

"Never will I interfere in your love life." She crossed her heart. "However, right now, you don't have one. Get a love life, and I promise to stay out of it. "

Patrick leaned across the desk and kissed her cheek. "Semantics, little sister. You should have been the attorney." He ambled toward the stairs and climbed. No love life. Pretty accurate description in the year he'd lived in Creekside. He lifted his hand to knock on Tara's door and stopped. How do you invite a woman to another family wedding at the last minute? Especially when they still haven't been on a date. He knocked.

The door swung open, and Tara greeted him with, "So you decided to pretend you had a choice and ask me to the wedding. Did you figure out I was your plus-one whether you asked or not?"

"Yep. How's Makenna?"

She ushered him inside. "She's fine, a little battered and unhappy she lost the race, but fine."

"Hi, Mr. Benton. I have Band-Aids on my knees. See?" piped Makenna.

Patrick admired the colorful dressings and sympathized with Makenna's loss. When Tara accompanied him to the door, he asked, "You're okay with being my date at the last minute? I gather some pressure was applied by my siblings."

"I'll enjoy the wedding, and my kids are excited about visiting Catherine and hanging out with their friends. Your siblings are persuasive."

As twilight tinted the sky a mixture of purple and lavender, Patrick sauntered toward The Station for the rehearsal dinner. The informal wedding didn't require a rehearsal, so the dinner was family. Ardy's family lived all over the world, and only his oldest daughter would be attending tonight. The others would arrive tomorrow for the evening wedding. Brave of Ardy and Constance to marry. Where did the previously married find the courage to try again?

Constance nursed her former husband through a terminal illness while working full time. Dr. Ardy Ament practiced medicine and shared custody of his children with his ex-wife until the children grew up and started their own lives, built their own families. Now at a time in their lives when they could focus only on themselves, Constance and Ardy chose to create a legal partnership. Why? Patrick climbed the steps to the door of The Station. A smiling host led him to a private room filled with family. A single empty chair waited next to Scott.

Couples filled the other chairs. Couples moving through life in tandem, partners facing the best and worst times together. If he found a partner, would he be less lonely? A vision of Tara flashed through his mind, laughing at him, teasing him about being set up by matchmaking siblings. Her laugh warmed his heart. The kindness she bestowed on everyone spoke to him. He'd never admit it, but a part of him thrilled at a second date, another wedding. On the slow meander back toward the hotel, Patrick found himself the last in a walking caravan. He enjoyed the couples' body language. Alex's arm lay across Nikki's shoulder, her arm around his waist. Scott and Casey held hands, occasionally bumping shoulders with a laugh. Andrea and James looped arms, their words indistinct, their voices a comforting background. Constance's heels clicked on the cement sidewalk, and Ardy guided her with a protective hand at her low back. Tomorrow night he'd be part of a couple. How would they fit together? Was he brave enough to pursue Tara for more than a casual relationship? Would she be willing?

****

Children at the small table focused on their game of Crazy Eights. Tara stared at the limited choices hanging in the tiny hotel closet. Her choice of outfit for the wedding was really no choice. The green dress she wore to James and Andrea's wedding her only option. Behind the small privacy screen, she slipped out of her robe and into the dress, the silk a caress against her skin. A caress, something she suddenly missed. Patrick's hands were long-fingered with short nails; how would they feel against her skin? Her body warmed. She forced the thought away and stepped into silver flats. After a last check of her make-up in the mirror, she helped the children put the game away. A knock sounded on her door, and a warm deep voice asked, "You ready, or shall I wait downstairs?"

CJ raced to the door and yanked it open. "We're ready."

Patrick held the door open, and Tara hustled the children into the hallway. The door clicked as CJ opened the stairway door. They trooped down the narrow stairs, Patrick at the end. When they reached the lobby, Nikki and Alex waited, surrounded by children. "James already took Dr. Ament back to Eckie House, CJ and Makenna can walk with us to Catherine's, and

Patrick, you, and Tara can accompany Constance."

Patrick led Tara to a small settee beside the front window. "Does this make me the father of the bride, or the two of us the bride's parents accompanying her to the wedding?"

"Hmm. Lately, the bride rides to the wedding with her bridesmaids," Tara teased. "Maybe you're the bridesmaid?"

The *click* of heels on the wooden floor announced the bride's entrance. "I'm ready," Constance announced. "Are you two my attendants?" Patrick and Tara rose, and Constance dropped a kiss on his cheek. "Thanks for being part of my wedding."

"You're welcome. I'd be hurt if you married without me," Patrick admitted.

The wedding similar to their last date yet different. The ceremony in Eckie House living room, reception dinner inside the dining room, dancing on the patio. Ronni and Nathan, cameras at the ready everywhere at once. No bridesmaids, Patrick stood with Constance, Dr. Ament's oldest daughter stood beside her father. The bride and groom promised respect, generosity, kindness, fidelity, and love. Beside Tara, Nikki sighed, the glint of a tear on her cheek. Alex's hand bumped Tara's arm when he wrapped his arm around Nikki's shoulder. Respect, generosity, kindness, fidelity, and love. Five words encompassing the best of an intimate relationship. The ultimate goal, five words defining a lifetime of hope.

Under a velvet sky lit by a full moon, Patrick and Tara strolled toward the hotel. Patrick placed his hand at the small of her back and guided her across the street, then took her hand. "Thank you for being my plus-one," he offered.

"I'm glad you asked. It was a lovely wedding."

The green dress flirted with Tara's pale skin. Patrick's blood heated, and his groin tightened. What was it about this particular woman that made his body respond like a teenager? Objectively, the dress was neither sexy nor revealing, yet each time she wore it, his body reminded him he'd been without a lover a long time. "Would you go to dinner with me next weekend? Dinner and a movie, with the kids too, after your move?"

"Owen and Jen will be here Friday and Saturday."

Patrick's cheeks heated in embarrassment. Of course, her brother would help her move. "Is he going home Sunday?"

"Yep. They'll leave right after breakfast."

"Then Sunday night?" He guided her up the steps to the front door of The Palace.

"Why, Patrick, are you proposing to go out with me to something other than a wedding?" Tara teased.

"Hey, it's not the first time. We shared lunch on my birthday."

She squeezed his hand. "We did. Spontaneous lunches at the office or away. We've had several dates that didn't involve weddings."

Patrick punched in the code and opened the hotel's front door. "Is that a yes or no?"

They started up the steps. "A yes. I'd love to go to dinner and a movie with you. The movie house is playing something both my children want to see, and by Sunday, we'll be ready for a break."

In companionable silence, they climbed the two flights of stairs. At Tara's door, Patrick took her key and slid it past the electronic lock. "Thank you for being my plus-one." His right shoulder propped the door open. He lifted her chin with his index finger and placed a brief kiss on her lips. His deep voice rumbled in her ear, "Been a long time since I left my date with a good night kiss at her door. Mind if I kiss you again?"

"Please do."

He wrapped his arms around her and deepened the kiss. Her hand touched the nape of his neck, fluffing the short hair, caressing the sensitive skin. He ended the kiss and withdrew slightly. "Good night, Tara." He stepped back, holding the door open with one hand. "Sleep well."

She whispered, "Good night." The door closed, and Patrick ambled the few steps to his room. He slid the key across the lock and opened the door.

Moonlight through the high window created a soft spotlight on the wood floor. In the space where light and shadow met, Victoria waltzed in the arms of a tall man wearing a white shirt and suspenders. Her delicately flowered dress floated with her movement. The spirits drifted to a stop. He tightened his arms around Victoria, drawing her against his chest. He bent his head, and their lips met in a long, slow kiss. "Ahh, Vicky. I'm grateful to be home." She placed her hands on his cheeks. They disappeared.

Patrick flipped the light switch. In the presence of Victoria and her lover, the warmth of their connection surrounded him. When they disappeared, the loneliness returned. Home. A few years ago, he made his home in San Diego, where a busy law practice filled his days, and raising Scott consumed his every moment. Now his days cruised between helping Nikki and a limited law practice. What did he need to feel at home in Creekside? Or who did he need?

Chapter Nineteen

Letters arrived at the office for Margaret and small gifts for Annabelle. Each night as I climbed the stairs to my apartment above the office, I wondered if tomorrow would be Margaret's last day. I understood the lure of family. I wrote and received letters from mine constantly. On the days I felt brave and hopeful, I'd offer to take Margaret and Anabelle to lunch after church or walking in the evening. If Margaret chose to move, would I follow? Was Faith right? Should I tell Margaret I loved her? Was it fair for me to add my desires to those of her family? What could a small-town attorney offer Margaret and Anabelle that they couldn't get from her wealthy family?

~Practicing Law in Creekside, A Love Story by Micah Henderson

****

Cell phone vibrating against the wooden nightstand woke Tara from a dreamless sleep. "Morning, Jen," Tara rolled over and glanced at the barely perceptible sunlight glinting through the window. Phone calls before dawn rarely meant good news. "What's wrong?" Her heart pounded.

"It's Owen. I'm on my way to the hospital. A drunk hit his patrol car. That's all I know. The girls are asleep, and Mrs. Hutchins next door is staying with them. I'll call when I know more."

Tara dropped her cell on the charger and ran for the shower. Fifteen minutes later, dressed in jeans and a T-shirt, she picked up the phone. No update from Jen. The suitcase clanged against the wooden floor when Tara yanked it from the closet shelf. She dropped it on the bed and started folding shirts, jeans, and underwear into the bag while she willed the phone to ring. It didn't. Bag packed, she slowed her breathing and focused on the next steps. She grabbed the cell phone. Ronni answered on the first ring.

"Hey, Tara. You okay?"

"I'm fine, but Owen's been in an accident." *Slow down, slow down.* She took a deep breath. "Could you pick CJ and Makenna up from Catherine's today?"

"You driving to Bisbee? I'm happy to keep the kids while you're gone."

"Thanks. I'll pack them a bag and drop it off on my way." Tara yanked another bag off the shelf and cringed at the folded boxes behind the desk. "Shoot. I'm supposed to be packing up for the move next weekend. Can't worry about that now."

"Don't worry. Ask Nikki to give us the key. We'll grab what the kids need after we pick them up this afternoon and start the packing. You keep us posted about Owen, okay?"

"I'll do that. Thanks, Ronni." She grabbed a small bag and headed for the bathroom. She tossed toothpaste into the bag and jumped when the phone rang. "Jen. How's Owen?"

"Hurt. He's in surgery now to set his arm. The doctor will be out in a while to give me an update. All I know at the moment is what the EMT told me."

"You're not there alone?"

"No. The guys who rented your grandpa's house are waiting with me. My sister's on her way from Phoenix. Are you coming?"

"Yep. A couple of loose ends to tie up, and I'm on my way. Hang in there, Jen."

Make-up and toiletries stuffed haphazardly in the bag, Tara finagled it into the suitcase and dialed Nikki's cell phone.

"Hey, Tara. Is everything okay? I think this is the first time you've called me on my cell."

"Owen's in the hospital, and I'm on my way to Bisbee," she answered, picking up the small suitcase and her purse. "The kids are staying with Ronni and Nathan; can you give them a key so they can get the kid's stuff from our room?"

"Sure thing. Anything else I can do to help? You driving to Bisbee by yourself?"

"Yep. When I have a better idea of what's happening with Owen, I'll let you know about moving out, okay?"

"No worries. You've got the room as long as you need it."

After thanking Nikki, Tara took a last glance around the room for anything else she might need, grabbed the phone charger off the nightstand, and stuffed the phone and charger into her purse. Two flights of stairs later, Patrick met her at the bottom of the stairs.

"Patrick, I don't know when I'll be back and how the move is going to work," Tara commented when he greeted her. "Owen's in the hospital in Bisbee."

"Give me a minute to grab a bag, and I'll ride along with you to Bisbee. I can pick up the moving truck and haul your stuff back," Patrick offered.

Tara gazed into his blue eyes. "That's going beyond landlord duty. Why?"

"Has nothing to do with being your landlord. Aren't we friends?" He took her hand and led her to a table. "Grab some breakfast. I'll be ready before you're finished." Frown lines appeared between his brows. "Unless I'm forcing too hard and you don't want my help?"

Nikki appeared beside them and set a mug on the table. "Accept his help, Tara. Bisbee's a long drive. At least he's company."

"You're sure you want to ride along?" Tara asked. At Patrick's nod, she added, "Okay. I'll wait for you."

Patrick climbed the stairs two at a time and disappeared. "Now, get some breakfast, Tara," commented Nikki. "Patrick only offers to do what he wants to do. He wants to help. That's his specialty, helping."

Tara walked to the breakfast buffet. "Owen's like that," she commented. "Always helping."

Nikki dashed behind the bar and refilled the juice carafe. "Guess it's a brother thing."

By the time Tara sipped the last of her coffee and placed her dishes in the bus cart, Patrick appeared beside her, holding a small leather duffle bag.

At four-thirty p.m., they approached the community hospital reception desk and were directed to the surgery center waiting area. Tara scanned the small, crowded room for Jen. Two large male bodies parted, and she rushed into Jen's arms. "How is he?"

"Hurt, but he's gonna make it. I came out of his room when you texted. He's sleeping now but spoke to me a few minutes ago and made a little sense," her voice broke, and tears streamed down her cheeks.

Tara drew her into a hug. "It's okay, cry. You've probably held that in all day." When Jen stepped back and dried her tears, Tara suggested, "Go freshen up and go home so you can tell the girls what is going on. I'll sit with Owen. When you get back, I'll go home to the girls. If that works for you?"

"Okay. I need to talk to the girls and decide what happens next for them. My sister picked them up from summer art camp. I'll call as soon as I know what I'm going to do. You'll call me if anything changes with Owen?"

Tara drew Jen into another hug. "I'll call if anything happens. You go home and reassure the girls." With a nod, Jen strode down the hallway and disappeared around a corner. A warm hand grasped hers, and Tara gazed into familiar blue eyes. "I'd forgotten you were here," she commented.

"You've other things on your mind," Patrick said. "You going in to sit with Owen?"

"Yeah. Jen's gone home to the girls."

"Okay if I take my bag to the bed-and-breakfast and check-in?" Frown lines appeared between her eyes. "Do you want me to stay here?"

"No, it's not that. Would you check at the B-and-B for another room? If Jen's sister is staying with her, the house is full."

"No problem. Go sit with Owen. I'll text you what I find out."

Tara kissed his cheek. "Thanks." And disappeared through a door.

Patrick yanked out his phone and strode away. *Kiss*

on the cheek, appropriate for a thank you to a friend. Does she see me as a friend? Do I want more than friendship? No question I'm attracted. When we return to Creekside, should I act on the attraction? Would that be stupid since she would be living upstairs from my office? By the time he opened the door to her car, the B and B confirmed a second room, and he texted Tara.

He followed the GPS directions, and after a turn down a narrow residential street, located the address. His home for the next few days was a two-story elegant residence fronted by an elaborate, multi-level garden.

Patrick found a small parking lot marked with the B and B name and parked. He yanked both bags from the vehicle and strode up a winding walk to the front door. Beside the bell, a small plaque indicated the building was completed in 1917, the same year Victoria opened The Palace Hotel. *Does this building also boast a benevolent ghost?*

Patrick yanked open the door and stepped into a beautiful room filled with artfully arranged antiques.

"Welcome, Mr. Benton," greeted a low voice belonging to a smiling man sporting a precision trimmed white beard. "Your rooms are ready." He held out a fountain pen and motioned toward the guest book opened on the counter. "If you'll sign in?"

Patrick dashed his signature across the old-fashioned guest book. When he glanced back at the desk clerk, two keys dangled from his hand.

"Thank you. Did the other clerk mention the two rooms share a bath?"

"No. But it doesn't matter. I'm sure we'll manage."

"Excellent." Two keys landed in Patrick's outstretched hand. "Up the stairs to the right, end of the hall. The bath is between the two rooms. Would you like help with your luggage?"

Patrick declined and strode toward the stairs. So they would share a bath. A mental image of Tara emerging from her bath flashed through his head. Nope, not going there. No lustful thoughts allowed for a worried sister. He set the two bags in the middle of the hallway and opened both rooms. Easy decision which should be hers since pastels and lace decorated room 4, and a crazy quilt in shades of blue, green, and deep purple adorned the bed in room 6. He placed Tara's bag inside the small closet in room 4. In his room, he yanked the shaving kit out of his bag and set it on one side of the double sink. As he shut the door, his phone rang.

"Hey Tara, how's Owen?"

"Confused. Doesn't remember the accident or the aftermath."

"Is Jen back? Are you ready for dinner or to check into the inn?"

"No. Jen's having dinner with the girls and her sister, so she'll return in a couple of hours. They took Owen for more tests, but he should be back in a half hour or so. Can you come to get me in two hours?"

Patrick agreed and disconnected. He glanced at a schedule posted beside the door. Another forty-five minutes available for "Sips and Snacks" in the front parlor. One glass of wine and a few snacks, and he'd still have time to shower and change before he was due at the hospital. Ninety minutes later, he strode into the waiting area and greeted Tara, "You been waiting long?"

"No, Jen just got here." She stood and led them

toward the door. The hallway rang with muted voices from the rooms and the clank of cartwheels on tile floors.

"How's Owen?"

"Broken arm, clean break should heal pretty quickly. The big concern is the head injury. Can't know for sure, but it looks like a long road to recovery, including cognitive therapy. He was unconscious when the rescue squad extricated him from the vehicle."

At the SUV, Patrick asked, "Okay if I drive?" At Tara's nod, he yanked open the passenger door. Tara climbed in. Patrick shut the door and loped to the driver's side. Seatbelts fastened, he asked, "Where to? Dinner first or B and B? Or do you need to stop at Owen's house first?"

"Dinner with a glass of wine."

Patrick drove to the B and B and drove into the lot. "You up for a walk to dinner? I noticed a little Italian place about a block away."

At Tara's nod, he shut off the engine. They climbed out of the SUV, slammed the doors, and strolled down the street to the sounds of summer in a small town; crickets, birds, and slow-moving cars.

Patrick yanked open the restaurant door and ushered Tara inside. Scents of spices, low conversations, and quiet music greeted them. Seated in a booth beside the window, Patrick touched his wine glass to Tara's and took a sip.

She sipped and set her glass on the table. "This was a good idea."

"What?"

"The walk, the wine, the squishy booth. I can feel my shoulders loosen and my jaw relax. I swear chairs in hospital rooms are the most uncomfortable." Her lips lifted in a slight smile. "Good idea having you along for the ride though I still don't understand why you wanted to come."

"It's a long drive alone, especially when you're upset." He sipped his wine and lifted his lips in a grin. "Anyway, I didn't have anything pressing on my schedule."

"Way I hear it, you haven't had anything pressing on your schedule since you relocated to Creekside." She winked. "Except helping out at the hotel."

"Practicing law in Creekside is very different from practicing in San Diego. Plus, unlike when I started in San Diego, I'm no longer hustling to prove something."

"What were you trying to prove?"

He gazed at the Chianti in his glass and pictured himself at twenty-five. "That I could succeed as an attorney, I could build a family." He shrugged, and one side of his mouth lifted. "That my mom didn't waste her money helping me pay for law school."

Their server returned with the entrees and replenished the wine. Conversation flowed as Patrick asked about growing up in her grandparents' home in a small town and how much the town had changed since her childhood. When the server returned and inquired about dessert, they declined, and Patrick handed over his credit card.

"I didn't mean for you to pick up the tab," Tara commented as the server disappeared.

Patrick sipped the last of his wine. "Mom's rules, always pick up the tab on a first date. Meant to take you on a date next weekend."

Tara's lips lifted at the corners. "What other dating

rules did Mom hand out?"

Patrick signed the check with a flourish and slipped the card into his wallet. As they walked out of the restaurant, he commented, "Never chose a restaurant you can't afford. If another person is picking up the tab, wait until they order, then choose something either the same price or less expensive. If the food's great, compliment it. If it's not great, keep your mouth shut."

"Bet you were a popular date in college," Tara commented as they climbed the stairs toward their rooms.

"Not so much. I was busy studying and working during undergrad. In law school, I dated Amy the whole time."

"Well, I like your mom's dating rules. I'll remember to pass them on to CJ and Makenna when they hit high school."

At the door to her room, he took her hand and turned her to face him. "Mom had one more rule, the most important." He caressed her cheek with a gentle hand. "Whatever you ask for, when a woman says no, she means it. May I kiss you?" he asked.

"Yes," she answered on a breath.

Patrick leaned in, and their lips met. He touched his tongue to the seam; she opened and wrapped her arms around his neck. Heat filled Patrick and answered a question he hadn't dared to ask. He recognized her attraction in the way she drew him against her body. A door slammed somewhere, breaking the spell. Patrick gentled the kiss, her arms dropped from around his neck, keeping hold of her hands. He stepped back an inch, and her eyes drifted open. "Thank you. Good night, Tara."

Her lips lifted in a smile. "You're welcome. Night." She disappeared through the door.

Lounging in the wing-back chair beside the window, Patrick listened to the shower run and then stop. He pictured Tara wrapped in a towel, her skin flushed from the shower. *No. No. No.* He picked up his phone and checked his email, deleting the junk. A knock sounded on the bathroom door, and Tara softly uttered, "All yours."

The scent of vanilla soap surrounded him when Patrick yanked open the door. He stripped and stepped into the shower, hoping to dispel the image created by his imagination of Tara after a shower. By the time he was ready for bed, he was under control. He climbed between cool sheets and drifted into sleep.

Chapter Twenty

On the warmest day in October, we strolled the length of Main Street, took a gentle left onto a dirt track, and meandered toward Whisper Creek. Though a breeze cooled my cheeks under my sweater, sweat trickled down my spine. Nerves. Yesterday I received a letter from my youngest brother. He asked me to come home for his wedding. Normally leaving my law practice for a week would be a small problem of lost income. But leaving Margaret now, when her whole family wanted her in Fortuna, was a chance I couldn't take. No more time.

Today I planned to speak my heart. If she said no, I'd accept it. What I couldn't accept was the regret of never speaking my feelings. How do I convince her that without her, my heart would die? There would be no one else ever. In a moment of unbridled optimism, I'd bought her a ring. Margaret shook the blanket and spread it near the creek's bank. I took her hand, and we watched Anabelle dance and prance near the water. She called us over to see the tiny fish, to help her find the frogs. Eventually, she slowed, and we congregated on the blanket to consume lunch. Annabelle settled on the blanket for a well-earned nap. Her head rested on her mother's thigh. When Anabelle's soft snore assured me she slept, I withdrew the ring from my pocket and grasped Margaret's hand.

~*Practicing Law in Creekside, A Love Story* by Micah Henderson

****

A scream startled Patrick awake. He sat up, flipped the light on beside the bed, and waited.

"No-o-o. Let him go!" Tara's voice traveled through the wall.

His feet hit the wooden floor with a thud, and Patrick dashed through the connecting bathroom. The streetlight filtered through lace curtains, barely illuminating the bed. The quilt and pillows lay haphazardly on the floor. "Tara, you okay?" Patrick asked in a whisper. A quick scan assured Patrick Tara was alone. He sat down beside her on the bed and lightly touched Tara's hand. "Wake up. You're dreaming."

Tara's eyes opened, and frown lines appeared between her brows. "What are you doing here? Are you sleepwalking?"

"Nope. You screamed in your sleep. I was afraid someone had broken in."

She propped herself up and blinked. "No, just a nightmare. Weird nightmare."

"Want to talk about it? Nikki claims that makes them go away; you won't dream the same thing again."

She lay down, and Patrick stretched out beside her. "They used an extrication tool to remove Owen from the patrol car. The car rolled six times and ended upside down. Owen so far doesn't remember the rescue or the accident. In the dream, it looked like the rescue squad was keeping him inside the car, holding the door closed. I demanded they let him out. I could see his face, and he was asking me to help him." She rolled toward him, her arm flopped across his chest, and her head rested on his bicep. Her breathing evened, and she drifted to sleep. Patrick closed his eyes. *Might as well rest here until she rolled back the other way. No reason to wake her.*

Tara woke to the sun streaming through the lace curtains and the feel of Patrick rolling away from her. His bare feet padded on the wood floor. The bathroom door softly thudded closed, and the lock clicked. They spent the night together. After the nightmare, his warm presence made her feel safe, and she'd had hours of dreamless sleep. A few minutes later, her phone chimed with a text: *—Let me know when you're ready for breakfast.—*

After breakfast, Tara arranged for Patrick to pick up the rented moving truck and meet her at Jen's at one o'clock. When he started to climb out of her SUV, she commented, "Thanks for offering to drive the truck to Creekside. I don't understand why you offered, but I'm grateful you did."

He released his seatbelt and faced her. "Because we're friends and neighbors? Creekside's a small town, and neighbors help each other." His lips lifted in a grin. "Because I was a boy scout."

"Well, thank you." She took his hand. "And about last night, thank you for waking me and stopping the nightmare. It's been a long time since I've suffered through one so vivid."

"Anytime." He opened the door, his feet made a plopping sound on the asphalt, the door slammed, and with a wave, he ambled to the rental office and disappeared through the door.

Tara drove out of the lot and headed toward the

hospital. He'd spent the night in her bed, the first man she'd slept the night with since her divorce. Since he didn't mention waking up beside her, she chose to keep her silence. Her scream made him think someone had broken into her room, and he'd come through the connecting bathroom intent on rescue. She hoped he didn't see her as a damsel in distress, a woman too weak to take care of herself. That wasn't who she wanted to be, and not how she saw herself.

After the assault, she'd worked hard on regaining not only her physical strength but emotional health. When she found out Trey was out of prison, she'd run, not her finest hour maybe, but she focused on protecting her children. Never again did she want to see the terror in CJ's eyes because Trey appeared. If CJ was ever to meet his father again, it needed to be planned, prepared for, and in a place CJ felt safe. Now they'd never find out if Trey changed,—if losing his freedom for five years was enough to straighten his life out, change his attitude. So that left CJ with his last vision of his father in the back seat of a patrol car on his way to jail.

She drove the car into the hospital parking lot, chose a spot away from the main entrance, hopped out of the car, and strolled into the artificial chill of the hospital corridor. When she yanked open the door to Owen's room, she stopped short. Jen lay on the hospital bed, cuddled against Owen. He lay on his back, eyes open. He glanced toward the door and winked. Tara strolled to the bed's opposite side and slid into the chair. Jen opened her eyes, slowly stretched, and climbed off the bed. "Morning, Tara. I'm going to freshen up," she mumbled as she glided out the door.

"Jen okay?" Tara asked.

"Worried and exhausted but generally okay. Last night, the girls crawled in bed with her, too worried to sleep alone," he answered.

"Meaning no sleep for Jen. How are you doing? You look a little better."

Owen scratched his stubbled cheek. "Thinking about growing a beard since I won't be at work for a while. Can't help with the accident investigation since I don't remember anything."

"From what I understand of the accident, it might be better you can't remember," Tara commented. "They arrested the driver of the other car, so it doesn't matter if you remember."

"It's weird, not remembering. That adage about seeing your life flash before your eyes is a lie. I not only didn't see a life rerun, I didn't see danger coming. My contribution to the report is I remember driving on an almost empty road early morning. Traveling slow and carefully because the ducks and geese that hang out in that pond think they own the road. Next thing I remember, I woke up in the ER."

The door opened on a *whoosh*, and Jen strolled to the bed. She leaned over and kissed Owen. "Morning, love."

His good arm circled her waist. "Morning, babe. You thinking about going home since reinforcements arrived?"

"Yep. Need to find out what's happening with our children. Unfortunately, they're good at wrapping Auntie around their fingers. Funny how she's so strict with her kids and such a pushover for ours."

"Same reason you're strict with your girls and a

marshmallow with my two," Tara commented. "No accountability. You don't live with them, so the results of your missing discipline aren't your problem."

"How are my favorite niece and nephew? In fact, where are they?" Owen asked.

"Staying with Ronni and Nathan, and they're fine. I talked to them last night, and they are staying busy but are worried about you. CJ was torn between being upset he couldn't come with me and looking forward to more hanging out with Zack," Tara answered. "Hanging out with Zack is the best."

"Zack. His dad's the artist, right? The big guy with the beard who can't keep his eyes off Ronni?" asked Jen.

"Sort of. Jude is Zack's uncle and guardian," Tara admitted. "And yep, I noticed the way Jude looks at Ronni. I don't think Ronni is paying attention, though."

"Okay, girls, no more gossip. Poor guy's suffering. Makes me feel bad remembering what that's like," complained Owen. Jen caressed his scratchy cheek, kissed him briefly on the lips, and sauntered out. Owen's gaze followed her until the door closed. He glanced at Tara, "I remember what it's like. Jen made me work for that first date, and the second and every step was an uphill battle."

"But she was worth the work, right?"

"Right. Worth the waiting and everything else."

His jaw clenched, and his eyes drifted shut, veiling his feelings. Tara recognized that tactic. She'd used it herself when something was wrong and didn't want to share the burden. She grasped the fingers sticking out of his cast. "That trick with clenched jaw and closed eyes won't work Owen. I learned that one from watching you. What else is wrong, big brother?"

"I know physically I was lucky, only a broken arm from an accident where the fire department had to extricate my unconscious self from the car. Could have been so much worse."

He doesn't sound like he feels lucky. "But?"

"But traumatic brain injury can mean a whole bunch of problems and a long road to recovery. What if I'm never the same man? The same father, husband, brother, cop? I know who I was, and I liked the man I'd become. Who am I now? Who will I be?"

"Trauma, anything changes you. I'm so different from the woman who married Trey and the one you hauled home to Grandpa's house after Trey beat me up. You will be different, not less than, just different. You'll still be Owen, husband, father, brother, friend, and cop. You got this, big brother. Not saying it will be easy, but I know you can handle it."

For a while, they talked of life-changing moments. Some were painful, losing their parents, moving in with grandparents, losing their grandparents. Others created nothing but joy, the day they held their children for the first time, their child's first smile. A hospital staff member opened the door pushing a wheelchair. "Time for your therapy session, Mr. Wilson." She set the chair beside the bed and helped Owen transfer. She glanced toward Tara. "He'll be gone a few hours." She whisked Owen out the door.

Tara took out her cell phone and texted Jen that she was leaving the hospital. She offered to pick up lunch. After placing the order online, she texted Patrick, offering him lunch if he was available in forty-five minutes to meet at Owen's house. In less than an hour, she drove into Owen's driveway, her mouth watering at the enticing scents of tomato, bread, and spices. As she yanked open the passenger door to retrieve the food, her nieces surrounded her, grabbing her in exuberant hugs. Tara handed the pizza boxes to the girls, and Patrick arrived, driving the moving truck.

Patrick jumped out of the truck and slammed the door. The girls disappeared through the front door. Tara yanked a large sack from the vehicle and slammed the door closed just as Patrick reached her side. "May I?" He took the sack.

"Yes. Your timing's perfect." She handed him the sack, and they strolled toward the door.

Balancing the large sack on his hip, Patrick asked, "What's in here? I noticed the pizza boxes disappearing through the door."

"The healthy portion of lunch and dessert," Tara admitted.

"Trying to hit all the food groups, were you?" Patrick quipped.

"Yep. Children do not grow by pizza alone, although sometimes they'd like to." She led him down the hallway and into a large kitchen where silverware, plates, glasses, and napkins were lined up on the counter. A bouquet of summer flowers decorated the center of a table surrounded by eight chairs.

Youthful voices announced Paige and Sofie's return, Jen and her sister right behind them. They finished off the pizza, salad, and cannoli in quick order and returned the kitchen to pristine condition. After hugs for her nieces, Tara followed Jen and Patrick out the door. By unspoken agreement, they waited for Jen to drive out of the driveway before they strolled to their vehicles. Ten minutes later, Patrick parked the moving van beside Grandpa's house, and Tara parked her SUV across the street.

They met on the sidewalk in front of the house. As they climbed the porch steps, Tara admitted, "Feels weird ringing the bell at a house I lived in up until a few months ago."

"Probably a good idea to ring, though. No telling what's going on in there. Could be a wild party," Patrick quipped.

The door opened, and a giant shadow filled the doorway. "Hey, Tara," rumbled a deep voice.

"Hey, Quinn. This is Patrick Benton, Patrick, Quinn Chauncy." Quinn opened the door and motioned them inside. "If it's okay, I'll take Patrick up to the kids' rooms and show him what we're moving."

"No need, Tara. Ben and I had time, so we transferred all the kids' stuff into the second parlor. Figured it'd be easier if everything was downstairs. Owen and Jen boxed everything, and we dismantled the furniture."

With help from Ben and Quinn, the truck was loaded. They decided to leave it parked beside the old house since there was plenty of room. Tara and Patrick climbed into her SUV.

As Tara started the engine, Patrick commented, "Having the boxes packed, furniture dismantled, and everything on the first floor probably saved us several hours of moving time."

"Yep. I didn't know Jen and Owen had already done so much prep work."

Patrick glanced at her. Frown lines appeared on her forehead; her lips turned down. "Was it harder packing it up without doing the boxing yourself? Did the prep work make leaving the house more difficult?"

"No. We'd been there five years and gone several months. No idea what we left behind. I dreaded sorting stuff since it's time-consuming, and as sure as I tossed something, one of my children would have missed it. This way, they can decide later, no pressure, what to keep and what to give away." She turned out of the business district into the residential area. "You relocated from a house to a hotel room. What happened to all Scott's stuff?"

"Storage. I knew I wanted to get rid of the house as soon as Scott decided on college in Arizona. In the final semester of his senior year, we did a whirlwind sort through the house, getting it ready to sell. Everything that mattered to Scott I put in a storage unit in Phoenix. It's still there."

"Do you miss your house?" she asked as she parked the car next to the B and B. "Big change from a house in a city near the ocean to a haunted hotel in a small town."

"The first summer Scott spent working at The Palace, I discovered the house was only a building. A beautiful building in a good location, but still just a building. Do you miss your grandfather's house?"

They strolled into the parlor, where wine and snacks were displayed on an old-fashioned buffet. Several guests lounged in small groups around the room. Their host appeared, offering them a choice of food and drink. Glasses and plates in hand, they settled in a pair of club chairs beside a small table.

"I do miss Grandpa's house sometimes. From the moment Owen and I moved in with our grandparents, the house surrounded me with a comforting mix of warmth and family history."

She sipped the wine and took a small bite from a cracker spread with cheese. Her face split in a smile. "When I'm feeling particularly sentimental about the house, I remind myself I do not miss the constant repairs. The weekends spent weeding, trimming bushes, waiting for the plumber because water leaked in the kitchen. Life in the old house seemed ideal when all the maintenance and repairs were Grandpa's problem. Different story when all that fell to me."

"At least while you live in the Henderson Building, maintenance problems will be mine rather than yours." He sipped the wine and set the glass on the table. "Because the building was recently renovated, I'm hoping there won't be much repair work required. Can I get you another glass of wine?"

At her agreement, Patrick gathered their glasses and strolled to the buffet. After a brief discussion with their host about walking distance restaurants, he returned to Tara and handed her a glass of wine.

As he dropped into the chair, he asked, "How did your visit with Owen go? Any idea when he'll be released from the hospital?"

"Tomorrow morning as long as nothing changes overnight." She gently swirled the wine in her glass, then took a sip. Her head lifted, and she gazed into his eyes. "Do you know anything about traumatic head injury?"

"Not much," he admitted. "Is that the diagnosis?"

"Yep. He started cognitive therapy this afternoon. He's worried he won't still be the man he was, that the injury will change his personality."

"Is that likely?"

"From what I could quickly find online, there isn't any way to predict the long-term effects." Tara frowned and sipped her wine. "Plus, any trauma changes a person, doesn't matter what kind. I discovered how much one event could alter a person's perspective and life after Trey's assault."

"Do you believe you changed as a person? Are you not fundamentally the same?"

"Fundamentally? I'm the same if what you mean is core values like loyalty, honesty, kindness, and compassion. My perspective changed, which altered some of my personality traits." She gazed into his concerned blue eyes. "Unless it involves my children's safety, I'm no longer guilty of conflict avoidance. I don't smooth things over to keep the peace. No more will I analyze something until I've worried it to death, and I discovered most things won't be perfect."

"And trauma forced those changes?"

"Trauma and therapy. Lots of therapy. When I first returned to Bisbee, I was afraid to leave the house," she admitted. "I claimed I felt lousy; after all, I was pregnant and bruised. I'd just gotten out of the hospital. Jen and Owen took turns driving me to therapy and waiting in the reception area during my sessions. They promised not to leave me there alone."

"And now Owen's starting therapy. Do you wish you were moving back to Bisbee?" Patrick asked as he sipped his wine.

"I think us staying in Creekside is better for everyone. Owen needs to focus on himself and Jen right now without worrying about how his situation affects his little sister. In some ways, I may be more help being someone he can talk to who is not really in the situation with him."

They gathered their glasses and plates and set them on the bus cart. With a thank you to the host, they started up the stairs.

When they reached their rooms, Patrick asked, "What would you like for dinner, or are you going back to Owen's? According to the host, Mexican and Greek are within walking distance."

"Let's do Mexican. Jen's sister is still there tonight, and Jen is at the hospital."

Ensconced in the reading chair beside the window, his feet perched on the hassock, Patrick answered emails and listened to the water running in the connecting bathroom. Again, an image of Tara rosy from the shower sent heat to his groin. What was it about her that made his body think he was seventeen instead of forty-two?

Today she looked like a college kid with her hair in a ponytail, her long legs defined by slim jeans, and wearing a T-shirt sporting "Kindness Counts." He wondered if the shirts bearing affirmative sayings were one of the changes after her trauma.

The shower stopped, and a moment later, the door opened then closed. Patrick tapped on the bathroom door. No answer, so he turned the knob and stepped into a room full of steam and the scent of vanilla. Would he forever smell vanilla and think of Tara?

By the time he'd showered, shaved, and dressed, he knew the relationship needed to go forward or end. His siblings found their mates. Scott was nearly grown. Did he want to spend the rest of his life alone?

He stepped out his door, and Tara greeted him,

"Perfect timing. You do like Mexican food, right? I didn't even think to ask."

"I do." He took her hand. "I was born in Arizona, hard not to like Mexican food."

A gentle breeze teased Tara's hair, tugging a few wisps from her ponytail. Sunset painted the sky in shades of orange as they navigated the GPS directions to the restaurant.

A yank on the door yielded scents of chilies and onions. They followed a hostess to a booth near the window and slid in opposite sides. When they'd ordered, Patrick asked. "Were you born in Arizona?"

"Yep. Bisbee. After they received their PhDs, my parents taught in New Mexico. When my mom discovered she was pregnant, they decided to have their children where my dad grew up. They moved in with my grandparents. Owen was born within a few months, and I followed when he was three. The story is he wasn't happy about a sister. He counted on a brother."

"But you weren't raised in Bisbee before your parents died?" Patrick tried to remember their previous conversations. He thought she mentioned coming from somewhere else.

She shook her head. "Nope. When I was three and Owen six, we moved. By the time my parents died, I'd lived in four states and attended seven schools. My parents taught at private colleges and universities all over the country. I spent my childhood in college towns. Sometimes we'd return to Bisbee in the summer as a family, and sometimes Owen and I would stay the summer with our grandparents while our parents taught elsewhere."

"Now that the choice is yours, which life do you

want for your children? The stay in one place childhood or the live everywhere." Patrick remembered Amy's determination not to stay in one place; her need to see the whole world. She offered Scott opportunities to travel in the summer, and sometimes he'd agreed, but mostly Scott declined. Did he decline because he didn't trust Amy's traveling partners or because he preferred home?

"From an adult perspective, I appreciate the experience moving frequently gave us. At the time, I hated it. New schools, new friends, not always fitting in are hard. I want to give CJ and Makenna the security Owen and I received from our grandparents. I'll save the traveling for vacations."

They finished their meal and the return stroll in conversation of places they'd visited beyond Arizona and dreams of places remaining on their bucket lists. When they climbed the steps to their rooms, a comfortable tiredness stole over Patrick. At Tara's door, he touched her lips with one finger and whispered, "A good night kiss?"

A smile tilted her lips, and she answered, "A perfect ending to our date."

He gently drew her against him and wrapped her in his arms. Her hands landed on his shoulders, and their lips met. He touched his tongue to her lips. She tasted of salt and lime, the margarita. Her lips parted, and he deepened the kiss. His body heated, and his groin tightened. Her fingers caressed the hair on his neck. He gentled the kiss and loosened his hold. He needed to end the kiss now. With two bedrooms to choose from if they continued on this path, the temptation was overwhelming to take the attraction to the next level.

Too soon. After a gentle hug, he stepped back and released her. "Good night, Tara."

"Night." She opened the door and slipped out of sight.

Patrick stood at the window in his room, staring out at the quiet night. From the bathroom, the sounds of Tara getting ready for bed drifted into his room. What were the odds he'd wake tomorrow sharing a bed with Tara? Not good. No doubt the situation with Tara was different from any of his dates in the last few years. He traveled a journey without a map, compass, or GPS. After Amy, he dated women he knew were not interested in a family or children. Women near his age either already had children they shared with an ex-husband, or they weren't interested in creating a family.

A knock sounded on the bathroom door, and Tara whispered, "Your turn."

Patrick got ready for bed, packed his small suitcase, and climbed into bed. Was getting involved with Tara a huge mistake? If things ended badly, more than the two of them were involved. Her children and his reputation in Creekside could be hurt, not to mention their mutual friends. Amy convinced him he was a much better parent than a spouse. She believed her needs and wants took second place to Scott's. If he married Tara, would he feel second, or would she? If their relationship ended, would Tara stay in Creekside or go home to Bisbee? He didn't want to be responsible for disrupting the lives of her children. He drifted to sleep.

Chapter Twenty-One

November blew into Creekside carried on a frosty wind. In order of age, Margaret's brothers visited me. Behind the closed doors of my office, they asked the same questions, expressed the same doubts. How could their little sister be happy married to a small-town lawyer? Their daddy raised her for better things than the apartment above a small office. I replied the same way each time, I loved Margaret. Everything I was, everything I owned belonged to her. Her youngest brother brought his news; he'd volunteered for service in the US Army. He didn't wait to be drafted.

~Practicing Law in Creekside, A Love Story by Micah Henderson

****

The scent of cinnamon and nutmeg greeted Patrick when he and Tara joined the other guests in the dining room. Munching baked French toast and sipping coffee, they planned Patrick's return to Creekside. Breakfast over, they checked out and loaded their bags in Tara's SUV. Through the quiet town they drove, the clear blue sky a good omen for moving day. At her grandfather's house, Patrick jumped out of the SUV, bag in hand. "I'll keep you posted on what's happening with your move," Patrick promised. "Are you okay with Ronni and Nathan deciding where stuff goes in the apartment?"

"Yep. Talked to Ronni yesterday and she claims moving furniture around is one of her favorite hobbies, especially when she can get someone else to do the moving."

"Take care, Tara. Keep me posted on Owen." He shut the door and walked toward the moving truck. When he'd thrown his bag in the passenger's side, Tara drove away. As he drove the big truck onto the street, he hoped the time they were apart would clarify his feelings. He didn't want a convenient relationship based on proximity. They'd lived across the hall from each other and shared office space for most of the last five months. Was that the attraction? Or did she represent the dreams he'd lost when Amy left? The dreams of a family built on lasting love?

By the time Patrick drove the moving truck into the hotel's parking lot, the sun started its descent, the air cooled. He maneuvered the vehicle around several unfamiliar cars. He hopped out, grabbed his bag, and slammed the door, grateful to be standing upright after the long drive. At the hotel's back door, he touched his key to the lock, opened the door, and let it close with a *click*. In the shadowy corridor, Victoria stood, her hand raised to knock. She looked toward him, dropped her eyelid in a wink, and glided through the door. The scent of lavender lingered in the hall. Victoria probably visited her lover in room 11. At least she had a plan for the evening. After long hours in the truck and letting his thoughts drift, he planned a shower, food, and a quiet evening reading. There was nothing he could do about Tara while they were apart; maybe by the time she returned, he'd know what he wanted and if the attraction was real or a product of proximity.

Stella Jayne Phillips

When he dropped the bag on the luggage stand, a message dinged on his phone. He glanced at the screen.

—*You home?*— Nikki texted.

—*Just dropped my bag in the room*— he responded.

—*Good. Dinner in the sitting room in an hour?*—

He agreed and headed for the shower. Two pieces of his plan were already arranged. By the time he arrived at the sitting room, he'd showered, changed, emptied his suitcase, deleted the junk from his email, and grabbed a glass of wine from the bar. He tapped once on the sitting room door, used his key on the lock, and stepped into his sister's arms. By the time the group was arranged around the table, Sam was regaling them with his adventures at art camp. Dinner over, he helped with clean up while Nikki changed Michelle and Alex changed for work.

When the boys were involved in their activities in the boy cave and Alex disappeared, Nikki asked, "How's Owen?"

"He's home as of today. According to Tara's text, the move went smoothly. He's happier in his own space." Patrick sipped the wine. "I'm back earlier than I expected because the tenants in Tara's house had taken apart the furniture, Jen and Owen packed everything else before his accident, and all of it was downstairs."

"Did they help you load?"

"Yep. Fastest move I've ever been involved in."

"Probably none of my business," Nikki admitted, "but why did you offer to go to Bisbee with Tara? It's not like you're a couple or she's family."

"Tara asked the same question. My answer is we're friends. I've helped lots of friends move, made airport runs to get them to family, and helped them with the process of settling estates." He set the glass on the coffee table. "Bisbee's a long drive, and I knew Owen planned to deliver Tara's stuff this weekend. Seemed like the right thing to do."

"And you like her, which thrills me." She grabbed his hand, and he gazed into her brown eyes. "Be sure the attraction isn't based on your white knight complex. She's a strong woman who has had some bad breaks the last few months, but she's capable of handling her life."

He stood, leaned over, and kissed her cheek. "Yeah, I know she's capable, but everyone can use a friend's support sometimes. Thanks for dinner." Patrick slipped into the hallway and strolled to the backdoor.

When he stepped outside, the light over the door blinked on, casting a white glow on the asphalt. He paced around the building to the moving truck. After he checked the vehicle's doors were locked, he meandered toward the square and the sounds of big band music.

At the oak tree, he plopped onto the grass, leaned his back against the trunk, and admired the way the Gallivanting Grandpas convinced the audience to get up and dance to "Blue Moon."

Would becoming a grandfather be my next chapter? Scott drifted farther away every day, anxious to be an adult, build his own life. Was the attraction to Tara because she and the children are a second chance to be a husband and father now Scott barely needs me? Can I start over as a husband and father and be more successful balancing the two roles? Nikki was right, Tara could handle anything life threw at her but that didn't mean having a partner wouldn't enrich her life. I don't need to be anyone's white knight, but could I be a partner to a woman with two young children?

The band moved into "I Got Rhythm." Patrick admired the dancing couples and strolled toward the hotel. At the parking lot, he checked the locks on the moving truck again and ambled to the back door. He touched the lock with his key and yanked open the door.

In the shadowy hallway, Victoria appeared outside Sam's room. She glided through the closed door and disappeared, leaving behind the scent of lavender. Patrick wondered if she visited Mitch and Colin in their basement room. She did keep an eye on the hotel's children.

****

When Patrick entered the lobby for breakfast, Nathan greeted him with a wave and a smile. Balancing a plate of omelet casserole and wheat toast in one hand and a mug of coffee in the other, he plopped into a chair across from Nathan.

"Morning. Besides my sister's excellent breakfast, what brings you here, Nathan?"

"I'm ready to help with the move whenever you say. I dropped Tina and Makenna off at sports camp a few minutes ago." He got up, placed his dishes in the bus cart, and refilled his coffee.

When Nathan sat down, Patrick commented, "Soon as I finish breakfast, I'll park the truck behind the Henderson Building, and we can start unloading. Scott and James will meet us there in about an hour."

"Perfect. I'll sit here and finish my coffee and text Ronni what time to be there. She's in charge of telling us where things go." He grinned at Patrick over the rim of his cup. "We need to haul all the boxes from Tara's room to the truck."

"Boxes?"

"Yep. Ronni and I and the kids boxed up everything in Tara's hotel room. I think the boxes are small enough for the dumb waiter," Nathan commented. "We wanted everything ready before you returned so we could finish the move in one day."

By the time they added the boxes to the moving truck and drove the few blocks to the law office, James, Scott, Chance, Ronni, and CJ lounged on the front porch.

Patrick opened the building's front door and led them up the stairs to the apartment. After a two-minute tour, he unlocked the kitchen door leading to the outside staircase. "So what do you think? Inside stairs or outside?"

Using the outside staircase, by the time they broke for lunch, the truck was empty, and the living room area was crammed with boxes and furniture. Patrick tossed the truck keys to Scott. "Since you need to clean up for work anyway, how about parking the truck behind the hotel?"

"Sure, Dad," Scott agreed. "I'm meeting Casey for lunch, so I'll drop the truck off now. You have enough help setting up, right?" At his father's agreement, Scott disappeared through the outside door. A few minutes later, there was the growl of the truck's engine.

After a pizza lunch delivered by Willie's, the beds were assembled, and boxes unpacked and broken down. As Patrick closed and locked the door, he glanced around the living room, making sure the French doors leading to the Juliet balcony were closed. A couple appeared standing in front of the door, their arms wrapped around each other. Patrick blinked, and the couple disappeared.

"When's the rest of Tara's stuff arriving?" James asked as they strolled toward the hotel at dusk.

"Friday, her bed comes from someplace in Phoenix. Everything else she plans to buy after she moves in. With all the antique shops in the area, she shouldn't have trouble finding what she wants," Patrick answered.

"She didn't want the furniture from her grandfather's house?" James asked as they dodged clumps of tourists on the sidewalk.

"The tenants rented the house furnished. Owen transferred the furniture with sentimental value into the kids' rooms and locked the doors. With five bedrooms, formal dining room, a couple of parlors, attic, and finished basement, the tenants didn't miss the kids' rooms."

"So she moved from a huge old house to a haunted hotel to an apartment over a law office. The apartment's better than a hotel room, but that's a big change." They turned the corner, and the hotel appeared. "Kind of like your big changes from house to hotel, beach city to a small town."

"Yep. See you." With a wave, Patrick climbed the hotel's front steps.

As he opened the door to his room, his cell phone rang, and Tara's name appeared on the screen. "Hey, Tara. How's your brother?"

"He just got home from cognitive therapy, so he's taking a pre-dinner nap. From what I could find on the Internet and what Jen learned from the doctor, the exhaustion is normal and will get better."

"How are Jen and the kids doing?"

"Jen's glad he's home." Tara sighed. "Paige and Sophie keep peeking in his room to make sure he's breathing. They're having trouble adjusting to a dad who naps in the afternoon. Doesn't fit with the dad they know."

"He did just get out of the hospital."

"Yep. He looks good, with a few bruises and a broken arm, but he has trouble focusing on anything for long, even conversations with his girls. Reading and processing require concentrated effort, meaning the therapy exhausts him. The doctors believe he'll get better but no timeline with a traumatic brain injury."

"How long do you plan to stay?"

"Jen's sister leaves for Phoenix in the morning, but their friends and neighbors are stepping up to carpool the girls. His fellow officers set up a system to manage Owen's trips home from therapy, so Jen plans to return to work on Monday."

"Sounds like they've got everything covered."

"Looks like it. I'll drive home on Sunday. Ronni says the move went well. If the furniture store delivers my bedroom stuff on time Friday, I can spend Sunday night in the apartment."

"Did you need me to check you out of the hotel?"

"No thanks. Ronni already checked us out as soon as you and Nathan loaded up the boxes. She promised to meet the furniture store movers on Friday and wait for the delivery from the department store in Flagstaff, too. By the time I get home Sunday night, we'll be set. Thanks again. You and your family are amazing. Hmm, sounds like my presence is required. I'll see you next week."

The call disconnected, and Patrick dropped his cell on the charger and yanked open the mini-fridge. He yanked out a bottle of water and read the note on the plastic container nestled next to a bottle of beer: *Chicken chili for dinner if you're too tired to go out.*

He guzzled the water and shut the fridge door; dinner could wait. Stripping, he headed to the shower, where the warm water eased muscles he rarely used. He ran and lifted weights at the community gym, but neither exercise prepared him for moving furniture up and down flights of stairs. He dried off and drew on sweats and a T-shirt, then popped the chili in the microwave.

Something to be said, living in Nik's hotel, he ate well. Scents of onion, chili, and tomato filled the room. He placed the bowl on the small table, hauled over a chair, grabbed the novel he'd started last night, and devoured the chili, smiling at the memory of his mom teaching Nik to cook. What a mess the first efforts were.

Probably a good idea not to see Tara for a few days. He didn't always agree with his little sister, but she made a valid point. Before he acted on his attraction, he wanted to be sure he was attracted to the real Tara, not to the damsel in distress. The real Tara raised two young children with no partner and ran her own successful business. The night she checked in to the hotel, her fear was obvious in the stiff set of her shoulders and the look she gave him when he offered to show her to her room. After five months in Creekside and the death of her ex, she was no longer afraid. He'd been attracted from the first moment.

Eleven o'clock, he shut the book with a snap,

disappointed in the ending. How could the author type the end when he'd left so many dangling threads? Life offered enough mysteries and unresolved issues without wasting his time on fictional ones. He dropped the book on the table beside the door and crawled under the covers.

In the dark hour before dawn, he woke to adult voices. In the weak shaft of moonlight from the skylight, a man and woman appeared, facing each other, their hands clasped. A deep voice asked, "You're positive I can't change your mind? You won't go with me?"

Victoria released one hand and caressed his cheek. "It's better for all of us if I stay here. Certainly, better for RJ."

He drew her into his arms, and their lips met. Stepping back, he whispered, "I'll miss you both. Be safe.

"We'll be here waiting," she responded. The scent of lavender filled the room, and they disappeared.

Patrick closed his eyes. What kept Victoria and her lover apart? When they appeared together, their love filled the room, replaced by sadness when they parted. Was he capable of loving a woman that way? Sleep claimed him.

Chapter Twenty-Two

Wedding–Friday, April 10, Margaret Curtis and Micah Henderson celebrated their marriage at Emanuel Lutheran Church. Rose Mosely, Anabelle Curtis, and Alexander Stark attended the couple. Pastor Joseph Martin officiated. Following the ceremony, Mrs. Faith Eckie and Miss Mary Beth Easley hosted a luncheon reception at Eckie House. Margaret and Micah created a beautiful picture, Margaret gowned in peach satin, and Micah wearing a traditional navy suit. Spring flowers filled the Eckie House parlor providing a fragrant backdrop for the sumptuous luncheon. Mr. and Mrs. Henderson and Anabelle will make their home above the Henderson Law Office after a brief wedding trip.

~The Creekside Reporter 1918.

****

The sunset painted the sky orange, yellow, and pink when Tara drove into Creekside on Sunday. Maneuvering her SUV through the residential area to avoid the busy town square, she turned onto Exeter Street and parked behind the Henderson Building. Illuminated from the inside, the second-floor apartment offered a warm welcome. Should she take the front entrance or enter through the kitchen? She glanced at the upstairs landing. Ronni leaned against the rail and waved. Suitcase in hand, Tara dashed up the stairs.

"Welcome home, Tara," greeted Ronni. "We held dinner for you, but the others can hardly wait." She grabbed Tara's bag and yanked open the door.

Tara stepped over the threshold to a chorus of "Welcome home." The scents of chili sauce, chicken, and spicy beans filled the small room. A selection of taco shells and fixings waited on the kitchen counter. An unfamiliar round oak table held plates, silver, and napkins. Plates filled, they lounged on the floor of the living room. "Where did the table and chairs come from?" Tara asked as she plopped on the floor.

"Nikki's basement," Ronni answered. "Unbelievable the amount of furniture stored down there."

As she munched on tacos, her children regaled her with detailed descriptions of their week's activities. CJ stretched out on the floor, and Makenna sprawled next to Tara, her head against Tara's shoulder. Listening to their high-pitched voices, hearing the enthusiasm in their voices, Tara's body relaxed, her shoulders loosened. Dinner over and leftovers stored in the fridge, Nathan, Ronni, and Tina chorused, "Good night," and disappeared out the door.

Patrick took her hand, and they walked to the panel door. He slid the door into its pocket and turned to face her. "Another exciting dinner date and this time no kiss good night?" he quipped.

"Nope. No kisses with our audience," Tara answered. "Thank you, again."

"You're welcome, again." He touched her cheek with the tips of his fingers. "I'm glad you're home." He slipped through the door. It closed with a quiet *click*.

Tara herded her children through their bedtime

rituals and tucked them in. When Makenna drifted to sleep halfway through her favorite book, Tara peeked into CJ's room. She glided to his bed, picked his book up off the floor, and turned off the light.

After a long, hot shower in the bathroom attached to her bedroom, Tara plucked a fresh nightshirt out of the drawer in her closet and dropped it over her head. She glanced around her room. Her own room with her own bath. A luxury after five months of sharing a hotel room and single bath with her children. She glided through the living area and kitchen, checking the doors were latched and locked. She climbed the stairs and gazed at her sleeping children. Each child was surrounded by the furniture and possessions they'd left behind.

She drifted downstairs into her room and crawled between new, soft, white sheets. When they chose food from the buffet in the kitchen, she'd joined Patrick in a deep discussion of the best taco fillings with Tina and Makenna. He'd crouched to their level and focused his attention on the two girls. They'd responded with smiles and giggles. She didn't need to guess what type of father he was to Scott. Patrick's core of kindness shone in each interaction with all children, no matter their age or parents.

When she met and married Trey, he was charming, kind, loving, and fun. Was it an act? Or the other Trey, the arrogant, greedy, violent one, was that behavior a product of drugs and alcohol? Or was the real Trey a combination, a complex man with many sides to his personality, not all of them good or bad? Was there more to Patrick, sides she hadn't seen yet? Darkness claimed her.

Soft voices woke her as early dawn peeked through the sheer curtains. In the shadowy corner, a man stood, unpinning the hair of a woman. Her dark hair dropped down her back in a long cascade, and the man wrapped his arms around her, tugging her back against his chest.

He nuzzled her neck, then turned her in his arms. "I've waited all day to hold you in my arms."

She turned in his arms, lifted on her bare toes, and kissed him. They slowly dissolved as the sun brightened the room.

On a sigh, Tara closed her eyes and drifted to sleep. Good to know she'd traded the benevolent Palace Hotel spirits for lovers.

At the chirping alarm, Tara woke to sunlight streaming through the curtains. After a dash to the bathroom, she headed to the kitchen, started the coffee maker, set the oven to 350, and took out the ingredients for her kids' favorite baked oatmeal.

After buttering the pan, slicing the bananas into the bottom, and mixing up the batter, she placed the dish on the oven's middle shelf and set the timer. She climbed the stairs and woke her children, stopping to help Makenna choose an outfit and matching socks. Returning to the kitchen, she removed the oatmeal from the oven to let it rest and set the table. Her children arrived in the kitchen as she poured her first cup of coffee.

After breakfast and clean up, she hustled her children upstairs to finish getting ready. Five months since they lived in something bigger than a hotel room, and they'd dropped back into their familiar routine. Ready, they clattered down the interior stairs into the office. CJ strolled onto the front porch to wait for Jude and Zack to pick him up for horse camp. Holding Makenna's hand, Tara joined him outside as the emerald pickup parked in front of the building. Zack opened the truck's back door, and CJ climbed inside.

With a wave, Tara gazed at the truck as it disappeared around the corner. "Let's get your backpack, almost birthday girl."

Makenna tugged the small pack over her shoulders, and they strolled toward the elementary school. "Will Tina and Hope be at camp today, Mommy?"

Tara glanced down at Makenna as they crossed the street. Makenna chewed on her bottom lip. "Yes, I bet you know most of the kids in your group."

"Will you pick me up after?"

"I can if you want me to," Tara offered. "But Nathan offered to walk you and Tina home."

"That's okay then. Uncle Nathan can bring me home."

They strolled through the elementary school's unlocked gate and cut across the grass to the cafeteria. They stepped inside and were stopped by a young woman wearing a T-shirt identifying her as *STAFF*. As Tara signed Makenna in, a teenage girl bounced up to Makenna and coaxed her into a conversation. By the time Tara completed filling in forms, Makenna and the teen were engaged in a game with other children.

Assured Makenna was comfortable at camp, Tara strolled toward the office. Today would be a perfect day to play hooky, slight breeze, clear sky, cool day for June. Unfortunately, last week in Bisbee meant she'd barely stayed even with her work. Grateful she at least had a short morning walk, Tara returned to the office and opened her laptop. A few minutes later, she startled when Patrick set a mug of coffee on her desk. "Hey, thanks," she commented with a smile.

"You're welcome. Kids off to their activities this morning?" he asked.

"Yep. How's The Palace without us? Do you have a new neighbor?"

"Palace is busy but no new neighbor." He dropped into the chair beside her desk. "How about dinner and a movie with the kids this Sunday?"

"Sounds good. You sure about including the kids?"

"You've been away a week. Figured you'd be hesitant going out without them so soon."

"I accept." Of course he understood she wasn't ready to leave the kids since she just returned from Bisbee.

"I'm meeting James for lunch; do you want me to pick you up something on my way back?" he asked as he stood.

"No, thank you. I'm making lunch from all the food in my very own refrigerator," she answered. "You've no idea how lovely that sounds. My own kitchen, a whole apartment."

"Later then." He disappeared out the door.

Where was this relationship going? Last night he flirted a little; in Bisbee, he kissed her. Now, he asked her out and included her children. He lived in a hotel surrounded by family, but sometimes she caught loneliness in his eyes. Loneliness she recognized since there were times a glance in the mirror reflected the same in her. Were they two adults looking to fill an empty space for now? Or was there more? She tapped a key on the laptop, and the screen returned to life. Right now, she needed to focus on her business. Examination of her personal landscape could wait until she crawled into bed tonight.

Four o'clock, her focus broke at the sound of familiar voices, Patrick's warm, deep tones joined with CJ's higher laughter. A moment later, CJ dashed into her office.

"Mom, I'm home." He dropped into the visitor chair.

She returned his grin and then grimaced at the dirt. "I'm glad you're here. How'd you get so dirty?"

"It's horse camp, Mom. Today we brushed the horses down, cleaned the stalls. Dirty work."

"I can see that. Head upstairs and shower. Put your dirty clothes on the washer, not in the hamper."

"Can I have a snack first?" he asked as he popped up from the chair.

"Nope. Shower first. No smelly, grimy boys in the kitchen." He disappeared, and a moment later, the sound of pounding feet announced his progress up the stairs.

Nathan appeared in her doorway, Tina and Makenna beside him. "Hey, Tara. Look who's home."

Makenna danced to Tara, wrapping her in a hug. "Did you have a good day?"

"Yes! We played games, painted pictures, sang songs, read books, and everyone said they were coming to our party, huh, Tina?"

"Let's go home to your mommy, T," Nathan commented. "See ya later." With a wave, he disappeared, the *click* of the front door confirming they were gone.

Tara shut down her computer and locked it in the drawer. With a quick farewell to Patrick, she and

Makenna climbed the inside stairs. "Mommy, there were still kids at the school. How come Tina and me had to come home?"

"I thought you'd be tired by now. Today was a longer day for you than the time you spent at preschool." Tara slid the pocket door into its space, and they stepped into the apartment. "You're not tired?"

"No. We were having fun. I didn't want to miss anything," Makenna whined.

"Let me talk to Ronni and see what she thinks. Sounds like your brother's out of the shower. Go wash your hands and face." She hustled Makenna to the stairs. "When you're done, snack will be ready." Makenna climbed the stairs, her steps slow.

After a snack and indoor playtime, Tara served crockpot lasagna and salad. When the dishes were loaded in the dishwasher and the kitchen cleaned, she sent CJ to his room to read and hustled Makenna into the tub. Wrapped in a towel, Makenna skipped into her bedroom.

As she drew the pajama top over her head, Makenna asked, "Can we have a dog now? We're not in the hotel anymore."

"I'll have to ask Mr. Benton. He owns the apartment." Tara tucked Makenna into bed. "Don't you think it would be better to get furniture for the living room first?"

"We need both," Makenna answered as she handed a book to Tara and settled on the pillow with her stuffed dog.

Tara glanced up from page five of *Slipping Under The Sea*. Makenna slept; her body curled around her toy. After a kiss on her child's forehead, Tara placed the book on the shelf, turned off the light, glided out of the room, and strolled to CJ's room. He glanced up from his book when she sat in the chair beside his bed.

"You ready to call it a night, CJ?"

"Can I have a little bit longer? I'm not sleepy, and I just got to the good part," CJ asked, a pleading look in his eyes.

"Half an hour, okay? Then you put the book away and turn the lights off." Tara ruffled his hair and kissed his forehead. "You're okay riding home with Mr. Lynch tomorrow, right?"

"Yeah. Carson's dad is cool, plus Zack will be with us."

"Cool, huh. That's good to know." Tara stood and sauntered to the door. "Half an hour, then lights out."

"Mom?"

Tara stopped at the sound of his voice. "Yes?"

"Carson bought his dad a T-shirt for Father's Day. Zack bought his uncle a ball cap. What should I get Uncle Owen since my father's dead?"

Tara swallowed back her tears. "Let's talk about that in the morning, okay? I think Uncle Owen will appreciate whatever we get, but we should ask Jen what the girls are buying. Is that okay?"

"Yeah. I know he's not my father, but he's all I have, and he just got out of the hospital."

"Night, CJ," Tara whispered as she closed his door partway. *Some days your thoughtfulness is amazing.*

Tara strolled down the stairs trying to picture what furniture the living room needed. The furniture in Grandpa's house was in place when she moved home. She bought new for the kids' rooms but left everything else alone. Familiar furniture and decorations provided comfort when she returned with a five year old and a baby on the way. The apartment, beyond the bedrooms and the small oak table, was a blank slate. Whatever she bought needed to withstand constant use by children since they had one room for all family activities. She grabbed measuring tape, pen, and paper and created a drawing of the downstairs living space. Finished, she tucked the drawing in the kitchen drawer and climbed the steps to CJ's room. A peek inside found him asleep, the book on his nightstand, and the lights off.

She started down the stairs and glanced at the living room. A man and woman stood at either end of a small sofa.

"Is this exactly where you want it? We're done?" he asked.

The woman's lips lifted in a smile. "Yes, this is exactly where it needs to be. We're done."

"Oh no we're not," he answered as he strode toward her. "We're just beginning." He grabbed her waist and swung her in a circle. "Today is only the beginning." He drew her against his chest, and their lips met. As the kiss continued, they dissolved.

Tara slowly descended the stairs. The lovers were just beginning. She wondered how the story ended.

Ready for bed, Tara slid beneath the cool sheets. As she touched the switch on the lamp beside the bed, her phone beeped. A text from Jen.

—*Is it too late to call?*—

—*Nope. Should I call you or you call me?*—

The cell phone rang with Jen's ringtone, the chorus to Tim McGraw's "Humble and Kind."

"Everybody okay, Jen?"

"Yep. I needed to talk to the person who knows

227

Owen best. If I had a mother-in-law, I'd probably be bending her ear."

"Sister-in-law will have to do." Tara propped herself up against the headboard. "What's up?"

"Owen's exhausted. Wakes up tired, sleeps after therapy, and barely drags himself through dinner before he hides in his temporary room."

"Hides?"

"Yeah. He's not asleep, can't focus enough to read or watch TV. He's hiding and forcing himself to remember stuff. And Tara, he won't let me sleep with him. He says he's afraid he'll thrash around in a nightmare and hit me with the cast."

"You're not buying that, right?"

"No. All I have to do is sleep on the other side. He'd really have to work at it to hit me with the cast if I'm on the opposite side. I don't expect him to be exactly the person he was before the accident. Trauma changes you. But I miss my best friend, my lover, the father of my children. I feel he's shutting me out."

"What are you going to do next, Jen? I know you better than to think you'd give up or back off." *Do I break a sibling's confidence and tell her he's afraid he's no longer the man he was?*

"I have an appointment with a therapist on Thursday. I will not let him pull away from me without a fight."

"Sounds like a good idea. You know things will continue to change for Owen. Healing from trauma, any kind, is a process without a definite end date."

"Yeah. But I can't take a chance he'll get in the habit of shutting himself off from me. That's not how our relationship works. We're all about sharing the load, no matter how heavy."

"Please let me know if there is anything you think I can do to help. I'm willing to drive back to Bisbee anytime you ask. With or without the kids."

"Thanks. I needed to talk to someone who loves Owen even when he's being an idiot. Someone who listens with no judging and no advice. You do know that makes you unique, right?"

"I certainly like to believe I'm unique. Thank you for the compliment. I'm so glad Owen found you."

Owen must be scared. Only time can heal him, and there are no guarantees he'll be the same man who climbed into the patrol car the morning of the accident.

Jen wanted her partner back. Partner to share the load no matter how heavy. When Tara married Trey, she believed her future stretched before her; the heavy responsibilities ahead shared with a man she loved, the happy moments multiplied by their love of each other and their children. She turned a second lamp on and rooted in the closet. Under a box of sandals, she found it, the not-quite box of photos.

The pictures were a jumble of captured moments when the moment mattered, but the resulting photography wasn't quite well done enough to make it into either a photo album or a frame. About in the middle, she found the photo. The photographer, Jen's older sister, attempted a formal family shot. The adults, Tara, Owen, and Jen, sat on chairs. Sophie stood behind her mom, peeking over Jen's shoulder, Paige sat on her father's knee, pulling against the arm that encircled her as she tried to climb down, CJ stood beside Tara, his fingers grasping her summer skirt into a ball, and Makenna sat on Tara's lap, her hand in her mouth. The adults were laughing, the children ready to escape to something more fun. Not exactly the perfect portrait but a joyful moment filled with love and laughter. She propped the photo on her nightstand and returned the box to the closet. Stretched out under the cool sheets, silently she prayed for Owen's healing. Her eyes drifted closed.

Chapter Twenty-Three

Wear a Mask–Stop the Flu. Following the example of Red Cross volunteers in Phoenix and Tucson, the ladies of Eckie House joined with the Women of Creekside Family Support Foundation to create and distribute cloth masks to all residents. Influenza is tearing through our country, and in an effort to slow the rampaging infection in Arizona, Creekside Town Council asks that residents don a mask when in public. Residents and visitors may obtain masks at community churches, the elementary school, The Hickory Building Mercantile, The Palace Hotel, and the medical clinic on Exeter Street.
~The Creekside Reporter, 1918.

****

The cell phone alarm yanked Patrick's focus away from the contract displayed on the laptop screen. Three o'clock, time to dash to The Palace and change for his Friday bartending gig at Victoria's. Changes saved, he shut down the laptop and slid it into his desk drawer, dropped the cell phone into his pocket, and left the office. He peeked into Tara's office with, "We still on for Sunday?"

"Yep. Call me before and let me know the time." A chime announced the front door opening, and young voices filled the air. "Sounds like my children are home."

Patrick stepped away from the doorway. CJ and Makenna raced by him with a chorus of "Hi Mr. Benton."

With a wave to Tara, Patrick strolled out of the building and joined the throng on the sidewalk. Dodging clumps of dawdling tourists, Patrick meandered to the hotel. Blue sky and temperatures twenty degrees cooler than the valley enticed visitors to Creekside all summer. The hotel was full. The two small suites in the attic were rented. Just as well Scott stayed at Eckie House this summer. A family date on Sunday, his first ever that did not involve his family.

In San Diego, he rarely dated women with children, and when he did, they were usually enthusiastic about a night away from their responsibilities. It didn't occur to him to include Scott in a date, though the two of them went out, watched movies, attended sporting events, and surfed together often. Frequently, they included Scott's friends or his male friends who had children about Scott's age. Sunday would be a different date.

Patrick climbed the front steps to the hotel and yanked open the door. The lobby was empty except for Victoria standing behind the front desk. Their eyes met. She winked and disappeared as Nikki came out of her office.

"You're home with barely enough time to change," she commented as she strolled into the lobby. "Thanks for taking the bar tonight. I worked in the office all day, and I need a break."

"I live to serve, little sister," he answered as he placed his foot on the first step. "In more ways than one."

"Funny," she responded with a chuckle.

Dressed in a Palace polo shirt and jeans, Patrick poured the first glass of wine at exactly five o'clock. By six, the lobby was full, and only one small table remained empty on the front veranda. Conversation blended with Frank Sinatra's mellow tones crooning the final bars to "Summer Wind" when James and Andrea appeared beside the bar.

"Evening, my favorite sister-in-law," Patrick greeted them. "What can I get you?" At their direction, he poured two glasses of red wine. "You on your way to dinner without my niece?"

"Yep," answered James. "Carly and Whitney offered to babysit. An opportunity we couldn't pass up."

"Your giant house about full, Andrea?" Patrick asked. "Thought you were determined not to operate a bed-and-breakfast. Instead, you've three non-paying college student guests."

"They're family. Anyway, if they were paying guests, they probably wouldn't offer to babysit," Andrea answered. "Then we'd be home sharing dinner with Michelle instead of sipping wine at Victoria's with dinner reservations at Wellingtons."

"Ahh, a romantic adult dinner," Patrick quipped. "And you chose to spend part of it with me. Thank you."

"No. Spending part of it with you was a coincidence," James answered. "We know Victoria's carries our favorite wine."

Patrick chuckled and ambled down the bar to serve another couple. Good to know romantic dinners were still on the agenda for James and Andrea, even with toddler Michelle and three college students living in the house. The couple staked a claim to the small table on the veranda. As he served and bused tables, their body language caught his eye. They leaned toward each other, completely focused on their own conversation. Was that why his marriage failed? Did he not invest enough time and effort in keeping the romance part of the relationship alive?

After Scott's birth, he didn't want to go on vacation without their son. Filling every weekend with adult activities, golf, dinner with friends, theatre tickets seemed pointless. When Amy pushed back, he'd sometimes go along but not always. If he planned to go with her and their childcare fell through, he encouraged her to go alone. He believed he was being considerate until she told him she filed for divorce because being alone had to be less lonely than their marriage. He'd wanted to blame her for ending their marriage because she found someone else before they separated. But if he'd put as much effort into their relationship as he did into parenting, she maybe wouldn't have strayed. His failures as a partner were much easier to see from a distance of more than ten years.

Did he learn from his failure as a husband, or would he make the same mistake again if he found a partner? If he married again, what did he want in his future?

Nine o'clock p.m., the mournful sounds of Lee Brice singing "Mercy" filled the lobby, and Patrick closed the bar. As he gathered glasses and bottles from the veranda, Scott pounded up the three steps.

"Heard you had a busy night, Dad. Want some help?"

"That'd be great. The weather's so beautiful half of Creekside stopped in for a glass on the veranda. Couldn't keep up with the busing."

"Yeah. Looks kind of like breakfast when the hotel's full and everyone shows up at once," Scott commented. "Uncle James mentioned you were really hustling when he and Aunt Andrea stopped by." He grabbed a bus tray and filled it with plates, glasses, and empty bottles.

"Busy all evening. How do you like living at Eckie House? Does it feel like the dorm with three college students in residence?" Patrick yanked a small trash bag from his pocket and gathered paper napkins from the tables and deck.

"It's good, lots of room. Kind of weird though spending my summer without you or Aunt Nikki checking up on me all the time," Scott admitted.

"Without our supervision, how do you use your free time?" Patrick grabbed the outdoor broom and swept the floor.

"Mostly with Casey and friends I've made in Creekside on other summers." They cleaned the tables, carried everything inside, and loaded the dishwasher. "As I expected, Aunt Andi and Uncle James are quick to ask me where I'm going and when I'll be back."

"So nothing really changed with the move to Eckie House. The family's still keeping an eye on you."

"Like I said, I expected it. The only time I'll be without a supervising relative is when they're out of town." One last wipe of the tables, and with a wave, Scott strolled out the front door.

In the dimly lit lobby, Patrick leaned against the bar as his son turned a corner and disappeared. What happened to the awkward sixteen year old who worked his first summer at The Palace? Twenty a month ago, a man replaced the gangly boy.

Patrick felt a warm presence beside him. He slowly turned his head and met the gaze of Victoria. *How did she let her son go off to war?* Her lips lifted in a small smile and, though she didn't speak, he heard, *It's never easy letting go.* She dissolved, leaving behind the scent of lavender and a feeling of comfort.

Five-thirty a.m., Patrick woke to sunlight barely glinting on the wooden floor. He rolled out of bed and dressed for a morning run. He quieted his steps as he trod down the hallway and descended two flights of stairs. As he exited, he eased the door closed to minimize the noise. He loped three blocks to Eckie House, vaulted the low iron fence, and jogged the property perimeter.

Along the property line, he ran, alternating sprints with jogging. At the path behind the orchard, he slowed and smiled at the spirit children silently chasing each other through the trees. Beyond the shade of the trees, he jogged into the sunlit meadow, turned, and ran the final fence line. As he neared the back of the house, he waved to Andrea, who lounged on her patio, mug in hand. She greeted him with a wave, and he passed beside the house. With a final sprint, he arrived at the iron gate and let himself out.

Three blocks later, he tapped his key against the lock, opened the door, stepped into The Palace, and slipped up the stairs. Some days he missed the ocean, especially running on the beach and ending his run with a dive in the water. As the shower's hot water cascaded over tired muscles, he admitted gratitude for a morning run that did not require a drive to the beach first and a wet drive home after his swim.

He dried off and grinned at his reflection. Plus, his Creekside run included breakfast as a reward after his shower. Dressed in jeans and a green Palace polo shirt, he descended two flights of stairs and strode into the lobby in time to catch Eric putting a carafe of fresh coffee on the bar. The scent of coffee drifted through the room.

"Morning, Eric, what's for breakfast?" He filled the mug with coffee and a drop of French Vanilla flavoring.

"My personal favorite, the baked French toast." A timer pinged behind the bar. Eric dashed through the connecting door to the kitchen and returned moments later with a steaming casserole dish. "All I need is to cut this up, and breakfast is served." He grabbed a knife from the bar and deftly sliced the French toast into equal servings, exchanged the knife for a spatula, and plated the first serving, handing it to Patrick.

"Thanks, French toast is my favorite too." Patrick added a dollop of blueberry syrup and found a table by the window as footsteps sounded on the stairs, followed by the appearance of a couple of guests.

Patrick finished his breakfast, loaded his dishes into the bus cart, carried it to the kitchen, and unloaded it. When he returned it to the lobby, he gathered empty dishes and wiped the tables while making conversation with guests. Breakfast over, he and Eric cleared the lobby and veranda, stored the food in the kitchen. Coffee mug filled, Patrick plopped on the stool behind the front desk, and Eric slipped out the door.

Summer Jazz Festival in Creekside today, and

Patrick volunteered to man the hotel while everyone else enjoyed the entertainment at the square. The event ended tomorrow at four, in time for his date with Tara. By Sunday night, CJ and Makenna should be ready for the more sedate entertainment of dinner and a movie.

****

"I've never been to the Happy Dragon," Tara commented as they crossed the street and turned onto Thaddeus Blvd. "We've eaten mostly in the area around the square."

"Casey recommended the restaurant," Patrick admitted. "When you mentioned the Jazz Festival had every type of food except Asian, I figured your family might appreciate trying something new."

"Mommy, can I have pot stickers?" Makenna asked. "We used to get those in Bisbee."

"Let's see what's on the menu. If Mr. Benton agrees, we'll order family style, and you can try several things."

"Family style's the only way to order Asian food," Patrick commented. "Otherwise, you spend the meal passing around the interesting food on your plate or wishing you'd ordered something that looks better on someone else's plate."

"True," Tara agreed. "It's so much more satisfying to try a variety from the menu."

The Happy Dragon lived up to expectations, the food fresh and plentiful. Sated, they strolled from the restaurant to the movie theatre. The movie wasn't quite the hit with Makenna the dinner was. She fell asleep and missed the ending. When they left the theatre, Patrick wasn't the only adult with a young child asleep in his arms. They strolled past other families, parents holding children's hands, some being carried like Makenna. At the Henderson Building, he carried Makenna up the flights of stairs to her room, she woke before he could set her on the bed.

"Momma, do I have to go to bed now? I'm not tired," she whined.

"Of course you're not," Tara answered with a wink for Patrick. "Say thank you to Mr. Benton for the date. Go brush your teeth and put your pj's on."

"Thank you, Mr. Benton. That was a fun date," Makenna responded, and Tara hustled her into the bathroom and closed the door.

Patrick ambled to CJ's room and peeked inside the open door. CJ lounged on the bed, propped up on pillows, a book open in his hands. "Good night, CJ."

"Good night, Mr. Benton, and thank you for dinner and the movie."

"You're welcome." As Patrick stepped into the hallway, Tara appeared in front of him.

"Give me a moment to check on CJ, and I'll join you in the living room, okay?" she asked.

With a nod and smile, Patrick strolled down the stairs and settled on a love seat. What now? He couldn't take her out for an after drink leaving two young children in the apartment. He could suggest she take her monitor and adjourn to the conference room downstairs. Which was less weird, holding her on the love seat in her living room when the kids could show up at any moment, or holding her on the conference room sofa in the office where they both worked? Before he could sort out his thoughts, Tara appeared, a small monitor in her hand.

"Would you like an after-dinner drink?" She set the

monitor on the coffee table. "I've wine, port, brandy, and sherry."

"Let me help," Patrick answered and stood. They strolled to the kitchen, and Tara pointed out the top cabinet. "What are you having?" he asked.

"The chocolate port." She took two glasses from the cupboard, he handed her the bottle, and she poured a small amount into each glass. They returned to the living room and dropped onto the sofa. "Usually save this stuff for special occasions. It's a decadent dessert in a glass."

"Is tonight a special occasion?" Patrick asked as he sipped sweet but slightly bitter wine.

"Yep." Tara grinned. "My daughter's first date. By tomorrow, everyone in town will know you took her to a movie and dinner. Makenna's at the sharing age."

"I kind of remember that with Scott. His kindergarten teacher pointed out at meet-the-teacher night that by the winter holiday, she'd probably know more about our family life than our neighbors and friends."

"I'll bet Ms. Lake at the preschool knows just about everything that passes through Makenna's thoughts. She loves to talk." She set her empty glass on the coffee table and rose.

Patrick downed the last of his port and unfolded himself from the sofa. Taking Tara's hand in his, he gently tugged until they were face to face. "If this is where you hustle me out the door with a thank you, may I have a kiss for the road?"

Tara set her glass on the table, and her arms circled his neck. "Kiss sounds like the perfect good night at the end of a lovely evening."

Their lips met in a gentle caress. He touched the seam with his tongue, tasting the chocolate wine. She opened, letting him inside, answering his play with her own. The feel of her warm body against his sent blood to his groin. A tearful voice on the monitor startled him, and their lips parted, her arms dropped.

"Mommy, it's scary. Where are you?" Makenna's voice filled the room.

"Must be my cue to say good night," Patrick commented as he stepped back, retrieved the glasses. "I'll take these to the kitchen, okay?"

"Thank you. She hasn't adjusted to sleeping by herself yet." Tara stopped his progress with a hand on his arm. She brushed a light kiss on his lips. "Thank you for our date." She dashed up the stairs and disappeared.

Patrick rinsed the glasses, loaded them in the dishwasher, and let himself out through the office. He meandered through the business district toward The Palace, dodging clumps of people on the sidewalks. First time a date ended because of a child's nightmare.

Chapter Twenty-Four

In November of 1918, the Great War ended. Maggie's brother and mine both survived the fighting. We should have been celebrating peace, yet we were under attack from an enemy more deadly than war, The Flu. We kept Annabelle home and wore masks when we left the office. Maggie spent every spare minute making cloth masks which were available free to anyone who asked. Public gatherings were canceled, the movie theatre closed. No parades, no large parties. The military bases where our brothers returned were closed, no one leaving or entering.

~Practicing Law in Creekside, A Love Story by Micah Henderson

****

From the last step, Patrick admired the efficient way his sister arranged breakfast on the bar while answering a question from a guest.

She glanced his way and, with a tilt of her head, beckoned him over. "Morning, Patrick." She filled a mug with coffee and handed it to him. "You're just in time to take over."

He took his first sip, set the coffee behind the bar, and smiled at the guests filing by the bar collecting breakfast. "Go on. I've got this."

"Patrick to the rescue. Thanks." Nikki pecked his cheek and disappeared down the hallway. By the time breakfast was put away, the lobby straightened, and the departing guests checked out, it was noon, and Scott appeared for the afternoon shift.

After changing his shirt for one without The Palace logo, Patrick waved to Scott and strolled out the front door. For the first time in his adult life, he didn't have a laser focus on accomplishing something, no burning need to provide for Scott or build a successful law practice. His son was nearly on his own. He didn't miss his law practice in San Diego though he did miss the pro bono work he did for the women's shelter. The only reason he stayed in the San Diego house was Scott, and he was happy to be out from under the maintenance and repair bills. He spent so little money living in The Palace that even after purchasing and remodeling the Henderson Building, he could choose how much to work. He needed something to work for, invest himself in. Living in the moment sounded good, but in practice, it made him feel like a drifter, someone floating through life without purpose. He needed a dream and a plan.

Scent of coffee greeted him when he yanked open the office door. Mug in hand, he ambled down the hall. Tara glanced up and motioned him into her office. "Afternoon. Anyone drop by while I helped out my sister?"

She yanked a sticky note off the wall and handed it to him. "Yep. Mrs. Meadows dropped by and would like an appointment for tomorrow. That's her number."

"Thanks for taking the message and making the coffee." He saluted with his mug.

"You're welcome. Patrick, I'm taking the kids with me to Bisbee on Thursday."

"Something wrong?" he asked as he dropped into

the chair.

"Nothing new. Jen called, asking for reinforcements. She didn't explain, but I'm guessing Owen's pushing back on the therapy. It would be like him to think he could get better without help."

"How long will you be gone?"

"I'm planning on driving home on Sunday. The kids have activities scheduled for Monday." Her brows crinkled in a frown. "Owen's always been there for me. It's hard being so far away when he's hurt."

"Does your sister-in-law want you to return?"

"She's not pressuring me, but Jen and Owen rescued me after Trey's attack, and I'd like to return the favor."

"But you're not ready to uproot CJ and Makenna, right?"

"Yep. They have their hearts set on staying in Creekside. You lived in San Diego, but your family stayed in Phoenix, was it hard being so far away when there were problems?"

"Sometimes. They were good about telling me what was going on, asking my opinion, and convincing me they could handle whatever happened."

"Jen's been pretty good about keeping me in the loop. All I can do is respond when she asks for help and see what happens next. The advantage to working for myself is I can go to Bisbee when she asks."

"Let me know if you need me to do anything in the apartment, you know, water the houseplants or feed the cat." Patrick rose and strode to the door.

"Funny. We haven't lived in the apartment long enough to acquire houseplants or a cat. Don't be surprised if we come home with a dog. My kids are on a mission to get one."

"Hey, your generous landlord allows pets. I might be willing to fence off part of the lot behind the building for a dog play area if you asked." He ambled to his office and took the message from his pocket. Laptop set up, he called Mrs. Meadows and set up the appointment.

****

Thursday afternoon, Patrick unlocked the office and entered a silent room. How quickly he'd become accustomed to arriving at the office and being greeted with the scent of coffee and subtle sounds of Tara working. He walked into the kitchen and grabbed an iced tea from the refrigerator. As he stepped back into the reception area, he stilled.

The antique reproduction desk was gone, replaced by a square desk topped with an antique typewriter. A woman gradually appeared behind the desk, her fingers flying across the keys. From the hallway, a man stepped into the room, his focus only on the woman. He made a sound. Her fingers stopped, and she turned toward the man, a smile lighting her face.

"Is it finished?" he asked.

She turned back to the typewriter and took out the paper as he walked toward her. "Yes, I finished. Just a few signatures needed, and you're a father."

He took the paper from her hand, set it on the desk, and lifted her from the chair. "You're sure this is okay; what you want?"

She wrapped her arms around his neck. "Absolutely sure. You are her father, the only one she's ever known. We're just making it legal."

He enfolded her in his arms and kissed her, turning

them in a circle. Her laughter filled the room, and they disappeared.

The room returned to present with the desk and chairs he'd chosen. If he married again, would he adopt his partner's children if there weren't another father in the picture? Though not his lover, he felt a potential for love in his relationship with Tara. Was he willing to begin again with young children? Tara's children would always be her first priority; he understood the feeling. But could he be a priority too? Was there room in her life for a partner, another adult? Something to think about before he encouraged the relationship. He wanted Tara, wanted to hold her, listen to her, support her in whatever way she would allow. What did she want?

At the end of the day, Patrick climbed the stairs to the apartment. He checked no water was running, nothing leaked, the refrigerator hummed happily. As promised, no pet greeted him with a demand to go out, and no houseplants cried for water. The rooms were empty but lived in. They felt like a home. At the door, he glanced up at the stairs to the bedrooms. He locked up and strolled out the door. He skirted around the business district and meandered toward Eckie House for an appointment with James and Andrea. What did his newly married brother need with an attorney?

Dodging clumps of tourists on the sidewalks surrounding the square, Patrick made his way to Eckie House. He glanced at the front porch as he opened the iron gate. A red-haired woman rocked an infant in the chair on the front porch. Sitting at her feet, two children played a game. The front door opened, the woman and children disappeared.

Andrea waved from the doorway, Ella a wiggling

bundle in her arms. When Patrick reached her, James appeared, rescued Ella from her mother's arms, and they meandered to the book room. When they'd arranged themselves around the room, drinks and snacks in hand with Ella crawling at their feet, Patrick asked, "What's up?"

"I want to adopt Ella, and Andrea's agreed," James answered. "At first, we thought to work through the papers ourselves and then decided there had to be some advantage to having an attorney for a brother." He took a folder off the desk and handed it to Patrick.

Patrick glanced at the papers. "Let me do some research on what we need for stepfather adoption." He slipped the folder into his briefcase.

The next hour flew by while they talked of friends, family, and local events. The sun lit the sky orange and yellow as Patrick walked toward the hotel. James' desire to adopt Ella didn't surprise him, though it wasn't the request he expected when Andrea set up a meeting. He'd expected James to want to change his will. Now he had a wife and child. It made sense to create a parachute for Ella first. By making James her legal father, Ella would be immediately in James' care if something happened to Andrea. He knew Catherine's will included a provision for James to become Hope and Lilly's guardian, if necessary. Would she change the guardianship to Chance if they married? He'd convinced Amy that if something happened to the two of them it was in Scott's best interest to have James as guardian. Amy's brother was ten years older and living in Europe, his lived one state away. He climbed the hotel's front steps as the sun dropped behind the mountain and the streetlights flicked on. Nikki motioned him over from behind the bar.

"You available to handle the bar tomorrow night?"

"Yep. You have a better offer than work?" he teased.

"Mitch and Colin have a summer league baseball game, Alex is off duty, and we want to show support as a family. Doesn't happen very often that game night finds the whole family available," she admitted. "The boys are growing up so fast we need to grab every opportunity while they're still around."

"Don't blame you. Hard to believe I'm no longer dashing out of the office to make it to the baseball game to watch Scott play, loading part of the team in the car after, and hauling them to after-game pizza."

"Do you miss it, Patrick?" Nikki asked. "The hassles, the scheduling, the rushing from place to place, all the small pieces of parenting?"

"Yep. Life's easier but not nearly as interesting." With a wave, he strolled across the lobby and climbed the stairs. He missed it. Odd, he hadn't considered that was the underlying problem. He missed being a parent, talking with other parents at games and school functions, creating schedules, balancing his work and Scott's needs, making his son the priority. Talking about their days, Scott's friends, school, sports, plans, making their time together count even if that meant tossing a ball around in the backyard or surfing at the beach. He'd purposely raised Scott to be independent, but success was a mixed blessing. He missed being needed.

Is the answer to find a group that needs me, a charity maybe? Or do I need to open myself to a new beginning, a new love, the chance for a new partner?

Am I too old, too set in my ways to take on a family, especially one where I wouldn't be in charge, the best I could hope for an equal or semi-equal say?

He stepped inside his room, and his cell phone rang.

"Hey, Scott," he answered. "What's up?"

"Hey, Dad, could we meet somewhere for dinner? Need to bounce a couple of ideas off you."

"The Happy Dragon on Thaddeus Blvd., okay?"

"Sounds good. I'm already out that way, half an hour?"

Seated in a booth near the restaurant's front window, they ordered a selection of small plates and talked of the hotel, Casey's family, and Scott's plans for fall semester. When the plates were cleared, Patrick lounged in the corner of the booth, coffee cup in hand, and asked, "What ideas did you want to talk about?"

Scott dropped three letters on the table. "These universities accepted my application and scores for entrance into their MBA program. A couple of them have fast-track programs I could complete in about eighteen months. I checked with Grandpa, Cyrus. The trust would pay for graduate school. I'm not sure which one is the best fit for me or even if I want to go directly from university to university without taking a couple of years to work first."

"What's your end-game, Scott? Ten years from now, where do you hope to be? What will you be doing?"

"That's the problem, Dad. The end-game changes depending upon where I am and who I'm with. Working with Aunt Nikki, I want what she has, her own hotel, a business she built in a place where she has friends and family. Last semester I interned at a couple of the large hotels in Flagstaff and shadowed the managers. They make similar decisions to Aunt Nikki's but on a grander scale. Having an MBA might help me get into one of the big chain's training programs if I want to manage a large hotel. I can't see how it will help if I chose to go in business for myself. Plus, if I use the money in the trust for education, it's not available to help me finance my own property."

"What are your dreams for your personal life?"

"Dreams? A wife who is a successful artist, an excellent mother, best friend, and lover. And a professional life that not only encompasses my personal definition of success but allows me time to be an involved father and loving husband."

"Which professional direction do you think will allow you to realize your dreams?" Patrick paid the bill, and they strolled toward the square.

"Thanks, Dad. That is exactly the question I need to ask myself to make the best choice for me. Sometimes I become so involved in learning hotel management and how to be successful that I forget professional success isn't enough, at least for me."

"Whatever you decide to do next, you know I'll back you, right? And Uncle James will go over any financial questions you have—free consultation for family," Patrick commented when they arrived at the hotel.

"Yeah, I know. Thanks for dinner, Dad."

From the front veranda, Patrick gazed at his son dashing down the street, expertly dodging tourists and eventually disappearing around the corner. He yanked open the heavy front door and gifted his sister with a smile. "You closing up?"

"Working on it. Want to help? I pay in glasses of wine."

He grabbed the bus tray, cleared the tables, and hauled the tray to the kitchen. "Do I need to check outside?"

"Nope, did that already. How was dinner?"

"Good. Nik, the life you live now, how does it mesh with the dreams you had after college?"

"Brother dear, I could not have dreamed I'd own a haunted hotel, be raising two stepsons, an adopted son, and a baby girl. After college, I didn't have enough imagination to dream the life I have now."

"But you're happy?"

"Yep. The life I didn't know to dream is exactly the life I needed to be happy. I read somewhere you can only be as happy as you allow yourself to be. I'm embracing all the happiness I can find."

Patrick poured himself a glass of wine, pecked Nikki on the cheek, and whispered in her ear, "You deserve every bit of happiness you can find," and ambled toward the stairs.

As he climbed the first flight, on the landing, he spotted Victoria. She gazed at him over one shoulder and winked. When he reached the landing, she turned and disappeared through the closed door of room 15.

Only as happy as you allow yourself to be.

Victoria drifted through the hotel, appearing and disappearing with no pattern. Perhaps her presence was the result of her wish to find again the happiness she had in her family and the business she built. Her dreams.

Chapter Twenty-Five

July 1919
Henderson Law Office closed for two weeks in
July, the longest closing since I opened the office. The
Flu finally left the US after resulting in more deaths in
our country than the number of American soldiers lost
in the Great War. Our brothers both returned to our
respective families, and we spent the next two weeks
visiting family and celebrating life. Annabelle, age
seven, was an intrepid traveler, rarely moody or out of
sorts, making friends with the family she'd never met
and sleeping in strange beds didn't faze her. On our
way home, she began a refrain of "When do I get to
have brothers and sisters?"
~Practicing Law in Creekside, A Love Story by
Micah Henderson

****

Monday, when Patrick yanked open the front door
of the Henderson Building, the scent of coffee, the
high-pitched voices of children, and the yip of a dog
greeted him. Mug in hand, he wandered into Tara's
office.

"Morning," he greeted them. "Looks like you have
a new member of the family."

Makenna bounced to him, grabbed his hand, and
tugged. "Look, Mr. Benton, that's Samson."

In the corner, his tiny body leaning against the wall

and big eyes staring at Patrick, a puppy yipped. Patrick dropped into the chair and turned to Makenna, "What kind of dog is Samson?"

Her face scrunched in a frown, Makenna answered, "We don't know. Paige found him in the alley behind her friend's house. He was left there with his sister, Delilah."

He glanced around the office. "Where's Delilah?"

"With Paige and Sofie. Aunt Jen said they could only keep one puppy," Makenna answered. "We promised to include Samson next time we visit."

The front door chimed. "Sounds like Mr. Healy is here. Grab your stuff." Tara picked up Samson; CJ and Makenna gathered their backpacks, and Patrick followed their procession to the reception area. When the children were gone, Patrick ambled beside Tara back to her office. "Well, my generous landlord, I'm taking you up on the offer of a fenced-off area behind the building. Samson's puppy pad trained, but he needs to learn to go outside, too."

"How big is Samson likely to get?" Patrick asked as he dropped into the chair. "You've taken him to the vet, right?"

"Yep. Vet says he's probably a miniature poodle mix with that curly hair and the snout. He's slightly less than a year old, so close to full grown." Tara set the puppy in a dog bed and handed him a chew toy.

"Beyond making your children deliriously happy with Samson, how did your weekend go?" Patrick asked as he sipped the coffee. "How's Owen?"

"Struggling. He's terrified the Owen he was is gone. The therapy reminds him of what he still can't do. His emotions are not always under his control, and he worries he'll say the wrong thing and alienate his wife and children. He's exhausted. Actions he took for granted now wear him out." A weary sadness appeared in her eyes. "The worst part is there is no timeline for him getting better nor tentative date when he can go back to work."

"Owen's looking for a silver bullet," commented Patrick. When Tara raised an eyebrow in question, he continued, "Simple fix for a difficult problem. How's Jen doing?"

"She sees a counselor with experience in head trauma patients, so she's not freaked out by Owen's behavior. The counselor suggested I visit since I don't live nearby, and Owen could spew his problems and not worry about how I'd react. Guess it's a blessing I decided to stay in Creekside, I'm a safe listening ear, and he doesn't worry about appearing weak or ungrateful in front of me." Samson yipped, and Tara tossed him a treat from her desk drawer. "He doesn't have to worry about facing me the next day and being reminded of what he said."

The tension in Patrick's shoulders released; it sounded like she meant to stay. "Yep. It's a sibling thing, I guess. We trust nothing we say or do will change the relationship."

"I'm grateful I'm close enough to dash down there when needed and far enough away not be underfoot. Ronni and Nathan offered to take the kids whenever needed. Nathan volunteered to stay upstairs, so the kids don't have to move."

She's staying, might as well put my cards on the table. "May I tag along next time you go?"

"Why would you want to?"

What's the worst that could happen if I put everything into the open? She could reject me, but better to find out now. "Because it's a long drive, we're friends, and I'd like to see where this relationship can go." He took her hand. "I'm ready for a romantic date, a dinner out that could lead to more if you're willing. At least the first time, I'd like privacy and a whole night. I can't figure out how to make that happen when you live with two young children, and I live in my sister's haunted hotel."

"I've never pictured Bisbee as a romantic destination," she admitted.

"Hey, romance isn't where you are; it's who you're with. We could waltz in the dark to soft music in the reception area; wouldn't that be romantic? The photos of George and Faith dancing in the meadow are romantic, and they're outside behind their home." He released her hand and stood. "No pressure. Think about it, though, okay?" At her nod, he strode out the door.

As he worked on a contract for the sale of a local business, he accepted he might have pushed too hard. He was ready for more, but was she? His sister, Nikki, was wrong; he wasn't looking for someone to rescue. He needed new dreams and goals and a partner to share them with. He needed a lover and friend.

A few hours later, Patrick poked his head into Tara's office. "Lunchtime. You interested in the deli, you can include Samson and we'll sit on their dog-friendly patio?" At the sound of his name, Samson dropped his chew toy and stood up, tail wagging.

Tara gazed at the dog and laughed. "Well, Samson's ready. Let me get his leash and my bag."

Samson leading the way, they strolled through

town. Settled on the patio under an umbrella, they munched on sandwiches and chips and discussed the town and their mutual friends. As they meandered toward the office, Tara asked, "So are you considering this a date?"

"Yep. We ate lunch away from the office, got to know each other better, had a little exercise with a stroll through the community, and managed to walk the dog. Food, conversation, exercise, definitely a date." They climbed the steps to the front of the office. Patrick opened the door, and they stepped across the threshold. In the shadow beside an old, square desk, a couple stood locked in a passionate embrace. Patrick flipped the light switch, and the couple disappeared. "Only thing missing from our date was the end of date kiss."

Tara chuckled. "There was a kiss, just didn't happen to be between the two of us." She lifted Samson into her arms and disappeared into her office.

Patrick escorted his client to the front door as the clock chimed three. "I'll arrange a meeting between everyone involved, Mrs. Meadows. As soon as it's arranged, I'll let you know." He held the door open, and she carefully navigated the steps.

He poked his head into Tara's office. "Contractor's coming tomorrow to fence part of the back lot. Did you want a little doggie door on the back so Samson could exit on his own?"

"You sure you want to do that for a dog that's not yours?"

"Yep. I don't have a dog now, but I might someday. Less expensive to do the whole project at one time anyway."

"Sounds great," Tara admitted. "And Patrick, I'd

like a little romance too. Maybe I can figure out a way before my next surprise trip to Bisbee." She grinned.

"Whatever works for you." He winked and disappeared down the hallway.

****

A week later, Tara glanced up from her computer to find Patrick propped against the doorway. "You ready for the big unveiling?" He lifted a hand that held a dangling key fob. "Your private dog-friendly patio awaits."

She popped out of her chair, grabbed Samson in her arms, and followed Patrick to the end of the hall. "It really wasn't fair you wouldn't let us outside while the project was under construction. All we could see from the apartment was the shrubs planted along the back fence line. They look good, by the way."

"It was a construction zone, not a good place for pets or children." He laughed. "Anyway, it was fun making you wait. Anticipation is always half the fun, especially someone else's."

At the back door, he unlatched a small dog door, then tapped the electronic lock with the fob, turned the handle, and motioned her outside. A wooden deck stretching the width of the building replaced the three steps down to a dirt lot. The building's overhang now extended over the deck, two rockers sat off to one side, and a small table with four chairs sat on the other. The barren lot was replaced by artificial turf surrounded by a fence. A variety of shrubs grew inside the fence line and a fire pit embraced by gray paving stones sat off to one side.

"What do you think?" Patrick asked when they strolled down the steps into the yard.

"It's definitely not what I expected." She placed Samson on the grass, and he dashed about, stopping to sniff each plant.

"What did you expect?" Patrick asked.

"The dog door, a small fenced area, a few plants, maybe real or artificial grass," Tara admitted. "I pictured minimum requirements for dog business, and you've created a small oasis behind the office."

"Honestly, I pictured that too until I talked to Donaldson," Patrick admitted. "He told me why a large vacant piece of land is attached to an office building in the middle of town."

"And the reason is?" Tara asked as they returned to the deck and dropped into the rocking chairs.

"Micah bought the land with the idea he'd eventually build a second commercial building on the lot facing the opposite direction. Instead, when Micha married, he moved his wife and child into the apartment over his office. A few years later, his wife gave birth to twin boys. An old maple tree shaded the vacant lot, so Micah and his brothers fenced the lot and added grass, creating a play area behind the office." Samson and the artificial grass disappeared, replaced by a giant tree and three children racing about the yard. Patrick blinked; the children disappeared.

"What happened? There was no sign of tree or fence before."

"Time, changing attitudes. The next generation moved to separate homes, some left town. By the time the last Henderson lawyer retired, the upstairs apartment had become a storage area and the play yard a vacant lot. The old tree was hit by lightning and had to be removed at least one generation ago."

"And you let Donaldson talk you into restoring the yard to its former glory."

"Without the tree. Decided since I restored the apartment might as well continue the trend with the yard."

"Thank Donaldson for me, okay?" Tara picked up Samson, where he'd settled for a nap beside her chair. "We've ended up with the best of accommodations. An apartment with someone else responsible for repairs, my office where I live, and back yard safe for a puppy and children."

"Full circle, then. The Henderson Building has come full circle." They strolled inside. When they reached Tara's office, she set Samson in his dog bed, and at a motion of her hand in invitation, Patrick dropped into the guest chair.

"What are your plans for Saturday night, Patrick?" She put up her hand in the stop signal. "Wait, I hate it when people do that to me. Let me try that again." She grinned and gazed into his eyes. "Would you like to go on a date Saturday night? Just the two of us?"

"Yes."

"You don't care where? Or what I've planned? Just yes?"

He nodded. "Yes."

"Excellent. That's the first time I've asked a man for a date since college. You made it easy. The children have overnight social engagements, so it's adults-only limited only by our imagination."

"Tell me what time, and I'll be here." He rose. "First time a woman asked me out since college. I can hardly wait."

Chapter Twenty-Six

Welcome to Creekside, David Micah and Paul Curtis Henderson. Monday morning at ten, David and Paul joined parents, Margaret and Micah Henderson, and big sister Anabelle. Momma and the babies are doing well.

~The Creekside Reporter, September 1920

****

After surviving his sister's teasing about having a Saturday night date, Patrick strolled around the square, dodging clumps of tourists, and meandered the final block to the Henderson Building. He glanced at the building's front door.

On the porch stood a man and woman. Each adult held a baby in their arms, a young girl standing between the adults held a small dog in her arms. Patrick started up the front steps, and the vision disappeared.

Did he want to start over? Dust off his old dream of family? He slipped the key into the front door lock, and as he punched in the security code stopping the alarm, he admitted, yeah, he wanted a new version of the old dream. The Creekside spirits prove love doesn't have to die, and neither do dreams.

He climbed the stairs to the apartment. The door stood open, and Tara called, "Come in and sit down. I'll join you in the living room in a moment. You can pour the wine."

As he set the bottle on the table, Tara appeared with a smile of welcome on her face, a small plate of cheese and crackers in her hand, and Samson at her heels.

"Welcome to my first adults-only date in forever." She dropped onto the sofa beside Patrick and picked up a wine glass.

Patrick lifted his glass in a toast. "To a Saturday night date." Their glasses clicked, and each took a sip. "First date in forever?" Patrick asked, watching her toying with the wine glass stem.

"Really, first date in forever having the potential for more than a good night kiss." She set the glass down with a clunk. "Embarrassing. Food and wine, low lights, soft music, sounds like a seduction right out of a romance novel."

Wine glass set on the table; Patrick took her hand. "You've set a lovely scene." He touched her cheek, turning her face, so their eyes met. "Remember you're both the star and the director; whatever happens, tonight is your decision. No pressure, I'm here because I want to be with you, want to get to know you. How that happens is in your hands."

The timer dinged, and Tara rose. "Saved by the bell."

Patrick grabbed the wine glasses and snacks and followed her into the kitchen area. He placed the glasses and snack on the table, grabbed dishes, napkins, and cutlery from the counter, and set the table. Tara placed a plate of coconut shrimp, rice pilaf, and steamed vegetables in the center of the table. "Dinner courtesy of Wellingtons."

As the plates emptied, they spoke of foods they

loved and those they didn't, favorite places, their childhood dreams, their college experiences. When they'd cleared the table, they took their Irish coffee and a plate of tiny cheesecakes to the sofa. Conversation moved to people who impacted their lives and favorite memories.

Samson started bouncing around, so they took him down the stairs and out the back door. In the moonlight, they lounged in the wooden rockers as the puppy checked out his yard. Patrick took her hand. *Should I offer to end the night now? Thank her for a lovely evening?* The physical chemistry between them simmered, each touch added to the heat. As Samson trotted up the steps and plopped down beside Tara's rocker, Patrick asked, "Is this where I offer to take myself home? Or do you have other plans?"

She lifted Samson in her arms and stood, motioning Patrick to rise. "Oh, I definitely have plans." She grinned and led the way inside.

He followed her up the stairs; her scent, a mixture of vanilla and summer, drifted back to him. When she opened the door and set Samson on the floor, he commented, "I hope I'm included?"

He turned her to face him and gently drew her into her arms. "A kiss?"

At her nod, their lips met. Her hands lay on his shoulders; his circled her waist. He played with her lips. A touch of tongue on the seam, a gentle press followed by a little more pressure. She responded, her lips parting in a sigh, and their tongues played. She hesitated, he gentled the kiss, she dropped her hands and stepped back. Grasping his hand, she led him toward her bedroom.

Inside, a bedside lamp cast a low yellow glow. She motioned him toward a chair in the corner and dropped onto the bed. "Patrick, I believed I'd enjoy being the seducer, being in charge. Now I feel strange."

"You've set an excellent stage for seduction. A delicious meal, interesting and fun conversation, a moonlit night. I've enjoyed every minute."

"You get it's been a long time for me, right? That my last lover was Trey?"

"Ahh. First times with anyone can be awkward, no matter how many firsts there have been." He toed off his deck shoes, stood, and walked to her. Taking her hands, he knelt and took her right foot in his hand.

"Let's start by taking these off and making your feet comfortable, okay?" He gazed into her eyes, and when she nodded, he carefully tipped off both her flats and gently messaged her arches. He stood, drawing her to her feet. "Remember, it's all about you now. I promise any word from you, and we stop, change speed, change direction. Anything." As he spoke, his hands caressed her body. They slipped under her T-shirt and lifted her breasts.

"My turn," she whispered and removed his shirt from his waistband. Her hands roamed his chest; her fingers lightly tugged the hair.

Buttons were suddenly undone, and trousers dropped to the floor. She slipped between the sheets, and Patrick slid in beside her. He kissed her mouth, nibbled her neck, tongued her breasts, and all the while, her hands roamed his back and squeezed his butt cheeks. He moved between her thighs and kissed her intimately, tasting her passion. Then, he slid up her body, his lips touching her everywhere. He grabbed a condom off the nightstand, sheathed himself, and gazing into her eyes, slipped inside. When he was spent, he toppled to the side, drawing her against him.

"Lovely," she whispered. Her eyes closed, her breathing evened in sleep.

Patrick forced himself out of bed and made his way to the bathroom. He glanced in the mirror at a familiar face now sporting a satisfied smile. He turned off the light and quietly returned to bed. He understood how five years could have slipped by, and Tara hadn't slept with anyone. She lived in a small town with two young children. It hadn't been five years since his last lover, but this seemed different. New but familiar, intimate in a way he couldn't explain. He tossed the covers over them and drew her body against his. Could he convince her to take a chance on an older guy with a grown son? A guy currently living in the attic of his sister's haunted hotel?

****

Tara woke to the muted roar of the shower and sunlight through the window, turning the wood floor to honey. She stretched, relishing the slight ache between her thighs. After the first early coupling, they'd dozed only to wake in the very early hours and love again. Before she drifted back to sleep, she remembered promising him breakfast.

The shower stopped, and Patrick stepped into the room wearing only trousers, his cheeks sporting a morning scruff. He strolled to the chair, grabbed her robe, and tossed it to her before she could ask. He turned his back while she rolled from the bed, donned her robe, and scuttled to the bathroom.

By the time she dressed, the scents of bacon and

coffee drifted in the air.

In the kitchen, she found Patrick at the stove, turning the bacon, a mug of coffee in his hand. "I promised you breakfast, didn't I?"

"Yep. And you provided all the makings. I would have felt stupid waiting around while you took a shower when I know how to cook and make coffee." He handed her a mug and turned back to the stove.

She filled her mug poured a dollop of hazelnut syrup into the coffee. "Sometimes you remind me of Owen; if something needs doing, you do it." She withdrew bread and butter from the refrigerator along with a dozen eggs. "You don't sit around waiting for someone else to take the lead."

Patrick took the last of the bacon from the pan, placed it on a paper towel to drain, and took her hand, tugging her into his arms. "Please, don't say I remind you of your brother after last night." He nuzzled her neck. "That is not how I want you to think of me."

He returned to the stove, turned the burner on, melted butter in the pan, and cracked two eggs into a bowl. "Scrambled or fried?"

"Scrambled," she answered as she popped bread into the toaster.

A few minutes later, they sat at the table, consuming breakfast. "Patrick." He looked up from the coffee he'd been staring into. She loved that; the way he focused on her when she spoke and made her feel her words mattered to him. "How do you want me to think of you?"

He set his coffee on the table and took her hand. "As your friend, as your only lover for as long as we're together."

"How long, Patrick?"

He gathered their now empty dishes and carried them to the sink, grabbed the coffee pot, and poured them each a second cup. As he dropped back into the chair, he asked, "What do you dream? How do you see your tomorrows unfolding?"

"I dream of watching my children grow up, become thoughtful, productive adults who eventually build families of their own. And I'll be with them every step of the way, nudging, encouraging, supporting whatever they dream." An honest answer but not complete, the perfect dream would be a partner to share the ups and downs, the falls and successes. Did she dare tell Patrick that part of the dream? Would it scare him away?

"You sound like you've visited my dreams about ten years ago. If anyone asked, I would have answered exactly as you did with the addition of being a successful attorney."

She sipped her coffee and gazed into his blue eyes. "I'm asking, Patrick, what do you dream now? Your son is twenty; you sold the successful practice. What do you dream now?"

He looked down, took her hand, and rubbed her knuckles with his thumb. "I dream of sharing all my tomorrows with a partner. A lover and friend to love me when I'm loveable and when I'm not, to let me support her even when she could handle the ugly stuff by herself. Not someone I rescued, as my sister accuses me of, but someone who cares about us enough to include me in the problem and solution."

The room's silence was broken only by the refrigerator's whir and their breathing. *What do I say to a man who lays his heart on the table, no games, no hidden agenda?* "Patrick?"

His sigh was audible in the quiet room. "Too much information? Too soon?" He stood and cleared the table, loading the last dishes in the dishwasher. He returned to the table and tugged her out of the chair into his arms.

"Tara. I've been divorced fourteen years, and while I can't claim monk status, you are the very first woman I've shared my heart with. That was far more difficult than I believed it would be. I want you to know this isn't a one-night stand or friends with benefits thing. I'm looking for a forever dream, and I'm in love with you."

The chiming of her cell phone ended their passionate embrace. "Hi, Ronni, what's up? You'll be here in about an hour? That's fine. See you then."

Patrick gathered his things and, with a final embrace, slipped out the door.

Tara gave the kitchen table a final wipe down, flipped the switch on the dishwasher, and headed to the bedroom, Samson trotting behind.

As she changed the sheets and pillowcases, Patrick's scent drifted to her. Would she be comforted or aroused by his scent if she left the sheets on? She yanked them off and made the bed with clean white sheets. Last night's sheets bundled in her arms, she grabbed the bath towels and headed to the laundry. Patrick was a single parent; he understood the frustration and the fear that each decision could be the wrong one. Yeah, Owen and Jen were great resources when she asked, but at the end of the day, she was the parent, the one responsible. After six years of single parenting, could she share the load? The positive part of single parenting was her freedom to raise her children her own way. If she married Patrick, they'd have to learn to work together. Samson whined.

"Okay, boy. Let's take a quick trip outside." She gathered Samson in her arms and headed downstairs toward the back door. She released the bolt on the doggie door, and Samson slipped through. She yanked open the door and followed him outside. As she dropped into the rocking chair, she texted Ronni her location.

After watching Patrick with his siblings, nieces, and nephews, she couldn't imagine him being hands off. And what about Scott? There were sixteen years between her thirty-six and his twenty. Would that cause a riff if she became his stepmother?

She grinned as Ronni, Tina, and Makenna appeared through the gate, the girls in a rush to greet Samson and Ronni, wearing a sly smile following slowly behind.

Ronni plopped into the other chair and asked, "How was the dinner date? Did he have to rush off when I called? Was I too early?"

"Perfect timing."

"Hmm. You don't sound very enthusiastic about my perfect timing. At least share the details of your romantic dinner. It's been so long since I shared a romantic dinner with a man; I need to live vicariously through you," Ronni teased.

"Okay." Tara grinned and dropped her voice to a seductive whisper. "I set the stage with low lights, soft music, a flickering scented candle on the coffee table, appetizers artfully arranged on a plate, wine glasses sparkling. And then Patrick arrived, greeting me with a kiss." She grinned wickedly. "His male scent of soap and warm skin more seductive than my candle."

Ronni sighed. "I miss that, a kiss in greeting."

"The whole evening was delightful, he's wonderful company and one of the few men I've met who pitches in without prompting, knows what needs to be done, and does it."

"What do you mean?"

"After dinner, he cleared the table while I put the food away, we rinsed and loaded the dishes in the dishwasher together, and he wiped the counters. It felt normal, like we'd done exactly the same things together a thousand times. And, after a beautiful night sleeping in the embrace of a lovely man, I came out of the shower to find him standing in the kitchen, coffee made, table set, and breakfast almost ready."

"Do you think he'd like to stay with Tina and me for a weekend? Without the sharing in bed part, I could use a little time with someone else backing me up, doing what needs to be done without being asked."

"You're out of luck with Patrick. After breakfast, he put his cards on the table. He's not interested in a casual relationship, or short term. After fourteen years alone, he's interested in a forever partner."

"So did you grab him around the neck, place a smacking kiss on his lips, and shout, 'Yes?'"

"You called before I could even process what he said. Saved by the phone call."

"Does that mean you're not looking for forever, or not looking for forever with Patrick?"

Tina, Makenna, and Samson climbed the step to the deck and plopped down beside Tara and Ronni ending the conversation. Tara waved as Ronni and Tina strolled out the gate, then she picked up the sleeping puppy and hustled a chattering Makenna upstairs.

Hours later, as Tara and Makenna ate dinner, Makenna asked, "Where did you and Mr. Benton have dinner last night?"

"Here, Makenna. I told you he was coming for dinner."

"But if he ate at our house, why wasn't I invited? You weren't out at some grown-up dinner."

"Where did you go for dinner, Makenna?"

"To Uncle Nathan's for a bar-b-que. Tina's lucky her uncle lives next door. Uncle Owen lives too far away."

"Uncle Owen does live far away. Nathan is your uncle too, so you have an uncle nearby and one far away," Tara answered as they cleared the table and she loaded the dishwasher. "Let's take Samson outside again and then go up and get you ready for bed."

By eight o'clock p.m., Makenna slept; Samson curled into his dog bed on the floor in her room. Tara wandered through the apartment, checking the windows and doors were secure. She grabbed the mystery novel she'd started a week ago and settled on the sofa.

Instead of focusing on solving the mystery, her mind wandered. Patrick's confession haunted her, and combined with Ronni's question, her emotions were unsettled. What had she expected from their night together? What was she looking for? A short-term affair? A one-time lover? A casual relationship, sex included? He wanted forever. What did she want?

When she crawled into bed, she gave up on finding answers. No more sudden, impulsive moves. She liked her life as is. Was she ready to consider a change when she was finally in control of her piece of the world?

She woke to the sound of soft snores. In a shadowy corner of the room, a man with white hair slept sitting in a rocking chair, his chin resting on his chest. A young woman appeared beside him and whispered, "Dad, wake up, let me help you to bed."

He startled awake and answered, "I can't sleep in that bed. Your mom's not there."

"Then come upstairs. The guest room bed is made up. Let me help you." She took his hands and gently tugged him to his feet.

As they glided through the closed door, he said, "You know this is the first night since we married, that we've slept apart."

"I know, Dad." They disappeared.

Tara drifted toward sleep, her last thought, why did some relationships end and others last forever?

Chapter Twenty-Seven

In 1922 our family grew by one more. This time no announcement appeared in the newspaper. There was no christening planned. On a sunny Tuesday morning, a thirteen-year-old girl, Thelma Louise Curtis, appeared in front of Maggie's desk lugging an old suitcase. When I heard Thelma say, "I want to hire a lawyer, Aunt Maggie."

I strolled into the reception area. "Why don't we step into my office?"

Thelma's mom died several years ago. Her dad remarried a woman with three young children and was pregnant with another. Her dad worked all the time, her stepmom was overwhelmed, and Thelma struggled in school and was bullied because she had trouble reading. She wanted out. She left two days ago, and no one probably noticed (not true, her father was frantically searching for her). The result was, with her father's agreement, Thelma joined our family. By the time she started college in Flagstaff, we wondered how we'd survived without her.

~From Practicing Law in Creekside, A Love Story by Micah Henderson

****

Sunday morning from behind the bar, Patrick smiled at Scott, taking the steps two at a time, yanking open the front door, and joining the guests in line for breakfast.

"Morning, Dad," he greeted as he piled his plate with food and filled a glass with juice. "I'm your relief at eleven, figured I'd get breakfast first."

"You miss breakfast at Eckie House?" Patrick asked as he re-filled the coffee carafe.

"Yep. They eat early on Sunday, so they get to church on time. Takes time getting a squirmy handful like Ella fed and dressed for church."

When only a few guests remained drinking coffee, Patrick refilled the carafe and cleared the food from the bar. Scott set his plate in the bus cart and strolled out the door, where he gathered dishes and wiped down the tables on the veranda.

As Patrick finished loading the dishwasher, he heard Scott in the lobby explaining the easiest way out of town since several roads were blocked due to a festival on the square. There were ten years between Scott and Tara's son, CJ. Would that be weird for them to be stepbrothers ten years apart? Or would it be awkward for Scott to have a stepmother only sixteen years his senior?

If he and Tara chose to have another child, there would be twenty-one years between his oldest and youngest, and he'd be ready for retirement by the time his last child left college. He'd tried the empty nest when Scott left for college and hadn't liked it. Leaving Scott to his job at the front desk, Patrick climbed the two flights of stairs to the attic.

After trading jeans and a Palace polo shirt for shorts and a T-shirt, he donned his favorite tennis shoes, grabbed wallet, phone, and sunglasses, and hustled down the stairs for his date with Tara and kids on the square. He spotted Tara lounging on a blanket at the far corner, Samson on her lap, Ronni sat beside her. As he ambled toward them, dodging adults, children, and dogs, CJ and Zack dropped onto the grass beside Tara, and Jude sat down beside Ronni. Nathan appeared from the crowd around the soda stand, Tina on one side and Makenna on the other, all three of them with their hands full of drinks. He reached the group on blankets, with Nathan and the girls one second behind. He dropped beside Tara, leaned over, and dropped a kiss on her cheek, then nodded toward the sleeping dog. "Already worn out?"

"Yep. Too much noise. Too many people for a shy puppy. I have a feeling he wasn't socialized much before we found him."

"Mommy, how come Samson's still asleep?" Makenna asked as she handed her mom a plastic cup of lemonade.

"All the new smells and sounds wore him out." Tara sipped the lemonade. "Thank you for bringing me a drink, Makenna."

"Looks like we're ready for food," commented Ronni as she started to stand.

"Gather up the orders," answered Patrick, "and I'll pick up everything. Anyone who wants to help carry is welcome."

A few minutes later, list in hand, Patrick accompanied by Jude, CJ, and Zack strolled toward the food booths lining the edge of the square. By the time they'd gathered all requests, their arms were full of pizza, tacos, burgers, salads, sandwiches, chips, and Asian appetizers. Zack and CJ rushed ahead, weaving between groups of people spread on the lawn. Patrick and Jude strolled. "Should we try to catch up?" asked Jude.

"I think we're okay at our own pace. I can see the top of their heads, and they're on a straight course for the rest of the group."

"When Scott was young, you ever wonder if you were too protective or too trusting? I want Zack to feel free but also safe."

"Worried all the time about how tight to hold on. Now I haven't a choice. He's an adult, so I spend a lot of time holding my excellent advice inside unless he asks. I was lucky. Before I'd do something too stupid, I'd call my mom for advice." They dodged a couple of boys racing across the lawn. "Gotta be tougher for you and Zack. Who do you ask?"

"Jefferson Lynch, mostly. His son's the same age. Sometimes I ask Ronni even though her Tina is young."

"You two have so much in common I'm surprised you're not dating. Or are you dating, and I'm out of the loop?" Color infused Jude's face. "Sorry, none of my business. Guess I spend too much time with my family. Sometimes we lack filters."

"It's okay, just a touchy subject. Today's as close as I've managed to get Ronni to agree to a date."

Zack appeared in front of them. "Come on. Everybody else is eating."

For the next couple of hours, they enjoyed first lunch then the band. As the sun set, they gathered children, dogs, and blankets and trudged toward home. Makenna rode on Patrick's shoulders, and CJ carried a sleeping Samson.

"There's lasagna in the slow cooker if you're interested, Patrick," Tara offered as they climbed the front steps of the Henderson Building.

"Sounds great. Thank you." Patrick set Makenna on her feet, surprised he missed the weight of a child in his arms.

"CJ, hand Samson to Mr. Benton, please, and hustle upstairs to the shower. Patrick, if you'd take the dog out, I'd appreciate it. I'll get Makenna started on her bath."

The family disappeared upstairs. Samson in his arms, Patrick paced to the back door, let himself out, and placed Samson on the grass. While Samson checked out his environment, the sun slipped behind the mountain. Carrying a small child home, taking the dog out, working with a partner to provide safety, security, warmth, love for a family—that was the future he wanted. What did Tara want, and did she see him in her future? Samson bounced up the steps to the deck and plopped down beside the rocker.

"No question what you want, puppy. Time for you to go inside." He gathered the dog in his arms and slipped inside.

After setting Samson on the floor and slipping into the guest bath to wash his hands, Patrick joined the family in the kitchen. "What can I do to help?"

"You can set the table," Makenna offered as she carried the silverware to the table.

"No, Makenna," Tara answered, "tonight, that's your job. Patrick, you may carry the glasses to the table. CJ has the plates."

After dinner, when the food was put away and the dishes done, Tara sent the children to get ready for bed. She reminded them tomorrow was an early day with their summer activities. The children chorused,

"Goodbye," and Tara offered to walk Patrick out.

At the door, she dropped a light kiss on his lips and whispered, "We'll talk tomorrow." Patrick returned the kiss and slipped out the door.

****

The low hum of the dishwasher greeted Tara when she opened the apartment door. She climbed the stairs to the children's rooms and stopped at Makenna's door.

"Momma, can you read me a story?" Makenna asked.

"Okay."

Makenna handed her Chance's *Under the Sea,* and Tara began to read. When she finished the story, she tucked Makenna in and kissed her cheek. "Night, love."

"Mommy, are you dating Mr. Benton?" Makenna asked as her eyes drifted shut. "Tina says her mommy is dating Mr. Healy cause she caught them kissing."

"Yes, Makenna," Tara answered, fighting a laugh, so Ronni finally kissed him. Watching Jude's longing glances was painful. About time he made a move. She listened to Makenna's even breathing, shut off the light, and strolled to CJ's room. She stepped inside and dropped into the chair beside his bed.

"You about ready for sleep, CJ?"

"I want to finish this chapter," he answered without looking up.

Hmm. Something bothered CJ. She waited silently, admiring the way his room had turned out, a good cross between a little boy and young man. In one month, her little boy would be eleven.

CJ looked up from the book. "Mom, are you dating Mr. Benton? Is that why he came to dinner? Was that a date?"

"Yep."

"Why? Why are you dating him? Are you going to marry him?" CJ shut the book and dropped it on the bedside table; a frown wrinkled his brow.

"CJ, where are these questions coming from? You understood I went out on dates when we lived in Bisbee." There hadn't been many, but she was honest when she went out, that she was on a date, and that was why Jen or Owen stayed with the kids.

"Yeah, but I never met the guy, and he wasn't someone I knew. Mr. Benton is everywhere. He even owns the building where we live. He used to live down the hall in the hotel. You see him every day when you work cause his office is next door. He even took all of us on a date. It's weird."

"So you don't have a problem with me dating. You do have questions about my dating Mr. Benton, not because there is anything wrong with him; he seems like an okay guy, but because we see him all the time anyway. Do I have that right?

"Yep."

"If dating can lead to marriage, and you're right, it can, don't you think it's better if I only consider people I know well? People we see all the time, doing all kinds of stuff? That way, before we include someone in our family, we know if they are a good person all the time, not only on a date."

"But you lived with my dad for years. You thought he was a good person, but he came back and hit you."

Tara sat on the bed beside CJ and wrapped her arm around him. "For a long time, he was a good person, a good dad. But CJ, your dad got involved with some bad people and started using drugs. He lost his way." She released him, ruffled his hair, and straightened his covers. "I promise, CJ, before I add anyone to our family, I'll talk to you and Makenna. If you have a question about something Mr. Benton says or does, something that worries you, ask me or him. We'll listen. Night, Son." She stopped at the doorway and flipped off the light.

"Night, Mom."

She glanced again at Makenna's sleeping form and walked down the stairs. Both children with questions about dating and marriage. Was she the only one who hadn't considered a future with Patrick? She gathered bowls and cereal boxes for breakfast and set them on the table. As she stood under the shower's soothing spray, she considered how life could be different with a loving partner. There'd been an intimacy to sitting on the blanket at the square, even though they were surrounded by people. Patrick easily managed to be useful during dinner and clean up, not taking over the children's regular jobs but helping make the dinner go smoothly. As she slid the nightgown over her head and then climbed between the sheets, she accepted that Patrick easily fit into their life. Plus, their one night together proved he fit her, was exactly the lover she needed. Lights flipped off she drifted to sleep.

She woke in the darkest part of the night to the sound of whispered voices coming from a shadowy corner of the room. "Thank you for letting her stay with us," the woman said.

"As long as you think it's a good idea, a week, a month, a year, forever, she's welcome," he answered as the couple gradually appeared, sitting on a small settee.

"Not all men would take on responsibility for

another man's child, especially a brother-in-law's child you barely know."

"You, Maggie, are the heart of our family. If your heart says we add your niece to our household, we will. I trust your heart to guide us." He rose, drew her into his arms, placed his lips on hers, and they disappeared.

Tara closed her eyes. Trust your heart to guide us. Exactly what she needed to do.

Chapter Twenty-Eight

In my arms, darling Maggie cries frightened tears. Today our twenty-one-year-old son, Paul, was accepted into the flight school at Thunderbird Field. From his early childhood, Paul dreamed of flying, and he's found a way to make his dream come true. He's becoming a pilot for the US Army. As soon as he's qualified, he will become part of the war effort, flying into who knows what hell. We waved him off this morning. As soon as the car carrying our son and his best friend disappeared, Maggie's tears began. I comfort her, but my own heart bleeds. Our beautiful son has gone to war, protected only by a thin metal shell that flies. June 1941.

~Practicing Law in Creekside, A Love Story by Micah Henderson

****

The first hints of fall drifted in the breeze as Patrick propelled Michelle's stroller along the sidewalk toward Eckie House, Nikki beside him. "How'd you end up with me as an escort tonight, Nik? You have an abundance of males living in your household," Patrick asked as they strolled through the residential area.

"Except for Michelle, they preferred the company of friends to boring mom, so they offered to help James set up. Alex is covering for Osborne. His wife went into labor this afternoon. Laboring on Labor Day weekend," she answered. "What about you? No date tonight?"

"Tara and the kids are already there, went early to help."

"I promised to stay out of your love life, and I will. Just want to say I'm glad to see you dating someone."

"Hey, I dated." Patrick unlatched the front gate and rolled the stroller through. "We going in the house or around the back?" He motioned toward the small cooler under the stroller. "That need to go inside?"

"Nope. Let's go around to the back. Yep, I knew you dated; Mom told me. But from what she said, you carefully chose dates you knew wouldn't last."

They turned the corner, the meadow stretched before them, and children's laughter filled the air. He spotted Scott in a game of kickball, a herd of children chasing him. Leaving Michelle settled on the deck and Nikki helping Andrea in the kitchen, Patrick started toward James, Nathan, and Chance beside the grill. When he spotted Tara coming down the outside staircase of Ronni's apartment, a giant bowl balanced in both hands, Patrick turned her way.

He met her at the bottom of the stairs, and she handed him the bowl. "Thanks," she said, placing a light kiss on his lips. "Haul that to the kitchen, and I'll grab the rolls and join you, okay?"

He nodded his acceptance and ambled toward the house. CJ stood a few feet away, his eyes locked with Patrick's and his brows drawn down in a frown. *Looks like CJ's not happy with their discreet PDA.*

Streaking the sky orange and red, the sun set on the official end to Creekside's summer season. Patrick joined the clean-up crew. He grabbed one end of a long folding table and was immediately joined on the other end by Tara. "Can I walk you home, Tara? Or do you have another escort in mind?"

"Thought you'd never ask. Check out Tina and Makenna under the tree."

He glanced at the two girls barely sitting upright on a blanket, leaning against each other, their eyes almost closed. "Looks like someone needs a ride home."

Tables and chairs stored, meadow devoid of trash, Tara gently tugged Makenna to her feet. "Momma, I'm tired. Can Mr. Benton carry me?"

Patrick took Makenna in his arms, balancing her on one hip. "Where's CJ?" he asked.

She nodded her head toward a green truck. CJ, Zack, and Jude sat on the tailgate, Zack and CJ holding a dog each. "CJ," she called. "Let's head home." The boys jumped down and, with a shouted, "Good bye," CJ dashed toward them.

"I can carry Makenna, Mom," CJ offered as he placed Samson on the ground.

"I know you can, but Mr. Benton offered, and I accepted." She put her arm around his shoulder. "Makenna's almost too big for me to carry. You worry about Samson. I bet he's nearly as tired as Makenna."

They strolled through the quiet residential streets. Makenna whispered to Patrick, "Mr. Benton, are you my date?"

"Not tonight, Makenna. Tonight I'm your taxi." He felt her giggle against his shoulder.

They turned down the alley behind the Henderson Building. Tara unlocked the gate, and they trooped through the yard. "Set Samson free, CJ," Tara directed as she unlocked the back door. "You go up and take a shower quick." CJ released Samson's leash and dashed through the door. "If you don't mind carrying your package upstairs, I'll take it from there." Patrick followed her up the stairs and set Makenna down in the living room. "You, young lady, upstairs and get undressed for your bath. Soon as CJ's out, it's your turn."

"Thanks for the taxi ride, Mr. Benton," Makenna said with a grin as she turned to the stairs.

"I'll get Samson, okay? I can carry him up and save you a trip," Patrick offered.

At Tara's agreement, Patrick paced down the stairs and outside. Samson, his nose buried in a bush, looked up as Patrick closed the door, then turned back to sniffing his way around the yard.

When the dog bounded up onto the deck, Patrick led him inside, up the stairs, and opened the door. Samson loped inside as far as his water bowl in the kitchen.

Patrick climbed the stairs and immediately heard Makenna's piping voice, "I won't sleep, Mommy. Tomorrow's my first day of kindergarten, and I'm excited."

He peeked in her room. Makenna sat on the bed, a book on her lap. Tara sat beside her. "Night, ladies," he said. They chorused, "Good night."

At CJ's door, he tapped and called, "Night, CJ." At his mumbled response, Patrick left. Through almost quiet streets, he walked to the hotel. Another son besides CJ caught Tara's kiss in public. Scott noticed, but rather than a frown, he grinned and gave his father a thumbs-up before he went back to the game. Makes sense. At twenty, Patrick's love life, or lack of, would have no impact on Scott. Patrick backed away from his thoughts and glanced at the hotel, immediately spotting Scott lounging in the rocker beside the door. Patrick dropped into the chair next to his son. "You staying here tonight?"

"Nope. Just wanted a few minutes of your time. Figured you wouldn't be late since your date's a single mom. Not that you asked, but I like her. Nice to see you finally got a social life."

"Well, since I doubt you waited on the veranda to comment on my social life, why are you waiting? I figured I'd see you tomorrow at breakfast before you go back to school."

"You will. I wanted to let you know I won't be going into the MBA program in the fall. I got my acceptance a week ago, but after two weeks at the chain hotel, I'm sure that's not a direction I'm interested in. I have an internship scheduled next semester with another large resort, but I'm looking for a job at graduation somewhere smaller. I don't want to do what Mom did."

Patrick glanced at Scott's serious expression. *This was a first. They rarely spoke of Amy.* "What is it you want to avoid?"

"Grampa Cyrus claims Mom rushed to grow up, to finish school, to have a wedding, buy a house, work in a law firm, have a child. She had this plan and wanted it now. She never stopped along the way to figure out if each part was right for her at that moment. I don't want to wake up one day and decide I'm not living the life I want, especially if by that time I have a wife and kids."

"When I met your mom, part of the attraction was her certainty. She knew exactly where she was going and what the next steps were, so I'd agree with Cyrus.

But some of the failure of our marriage rests squarely on my shoulders. I was so happy being a father, I sometimes forgot about being a husband and a friend. I'm sad I didn't know Amy was unhappy until she told me she was leaving." *Plus, marriage to me was lonelier than being alone, and she found someone else.*

"Is that why you didn't marry again? Being unhappy in her marriage didn't stop Mom from trying. Did it stop you?"

"At first maybe, but later on, I don't know. By the time I was comfortable in the role of a single parent, I couldn't take the chance of adding someone into our lives who might not stay. I'm not sorry I didn't put either of us through that."

Scott rose. "Well, if Tara's the one, I hope she's not at the place you were before, comfortable with life as a single parent and unwilling to rock the boat. You're an awesome dad; even my friends think so. Tara's kids would be lucky to have you as a stepfather. Night, Dad."

Scott took the steps in a long leap and strode down the sidewalk, disappearing around a corner. Did Scott have the answer to Tara's hesitation? She'd hit her stride as a single mom, kids content, a job that let her be available for them, a new town with friends and family nearby. How could he convince her to take a chance on them? That the sailing through life would be better together? He rose from the chair, slipped through the front door, and climbed the stairs to his attic apartment. When he crawled in bed a couple of hours later, he drifted to sleep with his last thought, was he the right man at the wrong time, the wrong man, or was Tara simply afraid to make another change?

****

Sunlight danced on the front windows as Patrick put the finishing touches on breakfast. He snapped the lid on the coffee carafe as the chime on the front door rang. Scott and Casey stepped inside with a chorus of, "Good morning." Before they'd set filled plates on a table, the lobby filled with guests. As the lobby emptied, Patrick put food away, refilled the coffee, and cleaned the bar. Casey and Scott gathered dishes and, when the dishwasher was loaded, gave Patrick a farewell hug and slipped out the door with a wave as Nikki appeared behind the desk. "How'd the return to school go?"

"Good," she answered. "I probably won't need to walk anyone to school again until Michelle is old enough to start. I don't think Sam wanted my escort today. He enjoys having his brothers as escorts."

"It's tough letting go," Patrick agreed. "It's great school is so close to the hotel, and the neighborhood is safe, but it takes away your excuse to see him arrive on campus because you're the driver."

"Yep. Catherine at least still has a kindergartner who requires her escort. In fact, she offered to stop by for Sam, but I wasn't quite ready." At the sound of footsteps on the stairs, she said, "I got this, Patrick. Michelle's with Andrea, so you can head for your second job. Thanks for covering this morning."

After a dash upstairs to change, Patrick strolled out the hotel's front door. *How fast time goes, Sam is no longer the sad, scared four year old who suddenly found himself living with his godmother. Today he has friends, family, and the childhood freedom that comes with living in a small town. Does Tara realize how quickly her children will become independent?* He climbed the steps and opened the office door. "Tara, good morning?"

"In the kitchen," she answered.

He wandered into the kitchen, where Tara sat at the small table flipping through the newspaper. He grabbed a mug and dressed his coffee. "Kids get to school okay?"

"Yep. Jude dropped Zack off, and the boys walked together. Makenna and I walked all the way to her classroom since it was her first day ever. Stood by the door with the other parents while the kids found their seats. When she settled in her chair, she looked at me and said, 'You can go, Mom. I got this.'"

"Sounds like she's off to a positive start. What about you, you off to a positive start with your baby in kindergarten?"

"Mixed feelings. Glad she's confident enough to feel good about going to school but sad that it's one more moment that proves her growing independence."

"Let's celebrate the first day of school. I'll take you to lunch."

They strolled through town to the Station, Samson on a leash. One minute the puppy led the way, and then he stopped to sniff something. "He's getting better," Patrick commented. "You working with him?"

"Some. He spends time with Nathan's Cameron and Jude's King, both well behaved and adults. I should walk him around town more, new people are a distraction, and he is a town dog."

"I notice he stops and sits each time you stop. That Nathan's doing?"

"Yep. Cameron's prior owner was an elderly lady.

Cameron learned to wait beside her so she wouldn't trip over him."

They climbed the restaurant's steps and found a table on the dog-friendly patio. Through lunch, they spoke of school memories, their own experiences, and those of their children. When they paid the bill and walked away from the restaurant, Tara held Samson's leash with one hand and Patrick's with the other. Back inside the office, she released Samson, and he trotted toward her office. Tara followed Patrick to his office, where they sat on the small loveseat.

She took his hand. "I have a problem, and, according to your sister, solving problems is what you do best."

Please, don't let me be the problem she wants to solve. "How can I help?"

"Loan me a little of your emotional courage." She slid closer until their thighs touched. "I felt courageous asking you out, leading us down the path of spending the night together."

He wrapped an arm around her shoulder and used his free hand to turn her face toward him. "I admired your courage and appreciated every moment of being led."

Their eyes met. "You follow extremely well. Other than a sensual night with a lovely man, I'm not sure what I expected, but our time together exceeded anything I dreamed."

"Was it the breakfast?"

A smile lit her eyes. "That was unexpected, but your willingness to lay your heart on the table took courage. Though when we met, I was running scared, I've found my courage now and my dreams." She turned toward him, placed a hand on his cheek, and leaned in. Before their lips met, she whispered, "I love you, too."

The kiss changed from sweet to passionate, his arms wrapped around her, and he drew her body flush with his. The alarm on her phone dinged, and he released her. "Time to pick up Makenna?"

She straightened her clothing and stood. "Yep. You do know that's a forewarning of your life with my family? Snatches of alone time stolen between family obligations."

Patrick stood and took her hand. "I'll be grateful every day for both, the stolen moments and the family obligations. The combination describes my dream."

Samson leashed, they strolled to the elementary school and arrived as the bell rang. Makenna raced to the gate. "Hi, Mom and Mr. Benton. I love kindergarten!" Makenna bounced through the gate and took her mother's hand. For the entire walk home, she continued a monologue about everything that made her day perfect. When they reached the Henderson Building, Tara sent her upstairs to wash her hands and face, and the adults walked to Tara's office.

Tara took a juice box out of the mini-fridge by her desk and a granola bar from the drawer, setting them on the corner of her desk. "You don't have to meet CJ?" Patrick asked.

"Nope. He and Zack are walking here. Seems it's okay to be picked up in the truck or walked home in fifth grade but not when you are in sixth grade. Either you take the bus or walk home with friends. Jude will arrive in a few minutes and pick Zack up here. For the number of times CJ spent weekends with Jude and

Zack, I feel it's about time I returned the favor."

"I'm going to wait outside for Jude." Patrick slipped out of her office as Makenna clattered down the stairs. He grabbed an envelope from his desk and ambled out the front door. An emerald truck drove into the parallel space in front of the building, Jude rolled the window down, and Patrick handed him the envelope.

"Hey, Patrick, thanks for looking at the contract and answering my questions. It's a little different than the usual," Jude admitted. "Send me a bill for your time, okay?"

"Are congratulations in order? Is this your first solo show?"

"First one in years and the first one at this gallery."

Zack and CJ appeared; Patrick stepped back. Zack climbed in the truck, and with a goodbye, they disappeared around a corner. Patrick turned toward the front door. CJ stood at the railing, and the worried frown was back.

"How was school, CJ? You and Zack in the same class?"

"Yeah, school's okay. Can I ask you a question?"

Patrick motioned toward the small table and chairs. "What did you want to know?" he offered as they dropped into the chairs.

"Are you dating my mom? Are you going to marry her?" CJ sat up straight. "Cause if you are, you better never hurt her. I'll protect her just like I did last time."

"I promise to never hurt her the way your dad did, CJ. I don't hit women." *No wonder he frowned when she kissed me. He's scared, not for himself but for his mom.*

291

"And you can't be my dad. I had a dad, and he died."

"Legally, I'd be your stepdad, but whatever I am to you is up to you. Whatever you choose to call me, I'll be one more adult, like your Uncles Owen and Nathan, who is looking out for you. Another person who wants you to grow into the man you were meant to be. We all need people who are on our side, right?" Patrick waited in silence.

Cars cruised by; the first fall leaves floated across the sidewalk on a slight breeze. Somewhere a dog barked. Patrick waited.

"Yeah. I guess that'd be okay. I gotta go tell Mom I'm home." CJ jumped up and dashed through the front door.

A few minutes later, Patrick followed. He peeked in Tara's office and found her alone. "Hey, what'd you do with your kids and dog?"

"Sent them all out back for the dog's trek around the yard. You okay?"

"Yep. Wanted to give you a heads up. CJ asked if I planned to marry you. No idea what brought it up, but wanted you to know. I'm leaving. Want me to lock the front door?" At her nod, he walked into her office and dropped a light kiss on her lips. "See you tomorrow."

He strolled out the front door, locking it behind him. He empathized with CJ. His experience of dad ended badly, an understatement. The men in his life now were good ones, but none wore the title dad. He slipped through the back door of The Palace and climbed the steps to his apartment.

Later, when he crawled between the covers, he wondered how he would have felt if his mom married again. Would their lives have been enriched by adding another adult to the family? He drifted to sleep.

In the moments before dawn, he woke to the sound of quiet weeping accompanied by the rumble of a man's voice. In a shadowy corner, Victoria appeared. Beside her on a small sofa, a man sat, holding her hand.

"So this time, he's not coming back. I won't hold him again; hear his voice."

"This time, he's gone for good, Victoria. He died sitting at his desk, one moment talking to the family of a patient, and the next he collapsed. He saved so many lives, but no one could save his."

"He knew, Welles, he knew his heart was failing the last time he visited." She dropped her head against his shoulder. "I asked him not to go. In all the years we were together, it was the only time I asked."

"But he wouldn't. Too many people depended upon him; too much was left undone. Will you be okay, Victoria? Is there anything I can do to help?"

She stood, drawing him up with her. "Hug me, Welles, one hug. You lost your brother and best friend, and I lost my love. But he's not gone to us, not really. He'll forever be in our hearts." She wrapped her arms around him, her head on his shoulder, and they disappeared.

Patrick closed his eyes. Victoria believed loving was worth the risk of losing. She loved completely, and a hundred years later, that love still existed inside The Palace. He drifted off to sleep.

Chapter Twenty-Nine

On the longest night of the year in 1957, I held Maggie for the last time. Illness had stolen her breathing, each inhale and exhale a struggle. Doctors came but offered only medicine for the pain, no hope. Through this long night, I lay beside her in the bed we shared for so many years. I dozed, and in my scattered dreams, we were the young couple with the beautiful little girl, the busy family with a law practice, rambunctious twin boys, and an adorable teenage niece. Our family's love surrounded me. Maggie's heartbeat with mine. As dawn slipped through the curtains, I woke just as Maggie breathed her last. But I know the truth; Maggie's love lives on with me, our children, and grandchildren, with every life she touched with kindness. She was the heart of our family in every way. From the moment Maggie entered my office until the last time I held her in my arms as she slipped away, my heart beat only for her.

~Practicing Law in Creekside, A Love Story by Micah Henderson.

****

The scent of coffee greeted him when Patrick opened the Henderson Building front door. Samson bounded into the reception area, tail wagging, and collided with Patrick's legs.

"Good morning, Samson. Nice greeting." Patrick

leaned down and scratched behind the dog's ears.

Tara walked out of the kitchen, coffee mug in hand. "Samson, what are you doing out here? I'm going to have to put a gate up in my office if you insist on playing receptionist."

Samson whined softly, lay down, and put his head on his paws.

Patrick laughed. "He knows you're unhappy with him."

"If you'll pick the little miscreant up, I'll grab you a coffee, and we can adjourn to my office. I'd like to talk about last night, okay?"

Patrick lifted Samson in his arms and was rewarded with a lick on his chin. "Okay, but I warn you I can't remember a positive conversation that began with 'about last night.'"

They strolled to Tara's office. Patrick put Samson on the floor and placed a small sheet of cardboard across the doorway to discourage escape. He took the offered coffee mug from Tara and settled in a chair.

Tara plopped in the chair behind her desk and sipped her coffee. "Last night, both my children asked if we were going to marry. In their minds, dating is for people who don't have kids; people with kids should marry. I can see where Makenna's coming from since Hope told the entire class her mom is marrying Chance, and they were going to live in Sanders House all together with a new baby."

"Ahh. So that's why she suddenly said yes, or at least why the wedding is soon."

"Yep. But up until last night, as far as I knew, CJ was not enthusiastic about us dating, much less getting married. Had nothing to do with you, I don't think. He was little when Trey left, and his last memory of his father is awful and something I wish I could erase."

"I did talk to him about our relationship." *Hope I didn't confuse him.*

"You aren't the only one he talked to. He confided to both his best friends, Zack and Carson. The boys are being raised by single dads, but Zack and Carson remember what it was like to have two parents. Both hope their dads find a wife before they're too grown up to care. Zack says it's scary with one parent, that he doesn't know what will happen to him if Jude dies because they don't have any other family. Carson says if his dad dies, he goes to live with his aunt and uncle who already have four kids. He'd rather have a stepmother if she was nice."

"I gather the heavy conversation was the topic at yesterday's recess? That CJ did exactly what an adult would do, asked his friends for advice?"

"Yep. They're the ones who told him to talk to you first, but they like you, and Nikki's kids talk about their uncle all the time." She set the cup on her desk, stood, walked around the desk, took his cup, and encouraged him to stand. She placed her lips on his and her arms around his waist.

She tasted of coffee, Tara, passion, and dreams. Answering her slightly tentative advance, Patrick returned the kiss with all the longing in his heart. Before he was tempted to suggest they take their passion to the sofa, they separated, their breathing shallow and quick. As it evened, he said, "So your children and their best friends approve of me as a stepfather but not a date, and that kiss says you approve of me as a lover?"

She nodded. "Since I asked you on a date and seduced you first, I should be the one to ask, will you marry me, Patrick?"

He lifted her in the air and swung her around, "Yes, I thought you'd never ask."

Their joy filled the room and continued as their lips touched.

In the corner of the room, two white heads glinted in the sunlight, an elderly couple with their arms wrapped around each other. Their lips met; they slowly dissolved, leaving behind the warmth of a forever love.

A word about the author...

An Arizona native, I spent my childhood visiting small towns and campgrounds all over the state and entertained myself on long car trips writing stories. Married and living in Scottsdale, I still imagine every new acquaintance's story and spend my free time traveling, reading, walking my tiny dog, and practicing yoga.

http://stellajaynephillips.com

Thank you for purchasing
this publication of The Wild Rose Press, Inc.
For questions or more information
contact us at
info@thewildrosepress.com.
The Wild Rose Press, Inc.
www.thewildrosepress.com